Walk on the Wildsyde

Wicked Sons Book 8

By Emma V. Leech

Published by Emma V. Leech.

Editing Services Magpie Literary Services

Cover Art: Victoria Cooper

ISBN No: 978-2-487015-33-3

About Me!

I started this incredible journey way back in 2010 with The Key to Erebus but didn't summon the courage to hit publish until October 2012. For anyone who's done it, you'll know publishing your first title is a terribly scary thing! I still get butterflies on the morning a new title releases, but the terror has subsided at least. Now I just live in dread of the day my daughters are old enough to read them.

The horror! (On both sides I suspect.)

2017 marked the year that I made my first foray into Historical Romance and the world of the Regency Romance, and my word what a year! I was delighted by the response to this series and can't wait to add more titles. Paranormal Romance readers need not despair, however, as there is much more to come there too. Writing has become an addiction and as soon as one book is over, I'm hugely excited to start the next so you can expect plenty more in the future.

As many of my works reflect, I am greatly influenced by the beautiful French countryside in which I live. I've been here in the Southwest since 1998, though I was born and raised in England. My three gorgeous girls are all bilingual and my husband Pat, myself, and our four cats consider ourselves very fortunate to have made such a lovely place our home.

KEEP READING TO DISCOVER MY OTHER BOOKS!

Other Works by Emma V. Leech

Wicked Sons

Wicked Sons Series

Daring Daughters

Daring Daughters Series

Girls Who Dare

Girls Who Dare Series

Rogues & Gentlemen

Rogues & Gentlemen Series

The Regency Romance Mysteries

The Regency Romance Mysteries Series

The French Vampire Legend

The French Vampire Legend Series

The French Fae Legend

The French Fae Legend Series

Stand Alone

The Book Lover (a paranormal novella)

The Girl is Not for Christmas (Regency Romance)

Audio Books

Don't have time to read but still need your romance fix? The wait is over…

By popular demand, get many of your favourite Emma V Leech Regency Romance books on audio as performed by the incomparable Philip Battley and Gerard Marzilli. Several titles available and more added each month!

Find them at your favourite audiobook retailer!

Acknowledgements

Thanks, of course, to my wonderful editor Kezia Cole with Magpie Literary Services

To Victoria Cooper for all your hard work, amazing artwork and above all your unending patience!!! Thank you so much. You are amazing!

To my BFF, PA, personal cheerleader and bringer of chocolate, Varsi Appel, for moral support, confidence boosting and for reading my work more times than I have. I love you loads!

A huge thank you to all of my beta readers and cheering section! You guys are the best!

I'm always so happy to hear from you so do email or message me :)

emmavleech@orange.fr

To my husband Pat and my family … For always being proud of me.

Table of Contents

Family Trees

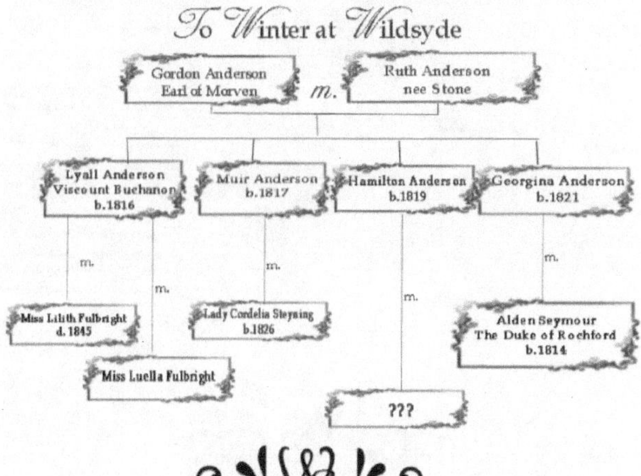

HOUSE OF BEDWIN

To Dare a Duke

Robert Adolphus
Duke of Bedwin
m.
Prunella Adolphus
nee Chuffington-Smythe

Lady Elizabeth
b.1815

Jules
Marquess of Blackstone
b.1819

Lady Victoria
b.1825

Lord Harry
b.1833

Lady Charlotte
b.1817

Lady Rosamund
b.1823

m.

Lord Frederick
b.1827

Lady Octavia
b.1838

m.

m.

m.

m.

Mr. Barnaby Godwin

m.

Cassius Cadogan
Viscount Oakley
b.1815

Sebastian Fox
Viscount Hargreaves

Agatha de Montluc

Miss Selina Davenport

Nicolas Alexandre
Demarteau

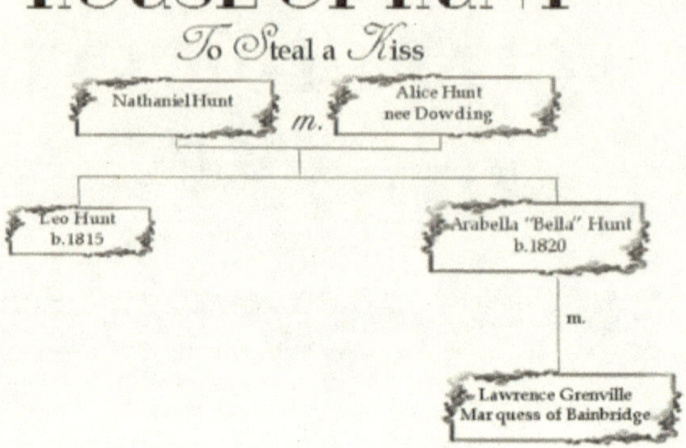
HOUSE OF HUNT
To Steal a Kiss
Nathaniel Hunt
m.
Alice Hunt
nee Dowding
Leo Hunt
b.1815
Arabella "Bella" Hunt
b.1820
m.
Lawrence Grenville
Marquess of Bainbridge

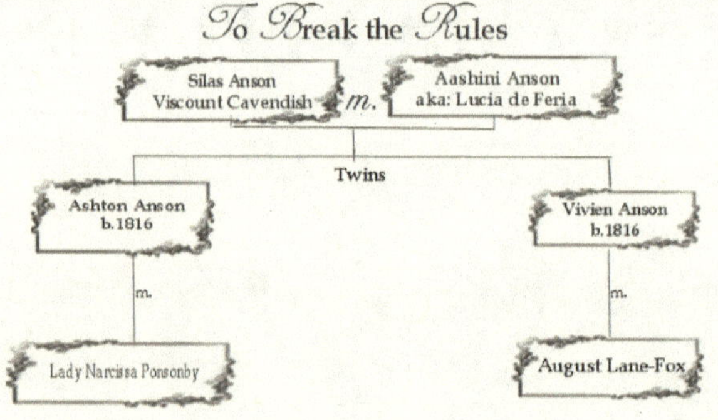
HOUSE OF CAVENDISH
To Break the Rules
Silas Anson
Viscount Cavendish
m.
Aashini Anson
aka: Lucia de Feria
Twins
Ashton Anson
b.1816
Vivien Anson
b.1816
m.
m.
Lady Narcissa Ponsonby
August Lane-Fox

HOUSE OF TREVICK

To Follow her Heart

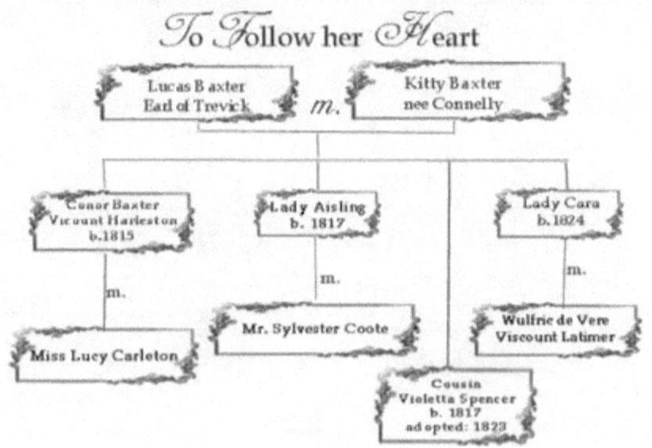

HOUSE OF ST CLAIR

To Wager with Love

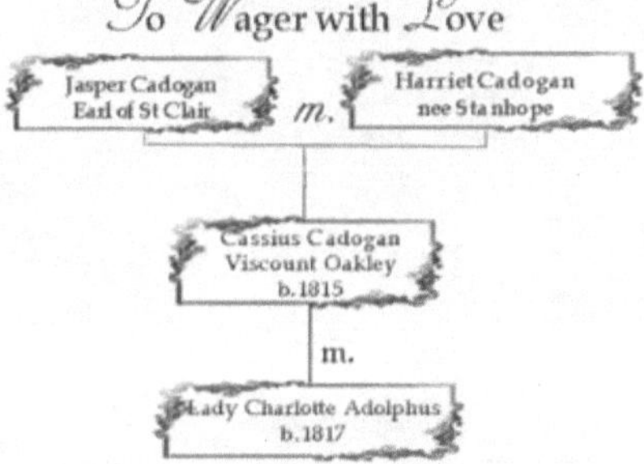

HOUSE OF CADOGAN

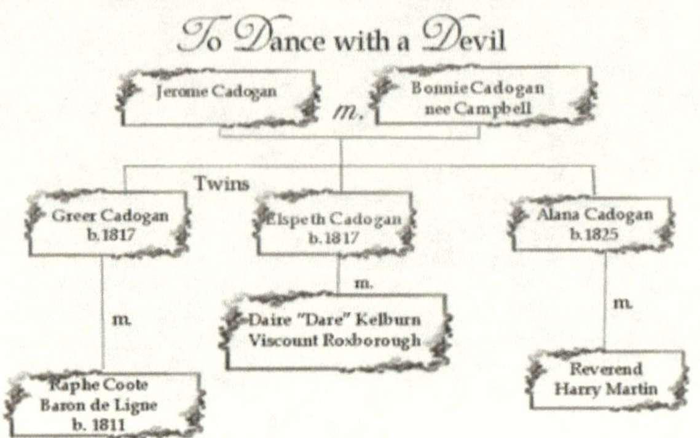

HOUSE OF DE BEAUVOIR

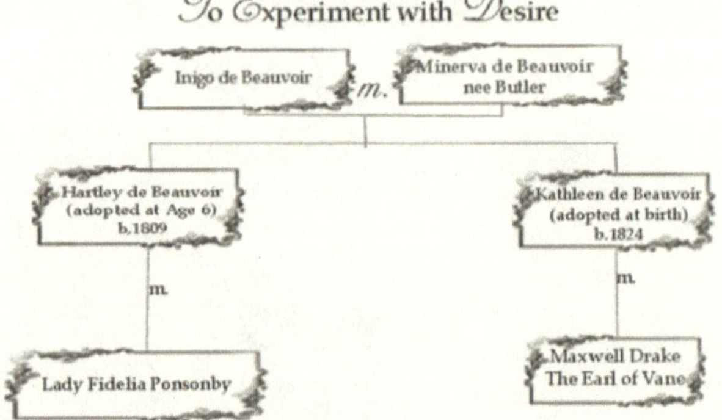

HOUSE OF ROTHBORN

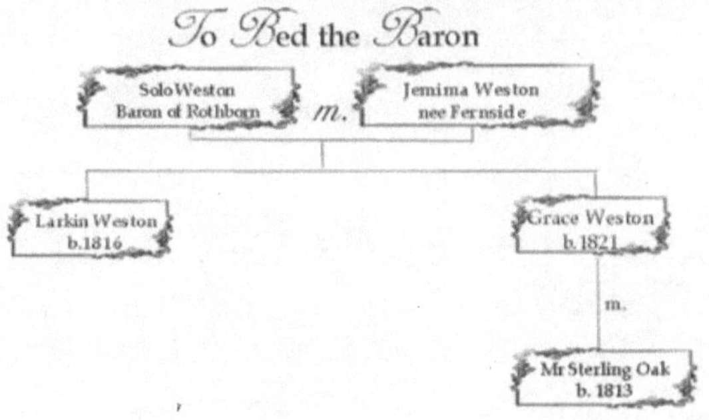

HOUSE OF KNIGHT

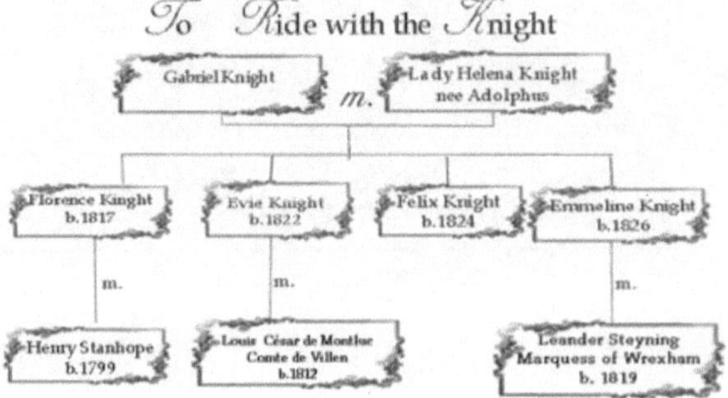

HOUSE OF MONTAGU

To Hunt the Hunter

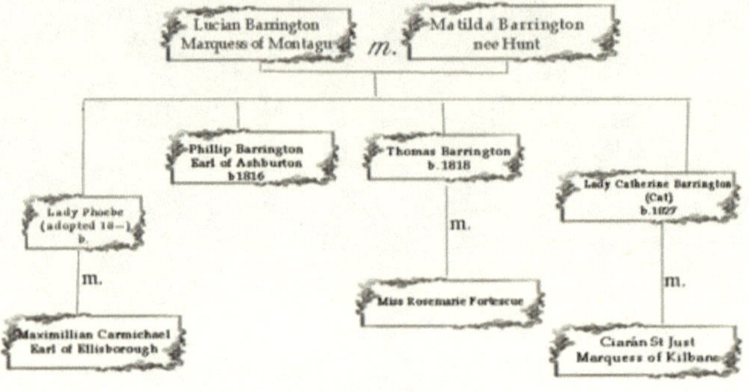

HOUSE OF ELLISBOROUGH

To Dance until Dawn

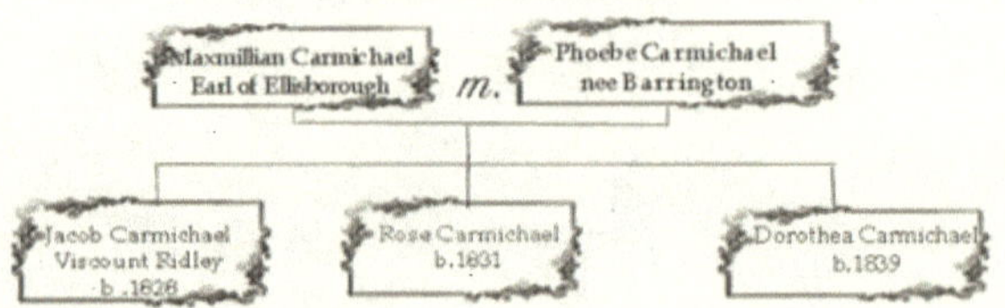

Prologue

Angus,

I've decided to buy that wretched hovel of a public house, the one on the corner of Argyll Square. See to it, will you?

—Excerpt of a letter from The Hon'ble Hamilton Anderson to his secretary, Mr Angus Stewart.

22nd April 1850, Cambridgeshire, England.

Clara looked about at the small stack of boxes and sighed. It had not taken her long to oversee the packing up of their home. Many thought the Reverend Halliday's lack of worldly goods showed what a spiritual man he was, concerned more with his duty than his own comfort. Sadly, Clara knew it was more that her father was a miserly muck worm. Muttering under her breath, she scolded herself soundly for thinking such an uncharitable thought, though that did not make it any the less true. As a small girl whose mother had died before Clara had a chance to remember her, she had believed much of her father's teachings. That had not lasted long. The trouble was, Clara was no fool, and one would have to be such a poor creature not to realise that the things the Reverend Halliday said and the things he did were quite separate entities. He was, in short, a hypocrite, and possibly the least Christian man she knew.

Still, today marked the beginning of a new adventure, and one Clara was looking forward to, though with some trepidation. She had longed to get away from the tiny village of Thorney. It was a quaint and quietly prosperous place where nothing ever happened, and she thought she might actually go mad if she lived the rest of her days there. So, when her father was given the church in Wick, it truly had seemed to Clara like a gift from the Almighty and the answer to her prayers.

According to her father, between Wick, the town that straddled the River Wick and extended all along the bay, and Pultney town on the Southside of the river, there were forty-five public houses. It was said that five hundred gallons of whisky was consumed in a single day, in Wick alone. Clara was well used to her father's view on the demon drink, though in this light, his predictions that they would find Wick to be a town sunk in depravity and vice did not seem wholly implausible. Clara could not visualise five hundred gallons of whisky or begin to consider how much one man could stomach on his own, but it seemed to be rather an excessive amount. Yet Wick was a place where things happened, where there was life and people and… *men.*

Clara did not blush at the rather unmaidenly thought, for she was made of sterner stuff than that. Vicars' daughters might have a missish and unworldly reputation, but she hardly felt she could be accused of that. Perhaps she had been sheltered, perhaps she had not seen much of the world outside of Thorney Village, but she had read a good deal, and she considered herself ready to take on whatever challenges life threw at her. Most of all, however, she intended to find herself a husband and get out of her father's house. This was her own mission, and a challenge it was, for her father viewed her as the perfect housekeeper and secretary, unpaid and duty-bound to do his bidding. She feared he would never give her consent to marry, not unless he gained by it. So, either she found someone who could do her father some good financially or in the church, or she married without his blessing.

Clara found she did not much mind which course of action presented itself, so long as one of them did. She needed a man. More than that, she needed a good, moral man of strong character, who meant what he said and did some good in the world, a man she could esteem for being everything her father was not. He ought to be generous with his time and charitable, kind and patient, educated and softly spoken. She pictured in her mind's eye a teacher, a tall, slender fellow, probably with glasses and a shy smile. He would read to her and ask her advice; he would admire her for her no-nonsense manner and encourage her to pursue her own ambitions, whatever they may be. Naturally, then he would sprout wings and fly about the town, scattering diamonds as he went, she thought sourly.

Her mythical beloved vanished like a soap bubble and Clara brought herself back to the here and now. There were things to be done, problems to be solved, one of which was currently hiding under the stairs. Checking that her father was still out in the front garden, lecturing the driver who was about to take them to the train station, Clara hurried along the corridor.

"Jimmy?" she whispered, before opening the door a crack.

A small boy of indeterminate age, but who she guessed to be of roughly nine years, peered up at her. "Is it time?" he asked, his eyes glittering in the gloomy cupboard.

"Nearly," she told him. "Now, are you quite sure, Jimmy? You're taking an awful risk, you do know that?"

"No, I ain't," he said stoutly. "I goes where you go. You're the only one who ever gave a tinker's—"

"Jimmy," Clara said, her tone warning him she would not tolerate his coarse language.

"Sorry, miss," he said, though she could hear the grin behind the words. "But you're the only one who's ever been kind, and you need looking after as much as I do, I reckon. 'Tis a wicked place you're going to, I heard the vicar say so. I know about living in wicked places and you don't."

Clara smiled, touched that the boy thought to take care of her. He was a kind soul, and though she knew it was wrong to smuggle him to Scotland with her, she feared what might become of him if he was left all alone. For he was quite correct, no one cared about Jimmy but her. He had arrived in the village one morning, having smuggled himself on the back of a carriage after having narrowly escaped a beating in the Seven Dials of London where he hailed from. He might have received another from the local boys if Clara had not stepped in and saved him. She had considered paying to send him to school, but he'd looked so terrified by the idea and sounded so determined in his assertion that he would run away and follow her to Scotland, that she could only believe him.

When her father had discovered Jimmy in the house, he told her the boy must be sent straight back to London, the kindly soul that he was. Clara had agreed meekly, pretended to do just that, and hidden Jimmy in the cellar.

"You have the sandwiches I packed?" she asked him now, wishing she could think of a better method to get him all the way to Scotland.

"Yes, I didn't even eat one. Not even a nibble," he said proudly.

Clara smiled at that. "And the money, just in case?"

"Yes, and I won't spend it unless I really have to," he promised, his narrow face grave with the responsibility of a sum he'd never seen in his life before.

"Good lad. Now once we're gone, the driver will come to collect our belongings and take them to Wick. Remember, we are stopping off to visit my uncle, so you'll get there a day before us. Do you remember what to do?"

"Yes, miss. Go to the church and hide there until you come and find me. And you paid the driver to take me all the way to

Wick, didn't you, miss?" he asked, and it broke her heart to hear the slight trace of doubt in his voice. He found it hard to trust anyone, even her.

"I did indeed, and don't you let him tell you otherwise. I also gave him extra to feed you on the way. You tell him that if he turns up without you or if he doesn't treat you kindly, I shall take him straight to the magistrate and sue him for theft."

Jimmy's eyes went round at that pronouncement. "Coo, would you really?"

"I would," she told him firmly. "Hush now, my father is coming. Good luck, Jimmy dear. I shall see you in Scotland." Closing the door just as her father entered the corridor, she sent up a silent prayer that Jimmy would arrive without mishap.

She turned to face her father. He was a robust man with a rather too full figure that spoke of a sweet tooth, the one indulgence he seemed not to mind spending money on. Indeed, anything that added to his own comfort was generally found to be indispensable.

"Ah, Clara, there you are. Are you ready to go?" he asked, giving her a critical look up and down. "We don't want to miss the train."

"I am, Papa," she said, reaching for her bonnet and tying the ribbons under her chin.

Without looking back, she strode out of the neat little cottage that had been her home since the day she had been born and climbed into the carriage. Excitement flickered in her heart as she settled herself down on the seat. It was finally happening. *Something* was finally happening, and she was going to make the most of it.

Chapter 1

Dearest Aunt Mabel,

We arrived safely in Wick this morning and I have taken a moment from unpacking our belongings to dash off this note. I can promise you, Auntie, that the town does not resemble a pit of vice and no indignities to my person were perpetrated between the carriage and our front door. I do wish Papa had not frightened you so, but really, you must know by now what he's like when he gets excited. Indeed, on a bright spring morning, Wick was a bustling place full of life and vigour. Our new home is a four-storey town house, a delightful place, bright and airy and with marvellous views over the town and even a glimpse of the sea from my bedroom. I feel we shall be very happy here.

I will write again soon, but do not fret about us, my dear. All is well.

—Excerpt of a letter from Miss Clara Halliday to her Aunt Mabel Halliday.

1st May 1850, Wick, Caithness, Scotland.

"Are you quite sure, sir?" Angus Stewart gave Hamilton a questioning look.

It was a look Hamilton had grown used to in the five years his secretary had worked for him and gently suggested that he'd lost his damned mind. Still, he'd got that look when he'd bought the run-down distillery too and see how well that had turned out. His gut told him this place had the potential to be a gold mine, and it had not steered him wrong yet.

"Aye, quite sure," Hamilton agreed, though he had to admit the place was a diabolical mess. The stench of stale ale and piss was enough to strip the paint from the walls, not that it needed the help. "Get quotes in at once. We'll have the place stripped and made sound before it falls down. Then I'll turn it into the best place in Wick. Somewhere the quality can go, for there's all sorts coming here these days, ye ken."

"Aye, sir," Angus said with a sigh. He was a mild-mannered fellow in his early thirties, soft-spoken, with only a trace of a Scottish accent after having been educated in England. He'd returned to Scotland with his brother when their father died and it had been Hamilton's lucky day when he'd knocked on the door, looking for work. "Did you see the new vicar arrived this morning?"

"Vicar?" Hamilton turned and frowned at Angus. "Why on earth would I take note of that?"

"Well, he is a close neighbour, sir," Angus pointed out, before adding with a quick grin. "And he's brought his daughter with him."

Hamilton snorted. "Ach, now it makes sense. Ye are nae gonna try to marry me off again, Angus?"

Angus laughed and shook his head. "I would not do such a thing to the young lady, but Malcolm was quite taken with her. Not that I blame him, she's a lovely wee thing."

"Malcolm?" Hamilton said with a touch of annoyance, for Angus' younger brother was a pain in both their arses. "He's nae business looking at vicars' daughters. He's going to the devil,

Angus. Ye ken he'll lose his position if he keeps on as he is. I supposed he's spent all the money ye lent him on whoring and carousing by now?"

Angus coloured a little and looked rather mortified, which was all the answer Hamilton needed.

"Ye are a deal too kind," he said sternly. "And it's nae a kindness ye do him by it. Ye have a promising family of yer own to think of now that ye have given Mary a babe."

"I know," Angus said wretchedly. "Only, I can't seem to get through to him. He is still so furious with me for dragging us back to Scotland, but we could not afford to remain in London. He misses the life we led there, though. He thought himself quite the man of fashion, you see. I believe he had ambitions to marry up. That's why I hoped if perhaps he formed a tendre for a young lady of worth, a sensible young woman, for she looked to be—"

"A vicar's daughter? *Sensible?"* Hamilton repeated sceptically. "She'll have seen nae more of the world than a church mouse and will be in nae state to deal with the likes of Malcolm. Ye keep him away. I'll nae have that kind of trouble on my doorstep, ye hear me?"

"Yes, sir," Angus said at once. "I'll see to it."

"Aye, ye will, or *I* will, and I promise ye, Malcolm winnae thank ye for that," he added, flashing a grin that was known throughout Wick to be one that promised devilry to follow.

"Are you quite sure, Papa?" Clara asked doubtfully. "It's just after everything you've said, it seems a little odd that you think it is safe for me to walk through the town unescorted."

"You are doing the Lord's work, Clara. *He* will protect you," the reverend said, not looking up from the sermon he was working on.

"Yes," Clara said, striving for patience. "I have no doubt of that, but a little practical, not to mention earthly protection—at least to my reputation—might not be such a bad thing, might it?"

"You worry for your reputation when there are souls to be saved?" the reverend said irritably, setting his pen down with an impatient sigh. "Clara, I thought you were above such foolishness. As my daughter doing God's work, all will recognise you to be above reproach. Reverend Thomson has made my name known in this town, and no one will dare to trouble you. Besides, you are not some society miss aspiring to make an advantageous match. Are you now?" he added sternly.

Clara avoided his eye, adopting a penitent stance with her gaze downcast. "No, Papa."

"Well, then. If you have ceased talking nonsense, pray do as I have asked you and take the pamphlets down to the boys' academy at once."

"Yes, Papa."

Clara left the study and returned to the kitchens where Mrs Macready was waiting for her. The vicarage's housekeeper was an older lady, small and pleasantly rounded, with pink cheeks and faded blue eyes. Clara had taken to her at once and been pleased to discover Mrs Macready equally charmed. She had not yet dared to push her luck far enough to explain about Jimmy, but she hoped the lady might be an ally there too. For the moment, Jimmy was ensconced in one of the disused outbuildings. He had arrived with the money Clara had given him—and handed it proudly back to her—and had suffered no ills on his long journey to Wick. Indeed, he seemed to have viewed it as a grand adventure and was in high spirits. As a boy used to sleeping rough, the little makeshift room she had created for him was a fine place indeed, but when spring and summer turned to autumn and winter, the poor fellow would freeze to death.

"Well?" Mrs Macready said expectantly as Clara walked into the kitchen, a cosy place that smelled of shortbread and seemed to always have a kettle boiling.

"God will protect me," Clara replied with a smile.

"Well, of all the daft," Mrs Macready began, only to turn pinker than usual and stammer an apology. "I do beg yer pardon, Miss Halliday—"

"Oh, please don't," Clara said cheerfully. "I'm quite used to my father's ways, I assure you and it is no more than I expected. I never had a chaperone in Thorney, you know. I'm quite used to going about alone. Pray do not trouble yourself on my account. In truth, I'm sure he's correct. I don't doubt everyone does know I'm the new vicar's daughter and that will be protection enough."

Mrs Macready looked doubtful and shook her head. "Perhaps I ought to go with ye," she said fretfully.

"Indeed, you will not. You have enough to do as it is without babysitting me," Clara said at once, finding she did not wish for the lady's company as she explored the town.

"Ye will nay go down to the harbour then, Miss. 'Tis a rough place. Sailors and fishermen and the like," she added, pressing her lips together in a disapproving line.

"I promise I shall not," Clara agreed easily, as Mrs Macready helped her into her cloak. Once her bonnet was in place and she had pulled on her gloves, Clara gathered the pamphlets her father had given her about the evils of drinking. "Even though I walk through the valley of the shadow of death—" Clara intoned solemnly.

Mrs Macready choked, shocked into laughter. "Stop that! 'Tis a sight too close to blasphemy for comfort, ye wicked creature."

Clara grinned at her. "Sorry. I couldn't resist. I'll be back before you know it," she added, closing the kitchen door behind her.

Hurrying through the back garden, Clara glanced over her shoulder to make sure Mrs Macready wasn't watching and tapped on the door of the small outbuilding. "Jimmy? It's me."

The door opened and Jimmy's freckled face peered out at her. "Here," she said, handing him a small parcel containing three currant buns and a wrinkled apple. "I'm certain Mrs Macready thinks I have a most unnatural appetite," she added ruefully.

"Well, me belly thinks me throat's been cut, so I don't care about that," Jimmy said frankly, biting into the bun with relish.

"You wretched creature, don't make out like you're starving when I gave you all that mutton pie last night," she said with a laugh. "You'll get no sympathy here, my lad. Not when you eat like a starved elephant."

"What's a heliphant?" he demanded, wrinkling his nose.

"A huge creature the size of a house," Clara told him. "I've a picture of one in a book somewhere. If I find it, I shall show you. Now tuck yourself back inside for now. Later on, we shall go on a little walk about the town, but I have an errand to run now."

"In the town?" Jimmy demanded.

"Yes. And no, you may not go with me, not this time," she told him.

"But, miss—"

"Later, Jimmy. I'm quite safe and do not need a knight in shining armour just now. Eat your breakfast and practise your letters or I shan't take you later either."

"Yes, miss," he said sulkily, before closing the door on her.

Clara let out a breath of relief. Though she knew a respectable young woman should never walk alone in a town, no matter her father's opinion, she could not deny a little thrill of excitement at the prospect. Walking alone in the little village she had grown up in had been quite unexceptional, mostly because there was nowhere to go and few people to socialise with. Here, though…

Picking up her pace, Clara walked briskly, following the directions her father had given her and looking about her with interest. The buildings were rugged and handsome, using the local Caithness sandstone, and the streets laid out in a grid pattern that made it relatively easy to navigate. Rather to her discomfort, people noted her progress as she walked, staring unashamedly, and the busier the streets grew, the bolder the interest. In Thorney, everyone knew everyone's business, but everyone made a pretence of not being the least interested in what their neighbours were up to. Though many of the friendly greetings and nods from the people of the town might gladden her heart, they also put her into something of a quandary about how to respond, for it was strictly forbidden for a young woman to acknowledge someone she had not been introduced to. Though Clara's upbringing had been sheltered, she had been well versed by the matrons of the village who had taken her under their wings in the ways in which a young lady comported herself in society. In their opinion, the vicar was ill-equipped to raise a proper young lady, and they had been quite correct. However, this was Wick, not Mayfair, and the place in which she was to make her home.

Having decided on her own course of action, as she generally did, Clara acknowledged the greetings from the ladies with an inclination of her head and a polite 'good morning' and ignored those from the men, for surely they ought to know better than to expect her to reply.

Having made her way to the boys' academy without incident, Clara knocked on the door and waited. After a protracted wait, the door swung open as if snatched, and Clara caught her breath. Before her stood the embodiment of her daydream. Tall and slender, with the look of a consumptive poet, the man regarded her with as much astonishment as she did him. What had at first glance appeared to be a look of deep irritation died on his face, and pushing his spectacles up his nose, the fellow hurriedly smoothed his tousled black hair.

"M-Miss Halliday," he stammered, in a voice far more English than she had expected, with only a trace of a Scottish accent.

"You have me at a disadvantage, sir," she said, once she could find her tongue again.

He laughed at that, and then hurriedly arranged his face into something a little more serious. "I beg your pardon, I am Malcolm Stewart, teacher here at the academy. It's only that everyone has been gossiping about the Reverend Halliday, and I was fortunate enough to glimpse you for myself yesterday at the moment of your arrival. I have been much in demand to recount what the beautiful Miss Halliday looks like, I assure you."

Clara opened and closed her mouth, uncertain of how to respond to this gallantry. On the one hand, she had never been called beautiful by a man she had only just met, which was rather gratifying, though she knew finding pleasure in such a thing was wicked of her. On the other, that people were gossiping about her made her feel like a goldfish in a bowl, though it was only what she'd expected. Deciding she had best ignore what was certainly flirtation—for the moment—she returned what she hoped was a friendly smile and held up the pamphlets.

"My father asked me to deliver these to you, to give to the boys."

Mr Stewart looked at them with a frown. Taking the stack from her hand, he perused the small, closely printed sheets.

She thought perhaps his lips twitched, though she could not fathom why. Admittedly, she privately thought her father's rather grandiose style of prose was entirely the wrong tack to take when warning people of the evils of drink, but she was not about to admit to that. She thought it wrong of Mr Stewart not to hide his opinion better, though.

When he looked up, there was a twinkle in his eye. "You understand, Miss Halliday, that I teach boys between the ages of six and twelve? They're mostly barely literate and, though there is a deal of wickedness in the creatures, I do not think they have yet succumbed to drink."

Miss Halliday regarded him, wondering if he was trying to be amusing to entertain her, or if he was simply a little dim. Deciding to err on the side of caution, she smiled and replied gently, "I rather think he hoped the children would give the pamphlets to their parents."

Mr Stewart coloured, pink cresting his high cheekbones, which answered her question. A shame. Though on closer inspection he looked heavy-eyed, as if he had slept little or badly for some time. Giving him the benefit of the doubt, for he did not look to be properly awake yet, she spoke rapidly to disperse his embarrassment.

"My father will give a lecture in the church hall on the subject on Friday evening at six. There will be posters going up around the town but perhaps you could relay the information to your class."

"Of course," he said at once, gathering himself.

"Thank you," Clara replied, before bidding him a good morning. She turned and walked away, content that her mission had been accomplished and determined to have a better look at the town. The High Street was a narrow, crooked street on the north side of the river and Clara was much struck by the number of shops selling far more luxurious goods than she had expected.

Indeed, the town seemed to be very prosperous. There were no shortage of dressmakers and tailors, milliners and the like, and she spent a happy half an hour window shopping and wondering how far she could make her meagre allowance stretch. The delicious aroma coming from the bakery was irresistible, and since her father wouldn't scold her for spending money on cakes and biscuits, as long as he got to eat most of them, she treated them all to something for their tea.

All in all, Clara decided she was well pleased with Wick, and felt certain that her new life would bring her much to look forward to.

Chapter 2

Lyall,

Thank you kindly for the invitation to young Gordy's birthday. I'd love to come and celebrate but I have not the time to spare for the moment. I have just bought a public house, and I intend to have it up and running by the autumn. Please give the bairns a kiss from their favourite uncle, and I hope the parcel that accompanies this letter will soften the blow of my absence a wee bit.

—Excerpt of a letter from The Hon'ble Hamilton Anderson to his elder brother, The Right Hon'ble, Lyall Anderson, The Viscount Buchanan.

5th May 1850, Wick, Caithness, Scotland.

"But whatever are we to do with him?" Mrs Macready said, staring at Jimmy as though he'd sprouted horns and a tail.

"Well, that is a dilemma, I admit," Clara said, praying she had not ill judged the depths of the lady's kindness. "But you must see that I could not abandon him to his fate."

Jimmy clung tightly to her hand, doing a grand job of making himself look pathetic and in dire need of charity. Though he was in need of kindness, Jimmy was not in the least pathetic and Clara recognised his demeanour as a wonderful piece of theatre on his part, for which she did not blame him in the least.

“Oh, yes, indeed… the poor bairn,” Mrs Macready said, her hand resting over her ample bosom in the vicinity of her tender heart. “But without the reverend’s say so,” she murmured, her agitation plain.

“There’s not in the least need for my father to know of it,” Clara said firmly. “Jimmy will be a grand help to you. He’s a hard worker and can fetch and carry and see to the fire, and all he asks in return is a warm, safe place to sleep, and his meals.”

“Is he clean?” Mrs Macready said sceptically. “I dinnae hold with grubby boys in my kitchen.”

Jimmy darted Clara a look of sheer panic, which was entirely genuine.

“He may need a little encouragement in that area,” Clara admitted. “But I am certain that will be a small price to pay in return for your kindness.” She gave Jimmy a long, stern look, and he subsided with a heavy sigh.

“Well, I could nae very well turn the laddie out when he’s come so far,” Mrs Macready said. “Very well. Jimmy stays, but he’ll mind me, or he’ll be sorry,” she said, wagging her finger at him, though the twinkle in her eyes made it plain she was not about to beat him with a rolling pin.

“I will, missus,” Jimmy said solemnly.

“Ach, and he’s all skin and bones,” the lady tsked, shaking her head. “Ye cannae work when ye have nae a scrap of fat between ye and the sky. Sit yerself down there and I’ll make ye a bite of breakfast, how’s that?”

Jimmy’s face lit up like Christmas morning and he wasted no time in planting his backside where Mrs Macready pointed. “That sounds like a grand idea,” he said, grinning happily.

“Ah, well, ye are a good fellow, I reckon.” Mrs Macready ruffled his hair and then grimaced slightly, wiping her hand on her apron. “Aye, well, one thing at a time,” she said with a sigh, and set about clattering pots and pans.

Satisfied that she had left her charge in excellent hands, Clara went back upstairs to hear the not uncommon sound of her father’s voice raised in anger. Wondering what had set him off, she went to the study to find him shaking his fist at something or someone outside the window. As his study faced onto the street, Clara moved to stand beside him, twitching the net curtain aside and seeing nothing to cause such outrage.

“Whatever is the matter, Papa?” she asked, turning to regard his flushed face with concern. “You will give yourself an apoplexy if you keep this up. Now, come and sit down. Mrs Macready has just put the kettle on, and I shall bring you a nice cup of tea, only do tell me first what has put you in such a pelter.”

“That… That devil!” he cried, shaking his fist again as she guided him firmly from the window. “And on my very doorstep! It’s a challenge, I tell you, and if he thinks I shall shy away, that I shall not face Satan himself and—”

“Goodness me, Papa! Which devil are you speaking of and what on earth is he guilty of doing?” Clara asked, more curious than dismayed.

“Mr Hamilton Anderson,” her father said wrathfully. “He’s not only at the heart of all the wickedness in this town, what with his supplying half the whisky that’s downed in this sinful place, but now… now he’s had the temerity to buy the public house just across the street there. I can see it from this very window! Drunkenness and licentiousness on my very doorstep, where my own innocent child could look out of her bedroom window and—”

“My window looks out onto the back garden, Papa,” Clara said calmly, too used to her father’s passionate outbursts to be overly alarmed by them. "And I cannot help but doubt that the man has done it expressly to annoy you."

"That just shows the nature of your tender heart," he said mournfully, allowing himself to be manoeuvred into a chair. "But don't you fret, my daughter. Despite his wealth and power, I shall rout the demon from his lair. I shall chase him out of Wick as good always vanquishes evil." Clara sighed inwardly, recognising at once the beginning of a sermon that might go on all afternoon if she let him work himself up again. "'And we know that for those who love God all things work together for good, for those who are called according to his purpose.' Romans eight, verse twenty-eight. And—"

Before he could take a breath and really get going, Clara patted his arm and said cheerfully, "Papa, please don't preach to me, for I am not the wicked man and have done nothing to vex you, not yet at least. Now, I shall fetch you a nice cup of tea. Would you like a slice of Mrs Macready's shortbread? She made a new batch this morning."

Her father glared at her with reproach. "I shall not be distracted from my duty by sugar biscuits, child," he said with indignation.

"No, Papa," Clara replied with a smile. "But I cannot help but think vanquishing demons is easier when one isn't peckish, and you've had nothing since lunchtime."

Huffing but amused despite himself, her father shooed her away with a last-minute admonition to bring a plate of biscuits, not just one if she really expected such tactics to work.

Clara returned to the kitchens, where Jimmy was making heroic progress through a plate of bacon, eggs and sausages that might even have defeated her father. Plucking the kettle from the range where it was boiling, she sloshed a little hot water into the teapot to warm it and turned to Mrs Macready.

"What do you know of Hamilton Anderson, Mrs Macready?"

"Mr Anderson?" Mrs Macready said, looking a little startled. Rather to Clara's surprise, the lady blushed and seemed somewhat flustered. "Oh, well, a charming rogue that one is. If ye winnae mind me giving ye a wee bit of advice, ye would do well to stay clear of him. There's many a lassie in these parts lost her heart to the dreadful creature."

"Really?" Clara said, instantly intrigued by this information. "Do you mean to say he trifles with their affections?"

"Oh!" Mrs Macready looked rather shocked by this and shook her head. "Nae, I dinnae mean to say anything of that sort, leastways, not that I ever heard of. It's only he has such a way about him. It's hard to explain, only, when he talks to ye, he… well, he has a voice like mellow honey and it's like ye are the only woman in the world and—" Mrs Macready blushed a deeper shade of pink and subsided into confusion, saying brusquely, "Well, he's a handsome fellow too, ye ken."

"My father seems to think he's the devil incarnate," Clara said, emptying the teapot before adding the tea leaves, turning her back on Mrs Macready to give the lady a moment to gather her scattered wits. Whoever this Mr Anderson was, he certainly seemed to be a dangerous fellow, if even a sensible woman of Mrs Macready's age could melt into a puddle of goo at the very mention of him. "As if it isn't bad enough, what with his business supplying whisky to the town, but now it seems he has bought the public house over the road too. Papa seems to think drunken orgies will go on in the street at all hours."

"Miss Halliday!" the lady said in shocked tones, covering Jimmy's ears. "Ye must nae say such things, especially before the wee laddie."

Privately, Clara suspected Jimmy's harsh upbringing had given him a sight more information about such goings on than she had herself, for her notions of what such a wicked gathering might involve were a little vague. Still, she apologised most sincerely and promised not to speak of it again.

Jimmy looked from Mrs Macready to Clara in confusion. "What's that?"

"Nothing, love," Clara said. "Eat up, or you'll upset Mrs Macready."

Jimmy flashed a grin that showed he had no intention of upsetting such a splendid cook and dove back in.

"Has he really bought the Fisherman's Retreat? Well, that's nae a bad thing if ye ask me. It was a dreadful place," Mrs Macready said, having got over her shock. She curled her lip at the thought of the last landlord. "I heard how as old Mr Brown was packing it in, and not before time in my opinion, but that was only a day or two ago. That laddie moves fast, I'll give him that," she said, and Clara detected a note of admiration in her voice.

"So, do you think my father is wrong to want to drive him from the town?" Clara asked, tugging a cosy around the teapot while it brewed.

"Drive him out!" Mrs Macready said in alarm, almost dropping the china bowl she'd just taken down from a shelf. She gave a crack of startled laughter and then covered her mouth with her hand. "I beg your pardon. How unladylike of me, I cannae think what came over me. Only the idea of the reverend… Oh dear. Dear me. If ye will forgive me for saying so, I ken the reverend has the best of intentions, and I am right behind him in believing there is a deal too much ungodliness and drinking in the town. Something must certainly be done, but I would advise him to stay clear of Mr Anderson."

"Why?" Clara asked suspiciously. "Do you think he would cause my father trouble?"

Mrs Macready pursed her lips, apparently searching for a diplomatic way of replying. "Lassie, if anyone succeeded in driving Hamilton Anderson from Wick, there would be a riot in the town, for he's the fellow everyone here looks to. He's popular and admired, and powerful too. And if a riot dinnae bring him back, *Himself* would come, and Lord, then we'd see fireworks."

Clara was about to ask who *Himself* was, but the bell rang, and Clara looked up to see the irritable jangle hailed from the study and was her father wanting his tea and shortbread.

"I'd best take this up to him," she said with a sigh, pouring the tea and arranging a generous selection of shortbread biscuits on a plate. On her way up the stairs, she reflected on all she had learned about the wicked Mr Anderson and admitted herself more than a little curious to meet the fellow in the flesh.

♡♧◇♤

"Christ," Hamilton said in disgust as he stared down at the crumpled heap snoring in the alley behind the Drovers where he'd been drinking.

He'd had a skinful himself, for the manager of his distillery had just become a father for the fifth time, finally a boy. The fellow had been so happy and excited, and so keen for Hamilton to share in his joy, he'd not had the heart to leave before the proud father had thoroughly wet the baby's head. He'd not seen Malcolm inside; he rarely spent time this side of the river, preferring Pultney town for his bad behaviour, but the place had been filled to the rafters so he may have avoided notice. However, for Angus' sake, Hamilton did not want the people of the town seeing the boys' schoolteacher howling drunk and out cold in the gutter.

"Up ye come, ye roaster. I've a good mind to toss ye into the river and have done with ye," he grumbled, grimacing as the stench of stale perfume wafted from his clothes and confirmed the kind of night the man had spent. Hamilton hauled the fellow to his feet, giving his face a couple of firm slaps. "Wake up, or I shall send ye to the devil and let him have the trouble of ye."

Malcolm groaned and swatted lethargically at Hamilton's hand. "Stop that, wassa trouble?"

"Ye are the trouble," Hamilton told him firmly and anchored an arm around his waist as he part carried, part dragged the fellow along the street. He was halfway to the academy where Malcolm's lodgings were when Angus appeared, his kindly face careworn and anxious. He'd clearly been out hunting for his troublesome sibling.

"Oh, dear," he said, hurrying forward to share Hamilton's burden.

"Aye," Hamilton said sourly. "I'd have put it a wee bit stronger than that, but the sentiment is close enough."

Between them, they carried Malcolm to the school, got him inside, and put him to bed.

"He'll be in no state to teach the bairns tomorrow," Hamilton said, raking a hand through his hair.

"No," Angus said, shaking his head. "Lord, what am I to do? I cannot afford for him to lose this position. If the children go home or get into mischief, it's bound to be reported."

Hamilton sighed, knowing that Angus, kind-hearted fellow that he was, would kill himself working two jobs if that was the only way to support his reprobate sibling. "Ach, I'll call in on the laddies in the morning. Reckon I can deal with them for an hour or two."

Angus stared at him as if he'd suggested he take holy orders. Hamilton bristled a little. "What? I'm nae an eejit. I went to university in Edinburgh, did I nae?"

"Oh, it's n-not that!" Angus said at once, colouring. "I… I just… You would do that for Malcolm?"

"Nae, I widnae do it for that sorry excuse for a man!" Hamilton said in disgust. "I'll do it for ye and for the bairns, though, just this once, mind. But they deserve a teacher, do they nae?"

"Yes. Yes, indeed they do and… and that's terribly decent of you, sir. Truly, I—"

"Stow it," Hamilton said irritably. "I'm away to my bed. I'm like to have a heid on me in the morning and I need my beauty sleep if I'm to face a schoolroom full of grubby boys."

"Yes, sir," Angus said, grinning, and clearly entertained by the notion. Shaking his head and wondering what on earth he'd just volunteered for, Hamilton wended his way home.

Chapter 3

Miss Halliday,

I beg you will forgive me for being so forward as to write to you in person. I only wished to ask, as I have not the courage to present myself to your father without an introduction, would you care to take a walk to the Old Man of Wick with me? That is to say, to the old castle ruins. It is a beautiful spot with spectacular views out to sea. I should be so pleased to show it to you, and perhaps give you a tour of our little town, such as it is. I beg your forgiveness for approaching you in such a way, but the truth is, I've thought of nothing but your lovely face since the moment you arrived on my doorstep.

—Excerpt of a letter from Mr Malcolm Stewart to Miss Clara Halliday.

5th May 1850, Wick, Caithness, Scotland.

Clara stared at the carefully penned note that Mrs Macready had handed her that morning with a disapproving sniff. Apparently, a boy from the school had delivered it the day before and Mrs Macready had spent the interval fretting about whether or not to give it to her.

"I ken the young have different ways than in my day, but I cannae think it right and proper that he send ye notes in such a way," the lady said sternly.

"No, Mrs Macready, I must say I agree with you," Clara admitted, though there was still a wicked part of her thrilled to have received such a note from a handsome young man. She had, after all, come here with her own agenda, and that was to find a husband. Malcolm Stewart was everything she had asked for, and he was a schoolteacher, too! That he had been thinking of her *lovely face* ever since their meeting was not an idea that dismayed her, either. Though it might be shallow, she was not beyond enjoying a little flattery. "What do you know of him? Is he well thought of?"

"Well, I cannae say," Mrs Macready said with a frown. "He's a quiet fellow and disnae mix much, but he seems pleasant. Polite," she added, though her tone was not exactly enthusiastic. "His brother is a nice fellow."

"I see," Clara replied, a little disappointed but not discouraged by this less than vibrant accolade. "Well, I shall go to the school and tell him to his face that he must not write such letters to me. If he wishes to further a friendship with me, he must present himself to my father," she said firmly, aware she was being just a little untruthful, for she was also taking it as an excuse to see the fellow again. If she were sensible, she would simply ignore the letter and pretend she never received it, but she doubted that course of action would end up with her getting married anytime soon. *Needs must when the devil drives*, she told herself, with a little thrill at the idea of doing something her father would certainly disapprove of.

He was not the only one, apparently.

"Oh, aye?" Mrs Macready said, folding her arms and giving Clara a look that suggested she had not been born yesterday.

"Well, I can hardly write back to him to tell me it is improper to write to me, now, can I?" Clara said reasonably.

Mrs Macready snorted and turned her attention back to the pastry she was rolling. "Whit's fur ye'll no go by ye," she said cryptically.

"I beg your pardon?" Clara said in confusion.

The lady clicked her tongue and lifted the rolling pin, wagging it at her. "If the fellow is fer ye, it'll work out. There's nae need for a pretty lassie like yerself to go a chasing him."

"But I'm doing nothing of the sort!" Clara retorted, stung by the implication but unable to hide a blush.

"Hmph," Mrs Macready said, and would not say another word on the subject.

It was with some trepidation that Clara approached the school, aware that Mrs Macready was not entirely mistaken in what she'd said. Certainly, if her father discovered either the letter or her visit, she would be in the suds. She had timed her arrival to just after the morning's lessons had ended and was almost knocked flat by a sudden rush of schoolboys as they ran down the road, forcing her to flatten herself against the wall to get out of the way.

"Mind where you are going, boys!" she called after them, to which not a one turned a hair. Shaking her head, she carried on up to the school to find the door ajar.

"Mr Stewart?" she called, knocking softly on the door.

No one answered and so she poked her head around the door, pushing it open a little wider. It opened onto a long corridor, with a classroom door on either side. One was closed, the other wide open, and showed a room filled with small desks and chairs. At the head of the classroom, in front of a large slate fixed to the wall, was an adult sized desk, at which was sprawled the figure of a man.

It was not Malcolm Stewart.

Clara took an involuntary step backwards, aware of a sudden prickling sensation up her spine. She had the most peculiar sensation of having disturbed a sleeping tiger. Steeling herself, she told herself not to be so fanciful. It was only a man, after all, though in fairness, he was like no man she had ever encountered before. Long, muscular legs crooked around the legs of the chair, the bare knees dusted with golden brown hair, quite visible from beneath the line of his kilt. Never having seen such a powerful young man's bare legs before, this sight was enough to render Clara speechless. Then her eyes drifted to his arms, which were crossed on the desk in front of him, serving as a pillow. He was in his shirtsleeves, which was shocking enough, but he'd rolled them past his elbows, displaying muscular forearms every bit as hairy as his legs. Clara gaped, a wash of heat flaring in her cheeks. But then he groaned, a deep, rumbling sound of distress that made all the hairs on the back of her neck stand on end. Despite herself, Clara gave a little squeal of alarm and was about to turn tail when the fellow's eyes flicked open and stared right at her.

He blinked. Then he closed his eyes and opened them again, and with what looked to be considerable effort, peeled his face from his arms.

"I beg yer pardon," he said thickly, pushing to his feet. He shoved at his hair, which was an untidy thicket of deep brown and gold, and only succeeding in making matters worse. "Can I help ye? Miss…?"

"Miss Halliday," Clara said, relieved to find she had not stammered when her heart was performing the most peculiar dance in her chest. A little voice was shrilling in her mind. It said, *run, run. Run!* For reasons best left unknown, she did not.

"Halliday?" he repeated, his rather bleary expression sharpening a little as he looked her over, interest flickering in his eyes, which were an unusual tawny shade, close to amber. He pushed to his feet and Clara took another step back, watching him warily. "I dinnae bite, lassie," he said, flashing a grin that showed strong white teeth.

"I never thought otherwise," she replied, annoyed with herself for having allowed her nerves to show.

"Ye are the vicar's daughter, then?" he said, leaning back against the edge of the desk and regarding her with open appreciation.

His gaze was direct, making Clara feel suddenly that she had gone out without putting her corset on, which was ridiculous. She knew she was wearing it because she had clearly laced it far too tightly. That would account for the fact she could not find a proper breath, she was certain. However, the man was insolent and ill-mannered. To find him sleeping in the children's classroom was bad enough, but he was barely dressed, and the way he looked at her! Quite shocking. Quite invigorating, too.

"I am, sir. I came to speak with Mr Stewart, but as I see he is not here, I shall leave you to your nap." She inclined her head and turned to leave.

"Nae, I was looking after the bairns for him as he's, er… indisposed. What were ye wanting with Mr Stewart?" he demanded, a curious glint in his eyes.

Clara swallowed, well aware the truth would do her no favours. Crossing her fingers within the folds of her skirts, she asked God to forgive her the lie and promised to make amends. "My father gave him some leaflets for the children. He asked me to discover if they had all been given out."

"Leaflets?" he repeated and then reached for one of the same upon his desk. "Oh, aye. I gave them out this morning. I'm nae sure what good they'll do, mind."

Clara had to admit she wasn't certain either, not when written in her father's condescending tone, at any rate. How many of the children's parents were literate was something her father had not considered either. She wasn't about to tell him that, though. "Well, it's easy to criticise and do nothing at all, I suppose," she said tartly, rather despising herself for her manner, but really, the man was clearly a reprobate. "If you will excuse me."

"Ach, dinnae run away so fast," he said, crossing the room to her. "We have nae been introduced."

"You, sir, are in no fit state to be introduced to a lady," she retorted.

He grinned again, and there was something about that charmingly wicked curve of his lips that was terribly endearing. It would be the easiest thing in the world to be charmed by him, but then he added, "Ah, snooty, are ye? That's a pity."

Clara stared at him in outrage, all the allure she had found in his smile vanishing at his words. "I am nothing of the sort," she said, shocked by the accusation. In truth, she ought to have turned and walked away the moment she laid eyes on him. No, worse than that, she ought never to have entered the building in the first place. This, then, was her punishment for misbehaving.

"Ye are, though," he said, folding his arms and leaning against the doorjamb. "Or perhaps ye are just a coward. Are ye too well bred to cross swords with me?"

"You sir, are rude, ill-mannered and… and quite outrageous." Much to her dismay, he laughed at that, and rubbed the back of his neck, his expression rueful.

"Aye, happens ye are right enough. Forgive me, lassie. I have the very devil of a heid, and a morning spent with those wee miscreants has nae helped a bit."

"You are a teacher?" she exclaimed, so shocked by this that she could not help the depths of her surprise show through. She could not for the life of her see this man as a teacher. A blacksmith perhaps, or wielding a broadsword at the battle of Culloden… *that*, she could imagine, but a teacher?

His eyes flickered. "And why not?" he asked, challenge in that warm, mellow voice, one tawny eyebrow quirking.

Clara swallowed. "I'm sure it's no business of mine what your profession is, sir," she blurted, and hurried from the room.

To her chagrin, he followed her.

"Ah, ye *are* a coward," he said, the satisfaction in his voice making her stop in his tracks. "I thought so."

Clara swung around, narrowing her eyes at him. "Why are you deliberately trying to provoke me?" she demanded, her breath catching when he took a step closer. Too close.

His voice lowered, so deep and dangerous it made her suddenly aware of her own skin, of the places where her clothing touched her. "Because ye are the prettiest sight I ever saw on waking and because yer eyes flash like diamonds when ye are vexed, and I dinnae want ye to run away too fast,"

Clara blinked, too breathless to speak, well aware she ought to be running away like the devil was at her heels, and finding she was rooted to the spot.

"They're grey," he observed, staring into her eyes with such intensity Clara could not help but return his gaze. His eyes were not just amber, she noted, but gold and bronze and copper and quite mesmerising. "Yer eyes are full of storm clouds, Miss Halliday. I reckon ye have a temper, have ye nae?"

"I am considered to be a perfectly placid and even-tempered creature," she retorted, putting up her chin.

"Liar," he said, flashing her that wicked grin again.

"How dare you!" she replied, glaring at him.

He only laughed, shaking his head. "Nae, dinnae fash. I like a lassie with spirit. I'm nae interested in these milk and water misses that agree with a fellow nae matter how daft he is."

"Oh, I'm so relieved you approve of me, sir. For your good opinion was all that was missing from my life," Clara said hotly, and then blushed, appalled at how rude she was being. "I beg your pardon," she said, immediately contrite.

"Nae, dinnae stop now, ye were just getting the hang of it," he said, winking at her.

Clara had the sudden childish desire to stamp her foot. She resisted. "You are the most… most…"

"Aggravating?" he suggested.

"Certainly that," she said furiously.

He grimaced suddenly a ran a hand through his hair. "Aye, I reckon ye are right enough. I suppose I owe ye an apology. Forgive me, Miss Halliday, I'm afraid I am nae at my best for my head is clanging and ye surprised me out of my wits – out of good behaviour anyway. But ye did well to give me a proper scolding, good on ye lassie."

Clara glared at him, refusing to be charmed by the rueful and far too endearing smile he sent her. "Good day to you, sir," she said, and turned on her heel, stalking away and wondering if he was so lost to propriety, he would follow her out of the school in such a state of undress. She was almost at the end of the road before she turned to check. The door to the school was closed, and she glanced at the window to the classroom, jolting as she saw him standing there, watching her.

"Oh!" Clara muttered, irritated that he'd seen her looking back. Now the odious man would think she was hoping he had followed her. Putting her chin in the air, she stalked off, determined that if she ever saw the vexing man ever again, she would not give him the time of day.

Chapter 4

Hamilton,

Will I see you tonight? You are always so busy of late, I fear you have forgotten me. Is there someone else? Come to me, darling. I am tired and bored and need you to cheer me up.

—Excerpt of a letter from Mrs Moyra Scott to The Hon'ble Hamilton Anderson.

8th May 1850, Wick, Caithness, Scotland.

"Look, Mrs Macready, that's my name," Jimmy said, holding up the piece of paper he'd been practising on.

"So it is! Ye are a clever laddie," the lady said with approval. "What else can ye write?"

Clara watched with pride as Jimmy ducked his head, carefully forming the letters of the simple words she had taught him over the past week. Mrs Macready had found him some clean clothes that her daughter-in-law had been about to donate to the church, and he looked very well in them. Though it had taken some persuading, Jimmy had also given in to the need to wash himself daily, though he still thought a bath once a week was an excessive punishment. Regular meals had already taken some of the gaunt, hollowed out look from his face and he looked pink-cheeked and healthy in the kitchen's warmth.

They both applauded and exclaimed over the surprisingly neat handwriting that Jimmy showed them, and Clara decided she'd not mention the back-to-front *d* on dog just now for he looked so pleased with himself. Clara set him to the task of illustrating the words he'd written and got to her feet, leaving the table to help Mrs Macready.

"I heard the reverend shouting this morning," Mrs Macready said in an undertone as Clara fetched the tray to lay out the meal being prepared for her father's lunch.

He was working on Sunday's sermon, and it did not seem to be going well, for he had asked for his lunch to be brought to the study.

"I know," Clara said with a sigh. "Please don't mind it. I'm afraid all the builders coming and going and the noise from the work over the road is making him rather tetchy."

That was an understatement. Though her father was prone to fits of ill temper, she had known nothing to get under his skin the way the renovation of the public house opposite was doing. He truly seemed to believe it was being done to spite him, that the devil was waving a red flag at him, goading him for the fun of it. He'd had several run-ins with the builders already, and Clara feared what might happen if the owner of the dreadful place ever dared show his face here.

"Aye, when I took him his tea this morning, I tried to suggest that it maybe wisnae a bad thing that place was being improved, that perhaps the clientele might be a wee bit more respectable than before. It wisnae well received," Mrs Macready said ruefully.

"Oh dear. I'm so sorry. I do hope he wasn't dreadfully rude to you," Clara said, horrified that her father might have insulted the poor lady.

"Ach, I am nae so feeble as to wither in the face of a few harsh words," Mrs Macready said stoutly. "But I cannae help but think it is nae good for him to get himself up tae high doh like that."

"I'm sure you are right," Clara said with a sigh. "I'll speak to him and see if I can't make him see sense. Here, give me the tray and I'll take it up."

Mrs Macready looked so relieved by this that Clara's worst fears were confirmed. The last thing she needed was to lose such a wonderful housekeeper, not to mention her only friend and ally. She must speak to her father about his rudeness before things got out of hand.

Hefting the tray, Clara carried it carefully up the stairs, setting it down to open her father's study door, before taking it inside to him.

"Here you are, Papa. Mrs Macready had made a splendid lunch for you, not that you deserve it after being so rude to her."

Her father set down his pen with such a clatter it splattered ink over the page he'd been working on. Scowling at it and then at Clara, she realised he was in no state to listen to anything she had to say. She would have to keep her mouth shut and wait until he was in a more receptive mood. If she kept on, she would only provoke him into sermonising at her and she did not think she could stomach that. He was not the kind of man who could endure an argument, or an exchange of ideas. If she had the audacity to disagree with him, he would just shout her down, not giving her the chance to speak or explain. Unbidden, the handsome face of the aggravating devil she had met at the school some days earlier came back to her and she smiled. He, at least, had not thought it wrong of her to speak her mind. Not that she was about to take such an ill-mannered fellow as that as a model for good behaviour, she told herself hastily and put him out of her mind again.

She had put him out of her mind several times since that day, but somehow, he always crept back in again. Vexing, odious man.

"I do not need you, Clara, to comment upon my behaviour when you have no notion of what you speak. Mrs Macready was ill-informed and is clearly prone to being led into wickedness by a lackadaisical and too tolerant view of the dreadful behaviour that is far too common in this godforsaken town."

"Surely it cannot be godforsaken, Papa. You are here," Clara said, counselling herself not to let her father goad her into losing her temper. "And I cannot agree that Mrs Macready is in any way lackadaisical."

"Really? I only hope her housekeeping is better than her moral judgement, for where one is lacking, surely the other must—"

"Your steak and kidney pie is getting cold," Clara said, strongly tempted to tell him to get his own lunch if Mrs Macready's efforts were not to his liking.

"Oh."

Clara watched dispassionately as her father quickly cleared a space on his desk so she could set the tray down in front of him. The aroma was quite delicious, and Clara had been looking forward to her own serving. Now she was so annoyed and out of sorts, she felt certain it would stick in her throat. "Bon appétit," she said, forcing herself to smile at him before she left the room.

She closed the door and let out a breath. That he believed kindly Mrs Macready was the one who needed moral guidance was one that made her question how, or more importantly *why*, her father had ever taken holy orders. Of course she knew the reason. As the third son, his choice had been the law or the church. When she was at her most uncharitable—now, for instance—she suspected her father had chosen the church because law had seemed rather too much like hard work. It was certainly not because he'd been called by God. Indeed, she sometimes wondered if her father actually believed in God, or if he really paid attention to the words he repeated by rote from the Bible. *Love thy neighbour*, for example, was one he seemed to be having a good deal of trouble with.

Frustrated by the situation, Clara went to the front door and stepped outside. She was not wearing a coat or hat and had no intention of leaving the premises, but she needed a breath of fresh air. Leaning against the front door, she looked across the street to where the sound of hammering and cheery whistling was coming from the open windows. The Fisherman's Retreat was a large building and a handsome one, though clearly in a state of some disrepair. The rotten windows had already been removed and several new ones put back in. To Clara, it looked a little as if the building was being woken up after many years asleep. The windows glinted like bright eyes, viewing this new stage in its life with interest and approval.

Clara tried to see the property from her father's point of view. Vast quantities of liquor were consumed in this town every day, and here was another public house, ready to supply the men with yet more whisky to throw down their necks. As she understood it, the fishermen were the worst culprits. The herring trade was booming and, when the men got paid, it was done in the taverns, as there was nowhere comfortable for such dealings by the harbour. So there they were, with their earnings in hand and temptation right before them. How much of that money ever got back to their wives and children, she wondered. She knew the men's lives were hard and dangerous at sea, and it was not surprising they needed to let off steam when back on dry land, but not at the expense of those who depended on them, surely? Yet if her father had made friends with the owner, if he tried to get to know and understand those men who lost themselves in drink, if he tried to extend a hand to them instead of lecturing them with such a lack of empathy… surely that would reap more rewards?

She could almost hear Mrs Macready murmuring 'more flies with honey than vinegar,' and wondered if a similar sentiment was one she had spoken aloud. If so, Clara could well imagine her father's reaction to it. He certainly preferred the fire-and-brimstone approach to leading his flock. Clara had seen often enough the expressions on some of those churchgoers faces after he'd been in a particularly vile mood, for his disposition certainly influenced his sermons.

Sometimes it had been all she could do not to go to some white-faced new mother or a sensitive boy and tell them not to listen to his harsh words and fear they were destined to burn in hell, not to take his judgemental views to heart, for her father was just a man like any other, flawed and full of opinions he did not need to share with the world but felt obliged to do so. Sometimes she was so constricted by the desperate desire to act, to speak up, she felt as though she were caught in a vice.

Yet, if she spoke, his attention would fall upon her, and she could not escape his ill temper once the sermon was over. On the occasions when she defied or challenged him, once he had grown tired of his own voice in proving to her why it was she was wrong—without ever listening to anything she had to say—she was treated to days of sulking, clipped answers to any questions she posed, and the house became so thick with tension that she feared it might smother her. Clara was honest enough to admit she was too cowardly to face that more often than she did already, too afraid to fight everyone else's battles for them as well as her own.

The afternoon was bright, though there was a swift chill wind blowing in off the sea, but Clara relished it, sucking in deep lungfuls of air as if they might cleanse her of the frustrated anger that simmered beneath her skin. She was so tired of this feeling of impotence, of never being able to act, to speak her mind. Once more, the wicked fellow at the school appeared in her mind's eye, provoking her and urging her to row with him. Never in her life had she met such a man. Though she had little experience with the opposite sex, they had all seemed as one in valuing a woman who was demure and softly spoken, who dropped her gaze if asked a direct question, who had no opinions past agreeing with the gentleman beside her.

Clara sighed and walked to the large camellia bush that filled most of the tiny entrance before the house. Gaudy red flowers were blooming there, exotic and bold in the environs of a town like Wick. Clara reached for one, stroking the silken petals gently.

"I always loved camellias, but ye cast the poor wee flowers in the shade, Miss Halliday."

Jolting, Clara dropped her hand as the deep voice startled her back to her senses. As if she'd conjured him with her thoughts just a moment before, the dreadful man from the school stood staring at her. This time at least he was neatly turned out—and fully dressed—his thick hair brushed into some kind of order, though the wind tugged at it playfully.

To her dismay, Clara could not think of a single retort to this, and it took her a moment to decide if the remark flattered or annoyed her. Both, she admitted ruefully, staring at the handsome stranger before darting a nervous glance at her father's study window. She thought they were just out of sight here, if he was still at his desk.

"What are you doing here?" she asked, intending the question to be tart and regretting the breathless way it sounded.

"Just passing by," he said, leaning against the railing that divided their tiny front garden from the street. "And what are ye doing here, staring at the flowers with such a dejected expression? Has someone upset ye, lassie? Do ye need me to thump someone for ye?"

Clara was so shocked and startled by this offer that she gave a choked laugh. "Indeed, I do not!" she replied, gazing at him in wonder. Would he really do such a thing for her if she asked it of him?

His lips quirked in a smile at her obvious outrage, but the smile dimmed, and he looked at her again. "But ye are out of sorts, I think? Is there aught amiss? I imagine it's hard to settle into a new place where ye have nae kin about ye?"

Clara frowned a little. She could hardly tell a complete stranger her troubles, though there was a warm, inviting glint in his eyes that made her believe he would listen if she were foolish enough to do such a dreadful thing. It was far harder than she could have guessed to hold her tongue.

His gaze remained on her, studying her with an intensity that made her stomach feel rather odd, all fluttery and uncertain.

"I reckon being the daughter of a vicar is nae an easy job either. Do ye ever get to laugh, Miss Halliday? Do ye dance and sing and get out to parties now and then?"

Clara bit her lip, knowing she should tell him not to be so impudent, for it was none of his business. But there was genuine interest in his eyes that teased away her usual reserve, inviting her to confide in him when she knew very well she ought not. "I sing in church," she said with a soft huff of laughter. "And… And sometimes in the kitchen, if there's no one around."

"And what about laughter and dancing?" he asked, his voice soft now, cajoling as he leaned on the railing. Without realising she was doing so, Clara leaned closer to him, her head inclined towards him in a manner that made their conversation seem intimate. Though she knew it was wrong, she was quite unable to make herself step back.

"I laugh," she said, a little defiantly. "I laugh with Mrs Macready."

"Ach, well, there's a lady born for laughter. She's a great gun, is Mrs Macready, a fine cook too, aye? Ye eat well, I reckon."

"We do," Clara replied, out of reason charmed by his approval of her only friend.

"And do ye dance?"

Clara shook her head.

"Not even in the kitchen when no one is by?" he teased softly. "Holding a broom in ye arms and dreaming of Prince Charming, aye?"

"Certainly not," she replied, blushing at the very idea.

"Does the reverend nae approve of dancing?" The question was grave, as if such a thing would be a terrible sin in his book. He looked so earnestly disapproving it chased away the wicked irreverence of his previous behaviour and made him seem a sensible man, one that would be a kind friend if she let him.

Clara considered this. "It's not that he disapproves of dancing exactly, he… he just doesn't like me dancing."

"Why?" he asked baldly, clearly perplexed by this reply. Clara heartily wished she had not told him what she had. She could not for the life of her understand why she had spoken so frankly. There was something about the man that invited you to tell him secrets, to put your trust in him, which was undoubtedly the stupidest thing a woman could do. There was something a little piratical about him, something wild and untameable, something she would do well to keep far away from.

"Ye are wool gathering, Miss Halliday," he chided her, a rueful curve to his lips. "Which is nae very flattering when I am giving ye my undivided attention."

Clara avoided his gaze. "I beg your pardon. I ought never… I should not be speaking to you," she said helplessly, glancing back at the study window again.

He noticed the glance and frowned a little, serious once more. "He widnae like it, I reckon?"

"Indeed, he would not," she said, laughing at that understatement.

"I hear he disnae like a good deal about our town. The builders have been made to feel like they are working for Satan himself, so I'm told."

"He is most upset about the renovations to the Fisherman's Retreat," Clara agreed. "He is determined to stop the excessive drinking in the town, and so the renovation of a public house on his very doorstep has been seen as something of a challenge, I fear."

"Wants to stop it, does he?"

Clara nodded, wondering if this man was involved with the project himself.

"I'd like to see him try," he said with a snort.

"Oh, I'm afraid you will. There's no question of that," Clara said ruefully. "And you are quite correct, he believes the owner, Mr Hamilton Anderson, is Satan made flesh. He intends to make him repent his sins or run him from the town."

The man's eyes widened at that, and he made a choked sound which he turned into a cough, but she suspected the idea amused him as much as it had Mrs Macready.

"Does he, then?" he replied, rubbing his hand over his mouth. "Well, I'm afraid he's in for a wee bit of a disappointment. There's nothing that will stop the work, and Mr Anderson will open his business the moment it is ready. He's going nowhere."

"Oh," Clara said in dismay. "Do you know Mr Anderson well?"

"Aye, lassie," he said, chuckling. "Very well."

Clara gazed at him, a slight shiver running over her skin at the way he rolled the 'r' in 'very.' His eyes glinted in the sunlight, shimmering bronze and copper catching her attention. Realising she was staring, Clara forced herself to look away.

"What kind of man is he?" she asked curiously. "I asked Mrs Macready, and she seemed to like him, though she told me I ought to stay away from him. He's… He's got a way with the ladies, I believe?"

"Has he now?" the man replied, his eyes twinkling. "Well, he is a handsome fellow, ye ken."

"That's what Mrs Macready said," Clara replied, frowning. "Though she gave me the impression it was his voice that charmed people." She almost added that *mellow honey* had been the description and that it made a woman feel as if she were the only one in the world, but that would have been a breach of confidence, so she held her tongue.

He leaned closer, the faint scent of something warm and spicy reaching Clara's senses, making her want to lean closer herself so she might breathe it in. "If the fellow has the least bit of sense, he will do all in his power to charm you, that much I do know. You'd best be on your guard around him," he said, a warm, teasing note to his voice.

His words made her heart thud rather too quickly. Forcing herself to straighten and get the conversation back on track, she tried to sound businesslike, though she felt rather odd, somewhat flustered and not quite sure of herself.

"Well, if you know the gentleman well, perhaps you could ask him if… if he would try to find a way to make peace with my father before things get confrontational."

"Do ye reckon that's possible?" he asked with interest. "In my experience, a fellow who has taken another in such deep dislike before he's even met him is nae in a reasonable state of mind."

Clara sighed, seeing the sense in this at once. She shook her head. "No. I don't suppose it is possible. Only it seems that Mr Anderson is a very popular man, and a powerful one. I should dearly love for them to come to terms. I like it here, you see, and I've not yet had the chance to make any friends and… and good heavens, why on earth am I telling you all this?" she demanded, blushing as she realised how terribly indiscreet she was being.

"Because ye like it here, and ye have nae had the chance to make a friend, except for Mrs Macready. And for me," he added gently.

"You, sir, are not my friend," she said, forcing herself to put some distance between them, to dispel the feeling of intimacy, of having found a confidant that had been growing out of all proportion. She might not have any experience with men, but surely, she knew better than to allow herself to be so easily beguiled.

"Aye, lassie, I am," he said, straightening. "Whether or nae ye are mine. If ye have need of me, ye need only ask, ye ken. I'll come running if ye call me."

"How can I? I don't even know your name," Clara retorted, folding her arms, though the thought that she could call on him if she were in need was strangely comforting.

Before he could reply, the front door opened, and Mrs Macready stuck her head out. "Well, bless me. Here ye are! I've been looking for ye all over the house. There'll be nae pie left for ye to eat if ye dinnae come soon, for Jimmy is outdoing himself. Oh! Mr Anderson, I beg yer pardon, sir. I did nae notice ye for a moment."

Clara gasped at the sound of his name, turning to stare accusingly at the devil who had failed to introduce himself to her properly. For good reason, it seemed. *"Mr Anderson?"* she repeated, unable to keep the annoyance from her voice, though in truth she was mortified rather than angry.

Oh, that would teach her to speak so unreservedly. What a fool she was for not realising at once.

He only smiled at her, a teasing note to his voice as he said just loud enough for her to hear. "Aye, lassie, the devil himself."

Too embarrassed and ashamed of herself to say another word, Clara turned away to hide her blushes and hurried back into the house.

"Oh, dear," Mrs Macready said, stepping aside as Clara hurried past her. She turned back and narrowed her eyes at Hamilton. Pulling the front door gently closed, she crossed to the railings and wagged a finger at him. "What are ye up to, laddie? Why was Miss Halliday blushing scarlet, eh? I'll nae have ye using yer wiles and making the poor lassie fall head over ears for ye. Are there nae enough girls breaking their hearts for ye in this town?"

"Mrs Macready, ye make me sound like some kind of villain. A regular Casanova, and ye ken very well, that's nae true," Hamilton protested. "I'm never anything but friendly. 'Tis nae my fault they like the look of me, I swear it."

Though he felt a twinge of guilt as he reflected upon his conversation with Miss Halliday. He had teased her wickedly, and he *had* been flirting with her, which was not in the least bit sensible. Especially not as it seemed her father was ready to burn him at the stake for witchcraft or some such nonsense.

"Maybe aye, maybe no," Mrs Macready said, crossing her arms over her ample bosom and giving him a look that told him he'd have her to deal with if he trifled with Miss Halliday.

As he had not yet met the reverend, this was a far more concerning prospect.

"Ach, I widnae trifle with an innocent lassie. Ye ken me better than that." He held her gaze, watching as her pale blue eyes softened as he'd hoped they would.

"Aye. Reckon I do, but she's a lovely child with a kind heart. And she has a deal to put up with," she added darkly.

"He's nae a kindly da, I reckon," Hamilton said, jerking his chin in the direction of the study window.

Mrs Macready pursed her lips. "I'm nae a nashgab, ye ken."

Hamilton, who was well aware Mrs Macready could gossip with the best of them when the mood took her, nodded gravely. "Aye, I ken that very well, but I'm nae about to blether their business about the town. Just between ye and myself, aye?"

Mrs Macready considered him for a long moment, and then, as he had hoped, unburdened herself. "He's a regular bodach," she said in disgust. "I've nae had the keeping of them for much more than a week, but I ken the type well enough. He keeps that poor girl on a string, and I reckon he intends to keep her there, too. She's nae said as much, but I think he disnae mean to let her marry."

"Not let her marry? A bonnie lassie like that?" Hamilton said in astonishment.

"I reckon," Mrs Macready said grimly. "She needs to get out of this house, and if ye ask me, she kens that very well. Which is why ye must nae play games with her. She's like to take it seriously, and what with the reverend considering ye are the devil made flesh—"

"Aye, aye, I hear ye," Hamilton said crossly. Damn the miserable ill-willie. He had enjoyed both his conversations with Miss Halliday very much, but he knew better than to dally with innocent girls.

Mrs Macready was right, he'd do well to keep everything businesslike between them. It would be hard, though, for there was something about the girl that made him want to tease her, to break through that serious exterior and make her smile. Perhaps it would be best if he stayed away entirely. He certainly had no wish to cross swords with some crabbit old vicar who he'd be forced to be polite to. There was no fun in facing an opponent you could not fight with fists or insults.

"Unless ye are serious about her, that is?" Mrs Macready added, a thoughtful glint in her eyes that made the hairs on the back of Hamilton's neck stand on end.

"Dinnae start yer matchmaking on me, Freya Macready," he told her, pulling himself up to his full height. She was a tiny woman that he could likely lift with one hand, but somehow she had the ability to make him feel like a snotty boy when she chose. "I've nae intention of wedding a vicar's chit, so ye can just take that look off yer face right this minute."

Mrs Macready shrugged, a smug tilt to her mouth that made Hamilton feel a little queasy. "I'll nae lift a finger, so long as ye behave yerself. But ye cannae be running around with the likes of Mrs Scott forever, can ye now?"

To his frustration, Hamilton felt heat creeping up the back of his neck. "Haud yer wheesht," he said, glancing around to be certain no one was by. "What do ye ken about her?"

The smug look increased. "Only that she's yer mistress and has been this past three months or more. Ye dinnae think ye could keep something like that entirely quiet for long in a town like Wick, did ye?"

"Well, there's nae need to repeat it," he told her sternly. "Moyra is a good sort, a good friend, and if there's more to it than that, it's no one's business but our own, aye? We're both adults and she gets lonely now her husband's gone to his maker."

"Aye, and nae a moment too soon," Mrs Macready said sourly. "I dinnae begrudge the lady a bit of fun after living with that old miser, but there's plenty who would. Have a care, aye? Talk of that kind will do ye no favours, especially if the reverend is trying to stir up trouble for ye."

"Aye, ye are a wise woman, I ken very well. I'll think on it, aye?" he said, suddenly out of sorts and irritable and wanting to get as far from the vicarage as he could.

"I'll be seeing ye then," Mrs Macready said, straightening her immaculate apron and going back into the house.

Hamilton glowered at the shiny black front door for a long moment before muttering a curse under his breath and stalking away.

Chapter 5

Dear Miss Halliday,

How glad I am to discover another young woman of quality in this dreadful town. I left my card with Mrs Macready yesterday morning, and if it pleases you, I should be delighted to call upon you again today at three pm.

—Excerpt of a letter from Miss Jessie Fleming to Miss Clara Halliday.

18th May 1850, Wick, Caithness, Scotland.

"I'm afraid you must be terribly disappointed by our little town," Miss Fleming said with a sigh. "I cried when I came back from London."

Clara smiled at the young lady's sincerity but shook her head. "I've been here such a short time I've not had the opportunity to see much of the town, but I confess I was impressed by how many dress shops and milliners there were. I'm afraid I'm something of a country mouse so I was delighted by the variety and quality of everything on offer."

Miss Fleming pulled a face. "It's hardly the kind of thing you see in the magazines, though, is it?" she said, smoothing her hand over the lovely royal blue gown she wore. It was obviously the height of fashion, and the lady wore it with a black and white cashmere shawl that gave Clara a most unwelcome stab of envy. "This came from Paris," she added, preening a little.

"Really?" Clara replied, impressed as she was supposed to be. "It must have been dreadfully expensive," she said wistfully, which was rather indelicate, but she was too curious not to ask.

"Oh, it was," Miss Fleming said with satisfaction. "But Papa says if I am to catch a husband of suitable standing, I must be properly outfitted. It's truly the only thing he and Mama ever agree about," she said with a tinkling laugh.

"Well, it is very beautiful. The shawl too," Clara said truthfully, a little dejected to consider what a dowd she must look in this lovely creature's presence. Miss Fleming was a delicate blonde with wide blue eyes and looked as fragile and sweet as a china doll. In contrast, Clara had heavy, unmanageable thick brown hair, grey eyes, and a figure that leaned towards the voluptuous.

"Thank you. And your…" Miss Fleming hesitated, obviously thrown into confusion as she realised there was nothing she could compliment Clara upon.

Her dress was good quality but plain and a dull shade of green, for her father disapproved of bright colours. Taking pity on the poor girl's fiery cheeks and mortification, Clara hurriedly offered her another cup of tea.

"You were born in Wick, then?" she asked, hoping to move the conversation on.

"Oh, no. I was born in Hampshire. My mother's family are still there," she said, which explained the rather cut-glass English accent. "My father is Scottish, though, and his family's business is here. When my grandfather died, he forced us to return so he could be close at hand. I think my mother never forgave him that," she added with a brittle laugh. "I was twelve at the time. We've been here ever since, and I longed and longed for my first season. I was rather a success," she murmured, lowering her eyes modestly.

“I’m sure you must have been,” Clara said frankly. “You are quite lovely. The gentlemen must have been buzzing around you like bees around a honey pot.”

Miss Fleming blushed a little and grinned, her cheeks dimpling. “They were,” she admitted. “It was quite marvellous. I’d never had such attention before, for there are so few eligible men here.”

“There are some, though?” Clara asked, trying not to sound too curious to discover them.

“Oh, yes. But few.”

It was on the tip of Clara’s tongue to ask for names, but she controlled herself. The urge to ask if Mr Anderson was among them was even harder to resist, but she remained silent, hoping Miss Fleming might be a little more forthcoming. She had neither seen nor heard anything from the provoking man since she had discovered his true identity, and she was heartily glad of that fact. Another encounter could only be mortifying on her part, and she would not know whether to ignore him or berate him for teasing her so dreadfully.

Clara was to be disappointed if she wished for news of the wretched man, though, for Miss Fleming only launched into a description of her favourite beaus in London, of which there seemed to be a staggering number, when Clara heard her father’s study door slam. Both ladies jolted, and Clara’s heart dropped as the sound of the front door slamming quickly followed.

“Oh dear,” she murmured, pushing to her feet and hurrying to the window to see her father accosting two burly builders who were carrying an immense piece of polished wood. Clara realised at a glance, this must be the bar top, and the sight of it had sent her father into a fury. “I beg you will forgive me, Miss Fleming, but I must leave you for just a moment.”

Ignoring the young lady's look of incredulity, Clara ran from the room, finding Mrs Macready in the hallway, twisting her apron in her hands.

"Oh, I didnae ken whether or nae to fetch ye, Miss," she said wretchedly.

"I'll deal with it," Clara said firmly. "Only, please see to Miss Fleming, for I've abandoned her in a dreadfully ramshackle manner."

"At once, miss," Mrs Macready said, hurrying away.

Clara ran to the front door, snatching it open and then taking a moment to compose herself. She would be no good at diffusing the row if she was not calm.

Taking in the situation swiftly, she realised that the two men carrying the enormous worktop were straining under the weight of it. There was a backlog of carts carrying materials that had parked in front of the public house, and they'd been forced to carry the bar top quite a distance already. The thing was solid oak, three yards long and as thick as her arm. It clearly weighed a ton, and the two men were being impeded by her father berating them for going about their work. She could see their difficulty, for they did not dare put it down and risk scratching the gleaming, polished edge.

"I dinnae mean to be rude, Reverend, but ye must let us by ye afore we drop this," one man said breathlessly.

"It is God's will that the thing be cut up and used for divine purposes instead of an altar to the demon drink!" her father said, raising his fist and gazing at the sky above. "Father, forgive these wicked men, for they know not what they do."

"Oh, mercy me," Clara said helplessly, picking up her skirts and hurrying closer.

"It's just a work top," the other man protested, looking perplexed. "It's nae an altar of any kind. We dinnae sacrifice virgins in Wick, ye ken?"

"Papa!" Clara whispered urgently, taking her father's arm. "This kind of scene is unbecoming in a man of God. Surely, another tactic is called for."

"When they wave such instruments of the devil under my very nose?" her father raged. "Indeed, I have stayed silent long enough."

"Ye have nae been silent since the moment ye arrived," the first fellow said indignantly. "This is nae the first time ye have interfered with us, and we are just honest working men. I dinnae drink myself, ye ken, saving for a wee dram on special occasions, or if I'm feeling a bit chilled. I'm just earning my wages. Now, let us by, Reverend."

"I would be failing in my duty as the voice of God in this town if I did not make a stand and tell you that you have fallen. *Ye are empty of the Christ, whosoever of you that justify yourselves by the law; ye are fallen from grace* –Galatians five, verse four!"

"Papa!" Clara said, tugging at his arm. "Truly, this is not the way. Please let the men go about their work."

"Let go of me, child!" her father said urgently. "You do not understand that this is a war against evil, against the demon drink that has taken a hold of this town and—"

"And can I help ye, Reverend?" the cheerful voice cut through her father's rant and the relief on the men's faces was almost comical as Mr Anderson arrived on the scene.

"Who are you?" her father demanded suspiciously.

"I'm Hamilton Anderson, Reverend, and I'm pleased to make yer acquaintance at last. I hear we have riled ye up a wee bit. Jock, Hamish, what are ye doing standing about in the street carrying that? Get it inside now. Excuse me, Reverend, I widnae want ye to get crushed. 'Tis a heavy piece, that," Mr Anderson said, sounding most solicitous as he deftly manoeuvred her father from the road.

Her father was not a small man, but his bulk was mostly fat, and it was immediately clear that Mr Anderson could lift him from the men's path without breaking a sweat if he chose to do so. The reverend could do little other than bluster his indignation as Mr Anderson gently but firmly forced him from the road and the two men hefted the heavy piece of oak towards the building site.

"There, now. We can have a proper chat with them gone, aye?" Mr Anderson said cordially, though Clara saw the challenging glint in his eyes well enough.

"Sir! You are impudent. How dare you lay hands on a man of God?" the reverend demanded, glaring at Mr Anderson.

"I didnae lay hands on ye, only stopped ye getting yerself crushed by a heavy piece of wood. Jock and Hamish are fine strong lads, but they couldnae hold that piece forever, ye ken. At best, it would have flattened yer toes if they let it slip."

"Are you threatening me with violence, sir?"

Mr Anderson gave a choked laugh. "I am nae. I just told ye I got ye out the way afore ye were harmed. It's nae in my nature to go about beating up men of God, ye ken. Lord, big as I am, my ma would skelp me good if she heard I so much as raised my voice to ye. I promise ye are quite safe," he added with that charming grin that laid waste to so many ladies' sensibilities.

Clara told herself sternly that she was made of sterner stuff and was not among them.

With any other man, she did not doubt he could have cajoled them into a good-natured discussion and come to terms, but sadly her father was driven by forces Mr Anderson did not understand. Clara didn't either if she were honest, but there was no denying her father seemed to have discovered the thing that motivated him to work. Never before had she seen him so passionate about writing his sermons, staying up late into the night and rising early. Never before had she seen the light of religious fervour shining in his eyes as she did now, and it rather frightened her.

"No man, woman or child is safe from your influence," her father shouted furiously, squaring his shoulders. "Do you deny your distillery is the largest in the town? Do you deny that the men of Wick are nightly inebriated, out of their senses with strong liquor whilst their wives and children go hungry?"

"Just ye hold on a moment," Mr Anderson said, and while her father's voice got louder with rage, Mr Anderson's seemed to do the reverse, but there was no denying he was heard well enough. To Clara's eternal humiliation, many of the neighbours had come out to stand on the doorstep to watch the entertaining scene. "Aye, my distillery is the largest, but it's also the most expensive. Little of it is drunk in these parts, but sent to Edinburgh and England, and exported too. I dinnae hold the men down and pour the stuff down their throats, ye ken. Every man is free to choose his fate, and aye, there's a good many that would rather drink than pay their bills and buy shoes for their bairns, but ye would do well to speak to them and understand why that is. Life is hard, aye, and men have demons of their own to wrestle with. Surely a man of God ought to listen to their troubles and discover what he can do to help them rather than putting the blame on one man's shoulders. I'll nae be your scapegoat, Reverend Halliday, and ye had best understand that at once."

Despite herself, Clara could not help but regard Mr Anderson with something approaching admiration, for he had voiced sentiments that she had not dared speak aloud to her father. Not that it would do him a whit of good, she realised with a sinking heart.

"'For such men are false apostles, deceitful workmen, disguising themselves as apostles of Christ. And no wonder, for even Satan disguises himself as an angel of light. So, it is no surprise if his servants, also, disguise themselves as servants of righteousness. Their end will correspond to their deeds,'" Reverend Halliday said coldly. "You may deny your sins to your last breath, sir, but God knows all, sees all, and you will be judged."

With that, he turned and stalked away, leaving Clara standing in the street with half the neighbourhood all agog. She did not dare look at Mr Anderson, but kept her head down, and hurried after her father.

"Miss Halliday."

She winced at the sound of her name, knowing she could not cut him in front of everyone. Steeling her nerve, Clara straightened her spine and raised her head.

"Yes, Mr Anderson?"

"I'm sorry, lassie," he said, his expression one of contrition. "If I caused ye any embarrassment, I apologise unreservedly. It was nae my intention, ye ken. I was about to tell ye my name, I swear it, only I was enjoying our conversation and I didnae want ye to stop speaking to me."

"That's quite all right," Clara said stiffly, not daring to believe him. Mrs Macready had warned her once more to guard herself against Mr Anderson's coaxing ways, lest people should gossip about her being yet another lovelorn female who'd given her heart to the fellow.

"I'm sorry too that yer da holds me in such dislike. I spoke true, though. I ken well enough there are men who think of nothing but the drink, but it's nae my doing. I pity them and if I could help them, I would. They were drinking themselves stupid long before I bought the distillery, though, and they'd keep doing it even if I were to close the business this instant. Ye understand me?"

Clara nodded but was too worried about her father to continue the conversation, nevermind giving the neighbours more to gossip about. "If you would excuse me, Mr Anderson, I ought to see to the reverend—Oh, Miss Fleming!" she exclaimed, having entirely forgotten her guest in all the excitement. "I do beg your pardon. How can you forgive me for abandoning you so rudely?"

"Do not consider it for a moment, my dear Miss Halliday," the lady said gently. "Miss Macready fed me the most delicious shortbread and in truth I was rather entertained by the spectacle, for I confess we watched from the window," she admitted, casting a shy look at Mr Anderson.

"Miss Fleming, good day to ye," Mr Anderson said politely.

"Mr Anderson. I hope you are well?"

"Aye, I thank ye," Mr Anderson said, opening his mouth and turning to Clara once more.

"And your mother is well?" Miss Fleming interrupted.

"Aye, she's grand," he replied with a smile, taking a breath.

"And the earl?"

Clara gaped at Miss Fleming and then turned to stare at Mr Anderson. Good heavens. Did her father realise who he was setting himself up in opposition to? If the man's father was an earl, then he was no schoolteacher, no humble tradesman, though looking at him now, Clara could hardly conceive how she had believed either of those things for above a moment. He carried himself with pride and confidence, such an aura of power and self-assurance that, in hindsight, it seemed obvious.

"Aye, Himself is well, as are my brothers and their wives and the bairns. I thank ye kindly for your concern, Miss Fleming."

"Oh, I am so pleased to hear it. I saw your brother, Lord Buchanan, in town during the season, of course, and Lady Buchanan, such a charming creature, and quite dazzlingly lovely, of course. Oh, she wore the most gorgeous green gown to the Countess St Clair's new year ball that—"

"I do beg your pardon, Miss Fleming," Clara said desperately, torn between agitation and the strong desire to laugh at Mr Anderson's obvious fight for patience in the light of such chatter. "I'm afraid my father is rather out of sorts, and I must go to him and see if I cannot calm him down. If you will excuse me."

With that, and ignoring Mr Anderson's obvious vexation with her for leaving before he'd finished whatever it was he wished to say, Clara fled.

Chapter 6

Lyall,

I'll admit it pains me to write these words down for you to read, but I need your advice. We have a new vicar arrived in Wick, the Reverend Halliday. He seems to think I am personally responsible for all the ills of the town and is on a mission to drive the demon drink from here and me along with it. He's taken offence at the renovations I'm making at the Fisherman's Retreat and is making a habit of interfering with my workmen. I had two quit yesterday saying their wives had told them if they continued to work in Satan's pit of vice, they'd turn them out of doors. I can hear you laughing from here, and truth be told, I was not too worried at first, but from what I hear the women of the town are flocking to listen to him preach on a Sunday morning.

I've tried speaking with him – that did not go well. His daughter is far more sensible and seems to have her father's measure, but I do not know how much influence she holds over him. I believe she has tried speaking sense to him, but so far, to no avail. I reckon he means to make mischief for me, and I do not know how to deal with such an attack from a man of God.

If you have any sensible advice, I should be grateful to hear it.

—Excerpt of a letter from The Hon'ble Mr Hamilton Anderson to his elder brother, The Right Hon'ble Lyall Anderson, Viscount Buchanan.

27th May 1850, Wick, Caithness, Scotland.

"He's rather splendid, isn't he?" Miss Fleming said in a whisper as she regarded the Reverend Halliday in full flow as his voice rose to new heights. Her pretty mouth curved in a conspiratorial smile as she slanted a look at Clara.

Clara sighed, knowing she would need to make her father a posset to soothe his throat after such a fiery sermon in which he had worked himself into a passion of righteous anger. Ironic really, as the brew contained sack wine, a tipple the reverend seemed to see as a purely medicinal element in his diet.

Clara studied her new friend, wondering how to take such a comment.

"Oh, don't look so anxious," she said with a laugh behind her fan. "We can none of us help our parents. My father mortified me daily during the season, the poor dear. His manners are not at all what one would like, despite Mama's best efforts."

"You are a comfort to me," Clara admitted, her own lips twitching with relief that her new friend was not about to abandon her.

"It's you who is the comfort to me," Miss Fleming said staunchly. "You have no idea how lonely I was before you arrived. Will you walk into town with me tomorrow? I saw a dear little bonnet I simply must have. It's not from Paris, of course, and I should not be seen dead in it in London, but for Wick it will be quite charming."

"I should be delighted to," Clara said, though she was more occupied with noticing that the church was full to bursting, and a large part of the congregation were women. Her father's teachings were not falling on deaf ears. The positive response received by the talk he had given on arriving in Wick had gratified him. His confidence had been further boosted when he had been asked to repeat it twice more.

It seemed there was a temperance movement growing in the town, and Reverend Halliday was leading the charge. Clara could not say she disapproved, either. Though she had not seen the results of such overindulgence first hand, both Miss Fleming and Mrs Macready had told her a few hair-raising tales that proved to Clara that it truly was a problem that needed a solution. The trouble was, she rather feared her father's confrontational style would only end in disaster.

A discreet cough to her right made Clara look to the far side of the aisle to discover Mr Malcolm Stewart smiling at her. He mimed doffing his hat, making her smile in return until Miss Fleming tugged at her arm.

"If you will forgive me for doing so, you'd do well not to encourage Mr Stewart. He's a poor schoolteacher with not a penny to his name," she said with a little sniff. "Not at all the kind of fellow you should aspire to."

Thinking this a rather unchristian, not to say somewhat mercenary attitude, Clara said nothing, but did not look at Mr Stewart again. She did not wish for the people of Wick to speculate about her.

Finally, the service was over, and Clara and Miss Fleming walked arm-in-arm down the aisle.

"My ears are ringing," Miss Fleming said with a giggle, once they were out in the fresh air again and away from the throng gathered in front of the church. "Come, I shall walk back to the vicarage with you."

"Oh, but it's quite out of your way," Clara protested, glancing behind at the little maid who followed Miss Fleming everywhere.

"Nonsense, a brisk walk will do us the world of good and put roses in our cheeks, won't it, Abigail?" she said over her shoulder.

"Aye, Miss Fleming," the maid said in a resigned tone.

"There, you see? Come along," she said smugly.

"Well, only if you will stay and take a cup of tea with me before you leave," Clara said with a smile.

"I would be charmed to do so," Miss Fleming said at once, and they set off along the road to the vicarage.

The spring sunshine had deserted them this morning and a steely grey sky glowered overhead, threatening rain. Miss Fleming contrasted remarkably with the scenery around her, for the gown of gold velvet figured silk she wore glowed in the sombre light. She appeared to Clara's eye to be a shiny penny among a pocketful of tarnished coins. Though she was happy and grateful to have a friend of her own age and station, she could not help a little stab of envy at being always cast into the shade. Her own gown was a sensible light brown velvet. It was beautifully cut, and the dressmaker had named the fabric 'marron glacé' which sounded very well, but there was no escaping the fact it was brown.

Her father's voice echoed in her ears for her envy, intoning 'Galatians five, verse twenty-six.'

Sighing, she slipped her arm through Miss Fleming's. "Must you always look so beautiful? It's very trying on a girl's moral fibre."

Miss Fleming replied with her tinkling laugh and cast an amused and rather gratified look at Clara. “Silly goose, whatever do you mean?”

“‘Let us not become conceited, provoking and envying each other,’” Clara recited, in a fair imitation of her father’s grandiose style of speaking. “I’m supposed to be a model Christian, you understand, and here I am, wanting to scratch your eyes out for wearing that gorgeous dress when I’m all in brown.”

Miss Fleming looked her over with a critical eye. “I have the loveliest yellow gown which I will give to you. I’m afraid it's last year's fashion but you won’t mind that, and we can furbish it up and make it look more *a la mode*. It’s just the thing for you.”

“Oh, no. I couldn’t,” Clara said, touched and rather embarrassed by the offer. She was uncertain what her father would think of her wearing yellow, too. Not that he had ever forbidden her to, she had simply never been brave enough to wear such bright shades. It had seemed inappropriate.

“Oh, Clara, don’t be such a peahen. I shan’t ever wear it again. Indeed, I’ve a wardrobe full of things I shall never wear again. Why ought you not have them if I wish to give them to you? For you’re already the prettiest creature in all of Wick. Well,” she added candidly, “*we* are the prettiest creatures in all of Wick.”

Clara snorted, which set Miss Fleming off, and as they turned the corner, they were laughing heartily.

The Fisherman’s Retreat was quiet on the Sabbath, thank heavens, but as they passed by, with Miss Fleming eyeing the building with interest, the door opened, and Mr Anderson stepped out and locked the door behind him. He saw them as he turned and smiled, giving a formal bow.

“Ladies, how enchanting to meet ye both, and dressed as fine as fivepence. Ye’ll have all the lads weeping into their whisky with heartache.”

"Mr Anderson," Clara reproved him sternly, remembering the run in he'd had with her father all too clearly.

"I beg yer pardon, Miss Halliday. It was a provoking remark, was it nae? I never could keep a still tongue in my head when there was a quip to be made," he told them with a devilish glint in his eyes. "May I walk ye home?"

"It's little more than a dozen steps," Clara said dryly. "I think we can manage it alone."

"Ah, but there are some desperate sorts in Wick, ye never know when ye will be needing a strong man to keep ye safe," he teased.

"Oh, then you had best accompany us everywhere, Mr Anderson, for I shall be afraid to set a foot out of doors without you from now on," Miss Fleming said, blushing and giggling, which Clara privately thought did her no credit. Likely, Mr Anderson thought it made Clara look crusty and ill-tempered in comparison. In the circumstances, she could hardly refuse to take his arm, though she cast him a dark look, so he understood the situation was not one of which she approved.

When the requisite dozen steps had been accomplished, Clara thanked him with ironic civility for his chaperonage, and turned to Miss Fleming, expecting her to release his arm.

"Are you coming, Miss Fleming?" she asked with a smile.

"Oh, no. I've just remembered Papa especially told me I must not dally on my way home from church, for we dine early today. And I could not possibly walk all by myself, now I know how dangerous Wick is," she added demurely, casting a flirtatious glance at Mr Anderson.

"Oh," Clara said, a little shocked by her friend's conduct. "Well, of course. I would not wish for you to be late for a family dinner. I will bid you both a good day then," she replied, and walked to her front door. Though she told herself sternly she must not, Clara could not help a glance back at them before she stepped inside.

Miss Fleming was chattering gaily as they walked down the road, but Mr Anderson looked back over his shoulder, casting Clara a rueful smile before winking at her.

Clara told herself sternly that she was not the least bit gratified by such ungentlemanly behaviour, but her wicked heart disagreed.

It took Hamilton longer than he would have liked to remove himself from Miss Fleming's company. While he had no complaints about walking a pretty girl home, especially one who exerted herself to be agreeable, he knew Miss Fleming was a dangerous companion. She had made it clear to him she was willing to be Mrs Hamilton Anderson, though he knew well enough she would far rather have married Lyall. Miss Fleming was ambitious and, if a better prospect presented itself, she would drop him like a hot coal. However, a bird in the hand and all that. Hamilton did not blame her for her attitude, which was purely practical, but he was in no mad rush to marry, and certainly not a girl like her.

While Miss Fleming was easy on the eye, there was something about her that set his teeth on edge, the nagging sense that she was playing a part to please him. He did not know what the real Miss Fleming was like, but he strongly doubted she was the amiable, bubble-headed female she presented to the world. His gut told him that Clara Halliday, by contrast, was everything she appeared to be. She was not only lovely, with looks of a kind that needed no artifice or paint to highlight, but kind and compassionate, strong-willed, but also a dutiful daughter. He felt she struggled with the position she was in, for he did not think she liked the confrontational stand her father had taken against the drinking men of Wick… or Hamilton himself.

As much as she might approve of her father's ambitions, it seemed Miss Halliday wished to change his tactics, although Hamilton suspected such a wish might be beyond her power.

Finding himself at a loose end, Hamilton considered his options. Moyra would certainly welcome his company but, as much as he liked her, he was not in the right frame of mind for bed sports. His mood was too meditative for that. The problem the Reverend Halliday sought to eradicate was not one he was unaware of; you'd have to be deaf, dumb, and blind not to see it. That he might really be adding to the problem was an idea he had dismissed at first, but one that nagged at his conscience as he wondered if he could do better.

He turned the problem over as he meandered through the quiet streets, but he had no lightning strike idea or solution and only gave himself a headache. He did not like Sundays in Wick. Most people gathered with their family on the sabbath to share a meal and whilst his family were not a million miles away, it was too far to go for the day. He missed them, though. He missed the messy, noisy family gatherings, and more than anything he missed the landscape around Wildsyde, the magic of the remote spot that seemed to be a world apart from the one he now inhabited. Foolishness, of course. Hamilton had everything any young man could want: financial success, popularity, and a beautiful and willing bed partner. It was daft to feel homesick. Besides, he had not long been with them, staying with his elder brother Lyall for their middle sibling's wedding.

Muir had done well for himself, a twist of fate no one could have predicted landing him a bride who was the daughter of a duke and came with a fat dowry, and who was also a sweet-natured and lovely young woman Hamilton had liked at once. Upon learning of the difficult situation she had been in, he had been rash enough to offer to marry her himself if Muir was not to her liking. In hindsight, he was glad she had rejected the offer., not least because Muir was clearly head over ears in love and would never have forgiven him. Hamilton's instincts had told him that Delia was a good woman with a kind heart, and would make an admirable wife, and he knew he'd been right in that estimation. However, he had not been in love with her, and he suspected that rare ingredient, unfashionable as it was, needed to be a part of any union he was prepared to make.

Quite out of sorts by now, after such unsettling thoughts of marriage and homesickness, Hamilton was relieved when he turned the corner and found himself presented with a mill.

"Gerroff! Take your 'ands off me or I'll draw your cork, jus' you see if I don't!" protested a small, skinny boy of about ten years of age. The claim seemed hopeful rather than likely, for the lad was outnumbered by six to one.

"Brody, Jack! What the devil are ye playing at?" Hamilton bellowed, shocking the boys into falling back and dropping their hostage.

The lad sagged, falling heavily on his backside as his captors let go of him like he'd burned them.

"He started it!" a lad Hamilton recognised as Jockie Dunbar's son piped up. "He's a Sassenach," he added indignantly, as if this were reason enough for a good hiding.

"Aye, what of it?" Hamilton demanded, glaring at the lads as he strode over and helped the boy to his feet. His coat was torn, and he'd have a grand black eye in the morning, but he seemed to be all in one piece. "My mother is a Sassenach, which ye would think on if ye had half the brains ye were born with. Would ye like to have a go at me, too?"

The lads exchanged nervous glances, and Hamilton snorted. "Aye, I reckoned not. It's all right picking on a wee laddie who cannae fight back, but someone bigger than ye is another matter. What kind of men are ye to become if battering someone weaker than ye is something ye take a pride in?"

Colour crept into the boy's faces, and they hung their heads, scuffing the toes of their worn boots.

"I'm not weaker than any of 'em," the lad Hamilton was holding up said crossly, with perhaps more spirit than sense. "If it were a fair fight, I'd show 'em."

"Aye, reckon ye might at that, laddie, but there'll be nae more fighting. Ye are all going to shake hands like gentlemen, or I'll skelp the lot of ye myself."

With this terrible threat hanging over them, the boys united in a common goal and needed little persuasion to shake hands and introduce themselves properly. The wee Sassenach was called Jimmy, and Hamilton watched with approval as the boys looked at each other with less hostility and something approaching a friendly manner.

"We sometimes play football," Jock said to the lad, giving Hamilton a wary glance. "There's a flat piece of ground over that way. Where that big old house fell down. We'll be there tomorrow if ye would like to play wi' us?"

"After school, aye?" Hamilton said, quirking one eyebrow.

"Aye," Jock said grimly, having plainly meant nothing of the sort.

"Reckon I might," Jimmy said. "If you play a decent game," he added with a challenging note.

"Ye will all play fair and there'll be nae violence, or I'll be hearing about it," Hamilton said firmly, knowing all too well that the Scottish version of football was closer kin to warfare than any game played in England.

"Aye, Mr Anderson," the boys replied in unison.

"Aye. Away with ye now. I'll see the lad home and ye can see how grand that black eye of his is developing tomorrow."

The lads grinned, tossed a few cheeky but well-meaning insults at Jimmy, which he took in the spirit they were intended, and ran off.

"Well, laddie. Ye are a sight and no mistake. Ye ma will likely tan ye hide harder than the lads would have done for turning up in such a state."

"That'd be a fine sight. She's been dead since the day I was born," Jimmy remarked, smirking.

"Yer da, then?"

"Don't have one," he retorted, with all the insouciance of a boy used to having no one to answer to.

Hamilton studied the lad thoughtfully. He'd never seen the boy before, and it was clear the lads beating on him hadn't either. Jimmy was new in town, and there was only one English family that had arrived in recent weeks.

"What about the Reverend Halliday?"

To Hamilton's dismay, the boy turned chalk white and looked like he might boke. He shook his head, his throat working. Hamilton frowned and crouched down, taking the boy by the shoulders.

"It's all right, laddie. Calm yerself. I winnae breathe a word to him. I swear it."

"It's not for my own sake," Jimmy replied, putting his chin up. "I'm no coward, right? But Clara… that is, Miss Halliday, she'll be in the basket if the old devil realises she brought me wiv her."

Hamilton's eyebrows went up. "Miss Halliday brought ye here, and her da disnae ken aught about it?"

Jimmy nodded. "She's a great gun. Reckon I'd be pushin' up daisies if she'd not taken me in. The reverend told her to send me back to London where I come from, and she pretended to do what he said, but she never. I lived wiv her at the vicarage in Thorney for a bit, hidden like, then she paid the driver what brought all their boxes and stuff to bring me too. Used her own money, and it cost a pretty penny. No one never did nothing for me before, not ever, but she did all that," he added in wonder, his voice wobbling a bit.

Hamilton stared at the lad, his estimation of Clara Halliday's character rising higher by the moment. Having been on the receiving end of the Reverend Halliday's particular brand of Christian charity, he could well believe the man would have sent a grubby street boy back where he'd come from without a second thought. That Miss Halliday had not only lied to her father but used her own savings to bring him with her, spoke of a woman of courage and one with a strong sense of right and wrong. Rubbing the back of his neck, Hamilton considered the situation.

"Reckon I ought to return ye to the lady, then, and explain ye had a bit of rough and tumble with the local lads but that's all's well, aye?"

"Oh, would you?" Jimmy said, the relief in his eyes plain to see. "I'd not want her to fret, and if I turn up all bashed about, she might not let me out again and I'll be queer in my attic afore the week is out if I have to stay cooped up in the kitchen all day and all night."

"Mrs Macready kens ye are there, then?" Hamilton asked with interest.

"She does, and she's a corker too," Jimmy said, grinning. "Merry as a grig, she is, and the grub she serves is like nothing I ever tasted afore." The lad put his fingers to his lips and made a kissing sound, which made Hamilton snort with laughter.

"Ye are a wee scoundrel, I reckon, and ye have fallen into clover, but I dinnae blame ye for making the most of it. Come along, then, Jimmy. I'll return ye to the lovely Miss Halliday and explain a bit. Reckon she might look kindly on me for having done ye a good turn?" he asked, giving the lad a sideways glance.

"Are you sweet on her then, mister?"

"Nae," Hamilton replied easily. "But it does a fellow nae harm to be in a pretty lassie's good book, aye?"

"Aye," the cheeky fellow replied, chuckling. "Reckon that's true enough."

They walked back to the vicarage and Hamilton hesitated as Jimmy led them around the back. “The reverend disnae come out here?”

“Nah,” the boy said confidently. “He’s never so much as stuck his nose in the kitchen since we got ’ere. Reckon he thinks his dinner arrives on a cloud sent by the Almighty.”

Hamilton fought a bark of laughter and arranged his face into something more serious. “Ye will mind yer manners,” he told the lad, who smirked all the same.

Opening the back door, Jimmy went inside, and Hamilton heard the feminine cries of distress before he set a foot over the threshold.

“Jimmy!”

“Oh, laddie, whatever befell ye?”

Hamilton entered in time to view both women hurrying over and enveloping Jimmy, each embracing him in turn and running hands over him to check he was whole and sound.

“There’s nae harm done,” Hamilton said, gaining himself a squeak of surprised alarm from Miss Halliday, who sprang to her feet, gazing at him like he’d appeared in a puff of smoke.

“Mr Anderson!” she exclaimed. “Whatever are you doing here?” He noted the way she glanced behind her, as if fearing his presence would somehow transmit itself to the reverend and bring him down upon them.

“I thought I had best bring him home to ye, since ye are the angel that rescued him from fate. I did a wee bit of rescuing myself today,” he added with a modest smile. “The local lads were getting a tad rough, but we had a chat with them, and all’s mended now, is it nae, Jimmy? They’ll be friendly the next time they cross paths, I promise ye.”

“Oh, no. You weren’t fighting?” Clara said, her expression one of anxiety.

"They jumped me! Weren't my doing," Jimmy objected.

"Good heavens!" Clara gasped, pulling Jimmy close again. "You poor dear."

"Ach, I'll lay money it was Jockie Dunbar's lad and his gang, the wee devils," Mrs Macready said, puffing herself up like an irritated hen. "Ye just wait, I'll be having a wee word with Jockie and—"

"Ye will do nothing of the sort," Hamilton said gently. "I told ye, did I nae, that it's all sorted. The boys were a bit out of line but they're all friends now. There's nae need to stir trouble with the lad's da, for it will only come back on Jimmy."

"I had nae thought of that," Mrs Macready admitted gruffly. "Aye, well, if ye say so, but ye mind me well, if they lay another hand on him, I'll be having words with Jockie myself and ye may warn the wee scoundrels to make certain they behave."

"That's fair," Hamilton agreed, knowing such a threat would certainly get Brodie and Jack's attention.

"Come, then, my wee warrior, let's see to that eye," Mrs Macready said, bustling Jimmy away amidst a deal of grumbling and leaving Hamilton alone with Clara.

"You saw Miss Fleming home safely, then?" Clara said, an amused glint in her eyes.

"Aye, I did. Are ye jealous?" Hamilton asked, grinning at her.

"Don't be impudent."

The look was stern but there was no heat behind the words, which he felt was an encouraging sign.

"I wouldn't ken where to begin," Hamilton replied with a shrug.

Clara sighed, shaking her head. "Can I offer you a cup of tea, Mr Anderson?"

"I'd prefer a wee dram after all the excitement, but aye. I'll take tea with ye, with pleasure," he added, taking a seat at the table. "Won't yer da be up in arms if he finds me here?"

"Certainly, so I shall thank you for leaving the way you arrived, but he never comes down here. You do not drink to excess, do you, Mr Anderson?" she demanded suddenly.

Hamilton blinked, a little startled at the bold question. There was a look in her eyes that told him she was concerned, not only about him, but about the situation in Wick.

"Nae," he said, his tone serious. "I would never do that. I'll nae pretend I dinnae have a drop too many on a special occasion. Like the day we met when my head was splitting in two. The night before, I'd been drinking the health of a friend's baby son. But I dinnae make a habit of it. I have too much work to do to be bevied at all hours of the day and night."

Clara studied him as she poured hot water onto the tea leaves. He was uncertain she was convinced but she said nothing more. Hamilton watched her with pleasure as she moved around the kitchen, admiring the sway of her lush hips and the thick knot of hair at the back of her neck. It was a very dark brown, and she had used a good many pins to secure it. He wondered how far down her back it would fall if he took those pins out and found himself momentarily distracted by imagining the feel of the silken locks tangled about his fingers.

"I did not see you in church," she said, with more curiosity than censure, jolting him out of his pleasant daydream and back to reality, which was all to the good.

"I didnae think it would be a good idea," he replied. "I usually go. You can't miss a service in Wick without the entire town believing ye are worshiping the devil, but yer da seemed likely to point at me and proclaim *I was* the devil, so I figured I'd give it a miss for once. I was nae up to mischief, though, I swear it," he added, giving her the benefit of a smile he knew had a pleasing effect on the ladies.

"What were you doing?" she asked, concentrating on laying out cups and saucers.

Hamilton shrugged. "Making plans, and I didnae pick up a tool nor write anything down so ye cannae accuse me of working on the sabbath," he added, a touch defensively.

"Do you think I would?" she asked in surprise.

Hamilton regarded her thoughtfully. "I dinnae ken ye well enough, but… but nae, I dinnae think so."

"I do try to be a good Christian," she said, frowning as she fetched the milk jug and set it on the table. "But my ideas of what that means always seem to be a little out of step with others. Especially my father," she said with a smile.

"He's hard on ye," Hamilton said, feeling a stab of concern as he wondered what her life was like.

"Oh, not really," she replied, sighing. "I help around the house and write up his sermons for him so they're legible, and I do the household accounts and such, but then so do many women. It's not like he works me to the bone," she said with a wry smile. "It's just a little…"

"Dull?"

"Yes, it is rather," she admitted ruefully.

"Aye, and perhaps I am in nae position to judge, but he's nae a man who finds much joy in life, I reckon."

Clara slanted a glance at him, apparently struck by the observation. "He does not," she said, a considering note to her voice. "Do you find joy in life?"

Hamilton grinned at her, which he thought was answer enough, and then delighted in the slow spread of pink that tinged her cheeks like a sunrise.

"I dinnae believe that God put us on this earth to suffer," he said, finding himself speaking earnestly now. "I know I'm blessed, and life is much kinder to me than to many folk around here who have it far, far harder, but when I'm feeling low, I make myself remember there's always a little good to be found in every day, some reason to smile or to be pleased to be alive. Perhaps it's just the birds singing, or the sight of the sun sparkling on the sea, or a pretty girl smiling at ye, but ye must hold on tight to those moments and keep them with ye, aye?"

She smiled at him approvingly in reply to his words, and Hamilton felt the heat of it, like standing before a fire on a cold night. It warmed him, sliding under his skin and settling there, and he thought it was a smile he would remember and hold on to for a good long time.

He held his tongue as Clara occupied herself with the tea, finding he enjoyed watching her. She was poised and lovely, her pretty hands both deft and elegant as she prepared the brew, adding milk and sugar as he requested.

"You have a sweet tooth," she reproved him after adding the three lumps he asked for.

"It's my one failing," he said, adopting a sheepish expression.

"Only one?" she repeated, her eyes flashing with amusement.

"Aye, other than that, I'm a paragon." Her lips twitched, and he decided there and then that he would not leave until he had made her laugh properly.

"So ye have made friends with Miss Fleming?"

"Yes, she was kind enough to call on me. I believe she has taken me under her wing," she added with amusement. "But I fear she will be sadly disappointed."

"Why?" Hamilton asked in surprise.

"Because she is lovely and terribly fashionable and… and I'm not," she said with a short laugh. Not at all the kind of laugh

Hamilton had been hoping for, either. "She offered to give me some of her dresses, which was so terribly kind of her and there's a part of me which would love to accept, but I cannot."

"Ye dinnae want to feel beholden to her?" Hamilton guessed.

"Does that sound terribly ungrateful?" Clara asked him anxiously. "She's been so very kind, but I really don't know her very well yet. Perhaps if we had been bosom bows for years, but…"

"I think ye are wise. Yer friendship is too new, fragile, aye?"

"Yes, exactly," Clara said, her expression one of relief. "I should worry whenever I wore it, and I can't explain why exactly, only I should not feel at ease."

"Then thank her kindly and say no thank ye. If she is a friend, she'll nae press ye. If ye did borrow them, I reckon she might nae like it overmuch when ye outshine her in her own gowns."

"That's mere flattery, and not at all likely," she observed, smiling. "But I shall do as you suggest. Thank you, Mr Anderson. I confess, I did not expect you to understand such a thing."

"I have a sister," he said with a chuckle. "I ken more than ye might imagine, and just so we are clear, ye have nae need of Miss Fleming's gowns, lovely though they may be. Ye brighten the day whenever I see ye, just as ye are, and I reckon I am nae the only one who sees that, and that's nothing but the truth."

The blush returned, a shade darker and she let out a little huff of laughter, which was closer but still not what he wanted from her. "You are a rogue, Mr Anderson, and flirting with me will get you nowhere, so kindly desist," she said reprovingly, but there was a sparkle in her eyes, and he did not think she minded it at all.

"Did ye nae leave a sweetheart behind when ye left yer home to come here?" he asked, curious now, for surely this beautiful girl had been remarked upon. If not, the men of her hometown must be blind and stupid.

Clara shook her head. "My father prefers a quiet life, so we have never had a great deal of society. And you are being impertinent again," she added, almost as an afterthought.

"So ye are hoping to find one here, I suppose?"

She bristled a little. "You just cannot help yourself, can you?" she said, shaking her head. "You ought not ask such questions of me."

"Why not? I'm interested," he objected.

"It's not done, and I think you know that very well. And if I am looking for a husband, what of it?" she demanded, a little defiantly. Her finger traced the painted pattern on the teacup, but she glanced up at him and away again.

"Nothing at all," he said, wondering if Mrs Macready was right about her father wanting to keep her by him. "Only if ye were at the school hoping to speak with Malcolm Stewart, I pray ye will look a little higher. Ye can do better than that, I assure you."

She turned red this time, a much less flattering shade which told him he'd not been wrong. Glaring at him and looking a little incredulous, she gathered herself and Hamilton knew at once he'd touched a nerve.

"Mr Stewart is a schoolteacher, an educated man, and one who has done nothing to deserve such censure. He may not be a man of means but he has an honest trade, teaching the next generation. I am not aspiring to marry a man of fortune, or—or any man," she added in confusion.

Hamilton opened his mouth to tell her the man was not at all what he appeared to be, and was gaining a dubious reputation in the town, and closed it again. He could not in all conscience slander the fellow, but neither could he leave her without a warning.

"Aye, well. As ye like. It's just my opinion, but ye will do as ye please," he said easily, pushing to his feet and regretting the fact he had not made her laugh as he'd hoped. "Just… just dinnae ever let yerself be alone with the fellow, aye."

She frowned at that, and he wondered if she thought it was jealousy on his part, making him say such a thing. Either way, it could not be helped, he'd had to warn her.

"I shall, thank you, Mr Anderson. You are always so considerate of my feelings," she replied, and he heard the thread of sarcasm behind the words. He smiled at her, pleased that she was bold enough to speak so to him and wondering if he been right to warn her off. Some women liked a fellow better if they believed he was a rogue, he ought to know. Maybe now she'd be on fire to see the wretched devil, which was an idea which bothered him more than he liked. Malcolm was a loose screw, and he did not think Clara had the experience to deal with such a fellow.

"Good day to ye, Miss Halliday, and thank ye for the tea," he replied, giving her a respectful bow before he saw himself out.

Chapter 7

Hamilton,

You did the right thing in asking me, for I have the best and most sensible advice you are likely to hear.

Marry her.

—Excerpt of a letter from The Right Hon'ble Lyall Anderson, Viscount Buchanan to The Hon'ble Mr Hamilton Anderson.

27th May 1850, Wick, Caithness, Scotland.

Clara walked to the kitchen door and watched Mr Anderson's broad-shouldered figure as he left. The kitchen seemed strangely empty now he'd removed himself from it. There was an energy about him, a presence that seemed to fill the room, and lingered in her mind long after he was gone. She told herself he was a dreadful man who could not stop himself from sticking his nose in where it did not belong. Yet he had been kind to Jimmy and brought him home safely, and most surprising of all, he had understood her not wanting to borrow Miss Fleming's dresses… though what on earth had possessed her to tell him such a thing, she could not fathom. Mr Anderson had understood at once what a position it would put her in, however, just as he had guessed the kind of life she lived with her father. There was a quickness about him, an understanding of human nature that made him at once very approachable, and very dangerous. For surely a man with such understanding would find it easy to manipulate a young woman who had seen little of the world. She certainly ought not to encourage him. It had been very wrong of her to invite him to take tea with her and yet she had wanted him to. There was a wicked delight to be found in talking to him and reproving him when he overstepped the mark… which was most of the time. If she'd had a bit of sense, she would have asked him to leave when he began flirting with her, but sadly it had not even occurred to her to do so. Clara bit her lip, wondering if she was really the well brought up girl she'd always believed herself to be. Either way, she must have a care around Mr Anderson. He was far too easy to like, despite his provoking ways. The last thing she needed was to put her trust in such a man, not when her father worked himself up at the mere sight of the fellow.

She wondered what on earth had made him warn her off Mr Stewart. Had Mr Anderson not been looking after the children for him when he'd been ill? Surely they must be friends. She could think of only one reason, and she did not know how she felt about it. He couldn't be jealous. Yet he had seemed genuinely concerned, and worry niggled at her.

Miss Fleming's reaction to Mr Stewart she could understand, for she was an ambitious young woman with an eye to her own future and she would assume Clara was of the same mind. Clara did not judge her for that. A woman's existence was a precarious one and, if Miss Fleming wanted to ensure her own comfort, Clara could hardly blame her for it. Indeed, she was no fool either, and did not wish to marry a man who could not afford to support her, for that would lead them both down a hard road, yet she hoped she would be prepared to do so if she loved and esteemed a man enough to tread such a path. She certainly could not entertain the notion of marrying a man simply for position or wealth. In those circumstances, she would stay with her father, though the idea did nothing to lighten her heart. He had left her provided for in his will, however, and whilst she would not be living the high life once he had passed on, she would be safe, and that would be something. Better that than a bad marriage that one could not escape from.

"Well, then, he's scrubbed and bandaged," Mrs Macready said with satisfaction, preceding Jimmy into the kitchen.

The boy did not look so satisfied, but he did look clean and rather less disreputable. Mrs Macready had given him a fresh shirt and carried his coat and the laundry over her arm.

"Give me his coat and I shall mend the tear," Clara said, taking it from her. "I expect Jimmy is peckish now after his adventures."

"Corr, I am famished," Jimmy said eagerly.

"Ach, ye have hollow legs and that's a fact," Mrs Macready retorted with a sniff. "Sit yerself down then, and I shall make ye something. Did Mr Anderson stay long, then?" she added, eyeing the teacups on the table with a canny eye.

"Oh, no. But after he was so kind to Jimmy, I could hardly send him away without a cup of tea or something."

"Could ye nae?" Mrs Macready replied, one eyebrow quirking. "Aye, well, maybe. He behaved himself, I hope?"

"Certainly, he did," Clara replied, unrolling the small mending kit that they kept in the kitchen and avoiding Mrs Macready's knowing gaze.

"He didnae flirt with ye?"

"He's not sweet on her, Mrs Macready, you don't need to fret none," Jimmy said candidly before Clara could reply, making both women stare at him with interest.

"Oh, aye?" Mrs Macready looked sceptical.

"He's not!" Jimmy protested. "For I asked him, and he said no. He said it was always nice to have a pretty lady think well of you, though."

"Sounds about right," Mrs Macready said dryly, and Clara was glad the lady did not look back at her again, for she was certain mortification burned in her cheeks.

Keeping her head down, she concentrated on her needle and thread and scolded herself for her arrogance in thinking Mr Anderson had the least bit of interest in her. Jealous, indeed. It was just as she had imagined from the start. Just as Mrs Macready had warned her, in fact. Mr Anderson was a wicked flirt and took nothing seriously. She would do well to keep that fact in mind the next time their paths crossed.

29th May 1850, Wick Village Hall, Caithness, Scotland.

"'Intoxicating wine is like the poison of serpents, the cruel venom of asps,'" the Reverend Halliday told his assembled audience as a murmur of agreement rippled through the room.

There were perhaps thirty women, some with children fidgeting on their laps, a few with babes in arms. Clara looked about at them, many of whom were of an age with her. She could have been one of them, might have carried that careworn expression and clothes that had been patched and mended times past counting. She looked then at her father, wishing he did not feel the need to bellow quite so much, but seeing the genuine concern in his eyes. Coming here had lit a fire within him, given him a purpose past his own comfort, and that gave her hope. If only she could find a way for him to take the anger and judgement from his dealings with the people here. The women came every Friday to hear him lecture about the evils of drink. 'Proverbs 23:21 – Drunkenness causes poverty,' had been thoroughly discussed last week. The men, however, were less amused by his interference. An angry fisherman had turned up on the vicarage doorstep just yesterday, telling Mrs Macready to inform the reverend to keep his nose out of things that did not concern him.

The reverend paused for a brief interval and Clara passed silently between the women, offering cups of elderflower cordial and shortbread biscuits. Once everyone had been served, she returned to pour a drink for her father.

"I saved you some shortbread," she said, offering him a small plate with three biscuits on.

"Thank you, my dear, most kind," he said, smiling at her. "A good turnout, eh? Three more than last week."

"Indeed, they seem most eager to hear you speak, Father." Clara hesitated, wondering if she ought to broach the subject. "Do you think perhaps you ought to invite their husbands directly to come with them? Perhaps if you visited the harbour and introduced yourself to them, if you got to know some of the men, not by preaching, just talking to them and getting to know their troubles. They might come and listen then."

Her father chewed on a biscuit, his expression thoughtful. "If there were no public houses in Wick, there would be no opportunity for the men to indulge in such vile behaviour."

"Well, that is true," Clara said hesitantly.

"That's the ticket," he said, waving a shortbread biscuit at her with approval. "We must go to the source of the evil and strike there. An excellent suggestion. Thank you, my dear."

"Oh… you're welcome." Clara watched him stride off with an extra spring in his step and wondered what she had unwittingly done.

"Ah, Mrs Cameron," he said, catching the attention of one of the women as she returned her empty glass to the serving tray and picked it up, intending to collect the rest. "Just the lady, and no surprise to see you tidying up after us all. What a comfort you are to us. Now, what do you think of my daughter's suggestion—"

Clara regarded him with some bemusement, surprised by the warmth in his voice as he spoke to the woman, even more that he was asking for her opinion. Still, it was good that he was on friendly terms with them, better than merely sermonising and never listening to a word they said.

"Miss Halliday? Coo-ee!"

Clara turned and smiled as she saw Miss Fleming in the doorway, waving at her. Glancing back at her father and seeing he was well into the second part of his talk, Clara quietly gathered her cloak and bonnet and walked swiftly to the door.

Miss Fleming chuckled as Clara slipped away, tying her bonnet strings as she went.

"Will you be in terrible trouble for running off?" she asked, slipping her arm through Clara's.

"No, not if I return before he finishes. I doubt he'll even notice," she replied ruefully. "But what a lovely surprise. I did not expect to see you."

"I know, but I was bored and so I thought I would stretch my legs. Papa is visiting my aunt. She lives down there," she added, pointing to the end of the street they were passing. "But she's a dull creature and I cannot abide the stuffy little house for above half an hour. So I excused myself."

"Oh, won't your father mind? If you're supposed to be visiting. I could come with you if—"

"Good heavens, no!" Miss Fleming replied. "Aunt Ailsa will only drone on about her ailments, some of which are quite mortifying."

Despite herself, Clara could not help a choke of laughter at the disgusted face Miss Fleming had pulled.

"Getting old seems a dreadful business," she said frankly.

"Yes, but perhaps better than the alternative," Clara suggested.

Miss Fleming gave a snort of laughter. "All the more reason to live while we are young, then. Oh, don't look. No, don't look!

Pretend you've not seen him," she said, suddenly clutching at Clara's arm.

Clara, who had never been adept at subterfuge, immediately looked in the direction she was told not to and saw Mr Malcolm Stewart walking towards them and smiling widely.

"Well met, ladies. I had no expectation of meeting such charming companions on my way home. Where are you off to? Might I escort you?"

"We are going nowhere in particular, Mr Stewart, just taking the air," Clara said politely. "Are you feeling better now?"

A look she could not read flickered in his eyes, but she thought he seemed uneasy.

"Better?"

"Why, yes? I believe Mr Anderson looked after the boys for you whilst you were indisposed."

"Oh," there was a flat note to his voice as he replied but he rallied swiftly. "Indeed, most kind of him, but it was nothing but a megrim. I suffer from them from time to time. Too much squinting at textbooks late at night," he added sheepishly, pushing his spectacles up his nose. It was rather an endearing gesture, and he had a sweetly boyish smile. Clara thought perhaps Miss Fleming noticed it too, for she stopped ignoring him and cast him a bright smile of her own.

"I hear you are something of a writer too, Mr Stewart, is that true?"

He huffed with amusement at the remark, looking self-deprecating, or at least trying to. "Well, I'm sure my poor work does not merit giving me such a title, but I do write, yes. Though… poetry, mostly."

"Have you anything published?" Clara asked curiously.

“Not as yet, but I am working on a something rather special,” he said hurriedly. “So, I hope in a year or so to give you a different answer.”

“How fascinating,” Miss Fleming replied, looking at him from under her lashes. “And do you have a muse that inspires you when you write?”

A pleased glint sparkled in Mr Stewart’s eye. “Mother nature is my muse at present, but I challenge any man not to find inspiration in the vision before me now.”

Miss Fleming gave her tinkling laugh, a light merry sound that Clara wished she could emulate, for it was quite lovely.

“Do you mean to write an ode to us, then?” Miss Fleming challenged him.

Clara groaned inwardly. Of all the bottle-headed things to do, inviting an aspiring poet to write an ode to oneself had to be way up the list.

“I might, at that,” Mr Stewart replied, a speculative expression on his lean face as he looked from Miss Fleming to Clara.

“Well, you’d best run along and put pen to paper. You would not wish to disappoint us, would you, sir?” Miss Fleming replied, one blonde eyebrow quirking.

Clara thought she detected a flash of irritation in his eyes at being so dismissed, but Mr Stewart bowed politely. “Indeed, I must. Miss Fleming, a pleasure as always. Miss Halliday, I thought I might call on your father tomorrow morning and introduce myself. I have some books that he might find of interest and thought perhaps he would welcome a visit from an educated fellow, as they are rather lacking in this town. Do you think he would be at home to me?”

Clara fought a blush, wondering if he was visiting her father as a means of seeing her, but she merely thanked him for his kindness and agreed that the reverend would be most pleased to welcome him.

"Dreadful man," Miss Fleming said with a sigh once Mr Stewart was out of earshot. "And really, Miss Halliday, I hope you will not take it amiss, but you really ought not to encourage him."

Clara blinked, wondering if she had heard correctly. "I did not encourage him," she said indignantly, for she had not been the one batting her eyelashes and inviting the fellow to write poetry about them.

"You ought to have told him your father was not at home tomorrow. Then he could not use it as an excuse to call on you."

"He's calling on my father, not me," Clara said, a trifle defensively for had she not just wondered if that had just been an excuse. "And it would have been wrong of me to lie. Besides, you were the one asking for a poem in our honour."

"A mere piece of nonsense," Miss Fleming said, waving this away. "This is the difference between us, for you have not had a season, my dear. You must learn the art of flirting and managing men to get what you want. Else you will be quite lost. The Mr Stewarts of this world are quite charming for a short while, but they are not the kind of man one wishes to marry. Not if you are to have any hopes of security and comfort. I tell you this for your own good, my dear. I know he's a pretty fellow, and he does have that romantic starving poet look about him, but really, he won't do."

Clara's lips twitched at this rather dreadful but ultimately sensible bit of scolding. "Yes, Miss Fleming," she said obediently, and decided she had best leave it at that.

Chapter 8

Dearest Auntie Cat,

When will you come to town? I'm feeling cross and crotchety and even Harris is at her wits' end. Papa is looking for a wife and I'm afraid I behaved rather badly yesterday. He took me to a garden party and though everyone was very nice to my face, I knew they were staring at me and gossiping.

Papa was talking to a lady, and she was very pretty but she kept giggling like a complete ninny and batting her eyelashes. If he thinks such a nincompoop could ever be a mama to me, he is much mistaken. So, I accidentally on purpose dropped my ice in her lap. You should have heard her scream!

I am in disgrace now, of course, and it's worse because today Papa has gone on an outing by himself, and I cannot even get a glimpse of the women he is making fall in love with him. I hate everyone. Except you and Harris. Please come.

—Excerpt of a letter from Miss Ottilie Barrington to her aunt, The Most Hon'ble Lady Catherine 'Cat' St Just, Marchioness of Kilbane.

30th May 1850, Wick, Caithness, Scotland.

"Good morning, Mr Stewart. My father is expecting you," Clara said, smiling as she took the man's hat and gloves.

"Thank you, Miss Halliday, and may I say how lovely you look this morning?"

Clara, who had spent much of the morning in the kitchen and knew she was flushed and sweaty, strongly doubted this, but she smiled politely and invited Mr Stewart to follow her.

"Did you never receive the letter I sent you?" he asked in an urgent whisper, making Clara start with surprise.

"I did, sir," she replied, feeling suddenly uneasy. She had forgotten all about the letter after her run in with Mr Anderson. "But you must know, it was very wrong to write to me in such a clandestine manner."

"But I want to see you," he said, surprising her by grasping hold of her hand. "I have thought of nothing but you since the moment I laid eyes on you. Won't you come for a walk with me? I promise there is nothing but respect for you in my heart, but I would give a great deal to have your company, even for a short while."

Cara tugged her hand free, a little startled by the passionate nature of his words. She supposed it was the poetic side of him that made him so easily excited but then she wondered why she was not pleased by such conduct. Mr Anderson had flirted with her, and despite his dreadful behaviour, she could not help but like him. Mr Steward's overtures, by contrast, made her skin creep, when he was everything she had thought she had wanted. Suddenly, Mr Anderson's warning came back to her, and she wondered if she ought to give him more credit. "If you wish for me to walk with you, I think you had better ask permission of my father," she replied coolly, surprising herself by feeling quite relieved to be able to do so. She wanted to marry, yes, but perhaps Miss Fleming had a point. She did not believe for one moment that the fellow had formed a passion for her in the instant of their first meeting. Not a real one, at least.

"I shall then," he said, standing a little straighter.

"Then we shall see," Clara replied, before knocking on the study door. "Papa, Mr Stewart is here."

"Ah, good. Yes, come in, come in, Mr Stewart, a pleasure to meet you. Do sit down. Clara, would you have Mrs Macready send up a tray?"

"Of course, Papa," Clara said, before excusing herself and leaving the two men alone.

♡♧◇♤

It was perhaps an hour later before Clara heard her father's voice as he saw Mr Stewart to the door. Passing the parlour door, her father knocked and stuck his head in, smiling at her as he found her sewing by the light of the window.

"Ah, Clara, my dear. Mr Stewart is leaving now, but we have arranged a little walking party for you young people to the Old Man of Wick. It's a charming setting, I understand. If the weather permits, of course. This Saturday afternoon, if you have no commitments already?"

"I should be delighted if you would come," Mr Stewart said, a triumphant gleam in his eyes.

Clara smiled, surprised by her father's agreeing to such a scheme, and amused and rather touched that Mr Stewart had persevered. For she did not doubt it had taken a good deal of persuasion. Indeed, she could not imagine how he had done it.

"A walking party, Papa? Who else is coming?" she asked, looking from one to the other.

Mr Stewart smiled at her. "I shall invite Miss Fleming, which I know will please you, and she has a neighbour, Mr Fraser, who will make up the numbers, and also my brother Angus and his wife, Mary, to chaperone so it will be quite proper. Do say you will come, Miss Halliday," he said, his expression so hopeful he looked like an eager puppy.

"I shall, Mr Stewart, and I thank you for your kindness in creating such a scheme. I shall look forward to it," which was nothing but the truth. A day in the company of other young people, out in the fresh air, and to such a romantic location as a ruined castle sounded lovely and a welcome change from her usual routine.

"Excellent!" Mr Stewart replied, beaming and looking like all his Christmases had come at once. "Then I shall see you on Saturday."

"Ah, but you will see me tomorrow," her father said, wagging a finger at him. "Don't forget. Six pm on the dot and bring the supplies you promised me."

"Aye. Of course. I'll be there," he said hurriedly, before leaving them with polite expressions of thanks for their hospitality.

"What's happening tomorrow?" Clara asked as her father closed the door.

Grinning, her father tapped the side of his nose, looking pleased with himself. "A little surprise, my dear. You shall just have to wait and see."

With an anxious feeling of foreboding, Clara had to be satisfied and watched as her father returned to his study.

2nd June 1850, Wick, Caithness, Scotland.

Clara did not have to wait too long to solve the mystery. It seemed the supplies her father had spoken of were paints and paper, now all affixed to thin sheets of wood and wooden poles to be held aloft. The messages emblazoned on the placards varied from bible quotes to heartfelt pleas to reject the demon drink. They lined the hallway of the vicarage, garish red paint stark against the pale sheets of paper.

"What do you mean to do with them, Papa?" Clara asked anxiously.

"We are going to stand in front of one of the public houses and shame the men who go in there. You gave me the idea, actually, that I should challenge the men directly, confront them with their sin."

"B-But that's not at all what I said," Clara protested. "I only suggested you speak to them. Papa, these men have hard lives, I think perhaps we ought to approach the situation with a little more delicacy of touch."

"Nonsense, one must fight fire with fire. It's the only way."

"But who will be holding these placards?" Clara demanded, following her father into his study as he gathered his pocket watch and folded up the speech he had prepared.

"My temperance army, of course," he said, sounding far too pleased with himself.

"But will not that put the women in conflict with their husbands? Surely that's a difficult position for them to take?"

"It's right and proper, to do the Lord's work and save their husbands from the devil."

"Yes, but the lord isn't waiting for them when they get home," Clara pointed out, worrying what kind of domestic scenes might play out in the light of such an event.

"Of course he is. The Lord is everywhere, Clara, have I taught you nothing?"

A sharp rap on the door galvanised the reverend into action and he pulled on his coat, reaching for his hat. "To battle," he said, grinning as he hurried to the front door. Clara recognised many of the faces of the women who attended her father's talks on a Friday as he handed out the placards.

"Ah, Mrs Cameron, I knew you would be the first in line," he said with satisfaction, sounding as merry as Clara had ever heard him.

"I'll proudly stand beside ye, reverend, when ye are doing such good work in the town," Mrs Cameron replied earnestly, giving Clara's father a look of such blatant admiration Clara wondered at it.

She hesitated for a moment. "If you will wait for me, Papa, I'll fetch my coat and—"

The reverend shook his head and hurried after her, catching hold of her arm. "No, child. It's no place for a young, unmarried lady, outside of a public house. I may not always have been the father you have deserved, but I know this much."

Clara stared at him, so shocked by such an admission she was momentarily speechless.

"Ye should listen to the reverend, Miss Halliday," Mrs Cameron put in, though her tone was kindly. "'Tis nae a place for an innocent lassie. If yer mama were, God rest her, she would tell ye so herself. 'Tis right and proper that yer da seeks to protect ye, though."

Clara glanced back at her, a little annoyed by her interference though her father was regarding Mrs Cameron with obvious approval. Clara turned back to him and tried again.

"But you said before the lord would protect me," she pointed out. "If it is right and proper for these women to stand up in such a battle, then there can be no wrong in me standing beside them, surely?" she said desperately.

"Yes, but he cannot stop you from hearing the language such men use. These women are used to such behaviour, but it would be wrong of me to subject a gently bred girl to such uncouth scenes. I shall see you later, Clara. Don't fret."

Clara looked around as Mrs Macready appeared at her elbow, watching the ladies walk onto the street, placards held proudly aloft.

"Oh dear," Clara said as her father closed the door behind him. "I don't know what to think of this. I can only admire the women for standing up for what they believe in, but I'm afraid it will cause trouble. Especially with Papa's dreadful lack of tact."

"Aye. That it will, but perhaps it's about time. Those women have taken all they can stomach, I reckon. Mrs Cameron lost her devil of a husband to the drink, and she's nae the only one. If my husband were still alive and drinking his wages, I'd likely be standing beside them. Happily, he wisnae the kind to indulge to excess, God rest him, but even decent men can go awry."

Clara frowned, accepting this. If the women were brave enough to fight for the cause, then she could only commend them for it, but it did not ease her worries all the same.

4th June 1850, Wick, Caithness, Scotland.

"What's all this?" Hamilton asked as he turned a corner and saw the crowd holding placards outside of Murray's tavern. They were on their way back from the harbour after Hamilton had overseen the loading of one of his largest ships with whisky and wool and barrels of herring.

"The Reverend Halliday," Angus said, giving Hamilton a wry smile. "And it's the third time this week. They were outside of Macrae's place on Tuesday. Reid's last night. Seems to have been peaceable enough so far."

"Aye, but they're reasonable men. Murray is a hot heid and a deal too fond of making money to take a scene like that in stride," Hamilton observed, frowning.

As he spoke, the man himself pushed outside, elbowing and shoving the women as he went.

"Ach, to the devil with him," Hamilton muttered. "Come on, Angus. I may have need of yer diplomacy skills."

"Get off my property and back to yer homes before I make yer sorry for causing such a spectacle of yerselves!" Clyde Murray bellowed, shaking his fist at the gathering before his tavern.

"You keep a civil tongue in your head in front of the ladies," Reverend Halliday said, with rather more spirit than Hamilton had credited him with.

"Ladies? Ha!" Murray said in disgust. "What do ye think ye are playing at, Janet MacDonald? Ye are nae better than a fishwife and ye need a slap."

"Try it!" the woman yelled back, as the reverend held onto her with difficulty.

"Stay calm, Mrs MacDonald! Do not let the devil temp you into violence and behaviour unbecoming to a lady."

"Will ye just pack it in?" Murray shouted, growing increasingly red in the face.

"Stop pouring that filth down Rory's neck and inviting him to bide in the gutter and I will," shouted a stocky, red-haired woman, shoving her placard in Murray's face. *"Woe to him that gives his neighbour drink!"*

Murray shoved back, and the woman staggered and would have fallen if not for those around her keeping her on her feet.

"Ye are a spineless little weasel!" she yelled angrily as Murray raised his fist.

"Ye'll nae be doing that," Hamilton said, catching hold of the man's wrist. "I should think even a sorry specimen as yerself would ken better than to lay hands on a woman."

"She's a damned harpy," Murray said, spitting on the ground in front of him. "And I'll nae have them bankrupt me by keeping my clients from my door."

"I dinnae think one night is gonnae ruin ye," Hamilton told the man.

"Not at the prices he charges," Angus muttered, gaining himself a glare from Hamilton, who did not think the comment terribly helpful.

"I'm an honest man, making an honest wage," Murray said, his ruddy face redder than ever in the light of his fury. "And they've nae right to stop me. The law says I can sell whisky, and I mean to do so."

"Aye, and what do you mean to do to stop them? For if ye lay a hand on any of the ladies here, I shall have to take issue with ye, Clyde," Hamilton told him frankly.

"And ye would nae mind if they were causing havoc in front of yer fancy new place, then?" Clyde demanded, glaring at him.

"Nae. They have the right to make themselves heard, but they cannae close every bar every night. Just haud yer wheesht and let them have their say, aye?"

Murray looked like he was gritting his teeth so hard he might break something, but he turned on his heel and went back into the tavern, slamming the door behind him. Hamilton let out a breath.

"Thank ye, Mr Anderson," said one of the women close to him, who he recognised as Aileen Carson.

"Nae bother," he replied, about to turn and leave.

"You, sir, are a hypocrite!"

Hamilton turned, eyeing Reverend Halliday with a sigh of dismay. "Oh, aye?"

"You pretend to support these women while you are no better than Mr Murray."

"Ye reckon?" Hamilton replied evenly, his temper rising. "For I have nae raised a hand to a woman in my life. Nor a man of God."

"You are sending the demon drink out into the world to destroy the lives of men," the reverend told him, his eyes alight with condemnation.

Hamilton reminded himself this man was Clara's father, and she would not thank him for getting into a public row. Taking a deep breath, he tried for reason. "I dinnae sell the cheap gut rot that passes for whisky in these places," he told the vicar. "I trade only in the finest, mature whisky, and there's little of that drunk here. It's nae the kind of thing a fellow swills by the bottle, aye?"

"So, you have no responsibility to the people of this town, then?" the reverend demanded. "You think opening another tavern to tempt them into spending their hard-earned wages in is a good business opportunity?"

Hamilton bristled. "I employ more men and women in this town than anyone else," he said, his voice rising as he felt Angus lay a steadying hand on his shoulder. "I do my bit, and I'm a fair employer. Generous, too. Aye, lassies?"

To his relief, the women agreed, remarking that there were few like him and that he did a good deal for the people of Wick.

"Not enough to satisfy God," the reverend retorted with satisfaction. He might have said more, but Flora Cameron took his arm.

"That'll do, Reverend. A row in the street when passions are high will help nae one. Why don't we sing a hymn, loud enough for God himself to hear us?" she suggested with a smile.

"A splendid idea as always, Mrs Cameron," the reverend agreed warmly, before turning his back on Hamilton and leading the women in a spirited rendition that ought to have Murray tearing his hair out.

"Well, of all the—" Hamilton began, only to be steered away by Angus.

"Leave him be. The reverend is ripe for a fight, and not the kind ye usually enjoy," Angus said, smiling at him.

"Ach, the wee bodach," Hamilton said in frustration.

"Come along. Mary will be pleased to see ye, aye?"

"Aye," Hamilton replied, frowning as he followed Angus home to take supper with him and his wife, yet the nagging sensation that the reverend might have a point left a sour sensation in his guts.

Chapter 9

Lyle,

That serves me right for asking your advice. I shall not do so again. Thanks for nothing.

—Excerpt of a letter from The Hon'ble Mr Hamilton Anderson to The Right Hon'ble Lyall Anderson, Viscount Buchanan.

4th June 1850, Montagu House, St James's, London.

"There's no point in looking at me like that," Regina Harris said, trying not to laugh as Tilly glared daggers at her. "This is entirely your doing and now we are both missing a visit to the National Gallery. It's me who ought to be glaring at you for making me miss out on such a splendid outing."

Tilly's beautiful face wobbled and then fell, and she ran to Regina, who hastily set her sewing aside before she stabbed the girl with her needle. "I'm sorry, Harry," she said contritely, hugging her tightly. "I know I was very bad, but that lady was such a—"

"Yes, well, we shan't go into that," Regina replied swiftly, who privately thought an ice in the lap was the very least the dim-witted creature had merited. Men were all the same, though. They just wanted a pretty nitwit on their arm, someone they could treat like a dress up doll and put away when they were tired with them. Not all men, she told herself severely, for she disliked injustice and she knew several men who were everything they ought to be. A slight cough in the doorway indicated the arrival of one such.

Harris leapt to her feet, dislodging Tilly as she saw the Marquess of Montagu, Tilly's grandfather, standing in the doorway. It was like looking at a more mature version of her employer, except those cold silver eyes seemed to see through her, which made her exceedingly uneasy.

"My lord," she said, dropping a curtsey as Tilly disengaged herself from her skirts.

"Pops!" the girl cried and ran to Montagu, throwing her arms about him so hard the man let out a soft huff of exclamation.

"Tilly, you little wretch. I do wish you would not try to incapacitate me every time you want a hug," he said mildly. He took the girl by the chin, gazing down at her. "You've been wicked," he observed.

"Only a little bit," she replied stubbornly.

"Tilly," Harris reproved, busying herself with tidying up her sewing so she could turn her back to Montagu. She did not like being near him, for the man was as sharp as a dagger blade and little got past him.

"Oh, well, yes, then. I was dreadful," Tilly said with a sigh. "But I was provoked," she added, folding her arms.

"What have I told you about how to behave when you are provoked, Ottilie Barrington?" Montagu asked gently.

"To imagine I am a block of ice and everyone around me feels the chill," Tilly recited dutifully.

"You allow no one that is not a close friend or family member to see your feelings, child. They do not deserve such intimacy. It matters not what they think of you, that is not your business, any more than what you think of them is theirs. You do not behave in a manner that is unworthy of the Barrington name. You are Montagu's granddaughter. You will behave as such."

Tilly's bottom lip quivered as she looked up at Montagu. "Yes, Grandpapa," she said, her voice tremulous.

Montagu sighed. "Don't try those tricks on me, you little devil. They may work on your father, but—" He paused and shook his head. "Oh, very well, they work on me, too. Fetch your coat and bonnet. I shall take you out and endure your father's scolding for spoiling you later."

Tilly gave a shriek of delight and hugged Montagu again, harder than before, making him suck in a sharp breath. "Thank you, Pops!" she cried, and ran off to fetch her things.

Montagu watched her go before turning his attention to Regina. "Are you going to scold me, too?"

Regina smiled and shook her head. "She's finding it very hard, knowing her father is looking for a wife."

Montagu nodded, a faraway look in his eyes. "Yes, I understand that very well. She fears she'll be set aside or replaced by his choice, or that his wife will not like or accept her."

"Those are valid concerns," Regina said, for she felt them on Tilly's behalf.

"The last is, the first are not. No one could ever replace her in her father's affections."

"No, my lord," Regina said respectfully.

"Lord Ashburton is of the opinion you neither like nor approve of him," Montagu said, startling her with such a direct statement.

Regina opened and closed her mouth before gathering her wits. "My opinion of Lord Ashburton is of no relevance. I do my job, and I do it well. So long as my work is of the highest standard, my private opinions are none of his business," she added, throwing his own words back at him.

Montagu's lips twitched. "Well done," he said approvingly. "Now fetch your coat and hat. You may accompany us."

“Oh, but—” Regina said, not wanting to do anything that involved spending time with Montagu.

“No buts, Mrs Harris,” Montagu replied, turning and walking away.

Ten minutes later and Tilly and Regina were ensconced in Montagu’s luxurious carriage, making the brief journey to Gunters. Tilly chattered happily to her grandfather, who seemed to delight in his granddaughter’s company. Not that Regina blamed him for that. Spoiled she might be, but Tilly was lively and clever, a quick-witted child who was an entertaining companion. She was also kind-hearted and loving, and she deserved a mother who would guide her through the coming years, for Tilly would be a beauty one day and then she would need careful handling. Regina could not help but worry, for both their sakes. She enjoyed her life as Tilly’s governess, though the realisation had come as a surprise to her. Once upon a time she had longed for a husband, some romantic figure to come and rescue her from a life where her future had not been her own. It was her own now, but it was by no means secure.

The elegant tea shop fell silent as Montagu walked in, every head turning to stare at him, and then at Tilly. He ignored the gazes as he always did, encased in the ice he was teaching Tilly to cultivate. A hushed murmur of voices rose after the initial silence, with women raising fans to whisper behind as they stared at Tilly. Regina hurried forward, about to take the girl’s hand, for she could see the blush rising to the child’s cheeks, but Montagu looked down at Tilly and their eyes met. Tilly put up her chin, adopting a cool, haughty expression that was an echo of her grandfather’s.

Montagu winked surreptitiously at the girl and took her hand, and Regina felt an unexpected lump in her throat at the silent exchange.

They enjoyed a lavish tea, with Montagu choosing a ridiculously indulgent selection of cream cakes and buns. Regina was rather startled to discover herself enjoying the outing. Once they had eaten far more than Regina thought quite proper for any of them, though she did not regret a single crumb, Montagu escorted them out again.

"I rather regret dismissing the carriage," he said with a sigh. "I thought the walk would do us good after such a disgusting display of indulgence, but I'm not sure I can make it," he said sadly, resting an elegant, gloved hand on a stomach that was as flat now as it had surely been in his youth.

"Silly, Pops. Of course we can," Tilly said scornfully, taking his hand and tugging on it as if she would drag him down the road.

"Child, I am not a dog on a lead, kindly stop pulling at me," he complained, though without heat.

"Tilly, you will walk like a young lady, please. We do not want your grandfather to think I have taught you nothing. He might have me dismissed."

Though she had said it merely in jest, a look of pure panic crossed Tilly's face, and she clung to her grandfather's hand. "You wouldn't do that, would you, Pops? Not Harry? I couldn't bear it if Harry left me. Not that. *Please?"*

"Calm yourself," Montagu said, gazing down at his granddaughter in surprise. "Of course I shall do no such thing. Whatever do you take me for?"

Tilly let out an uneven breath, struggling to calm herself. "I-I apologise, Grandfather. I just… I'm sorry," she said helplessly.

"It's all right," Montagu said, stroking her hair. "Go on now. Isn't that Lady St Clair up ahead? Tell her what a wicked child you've been. She'll enjoy that." He smiled at her and Tilly's expression smoothed out, the happiness returning to her eyes.

"Yes, Pops."

They walked on in silence for a while as they watched Tilly run ahead and catch up with Lady St Clair and her friends, one of whom was carrying a fat pug. The lady exclaimed with delight and then turned and waved at Montagu, who raised his hand in greeting.

"My granddaughter thinks a great deal of you," Montagu observed.

"I think a great deal of her," Regina replied with a smile, though her heart was beating hard as she felt Montagu's gaze upon her.

"I don't believe I know anything about you, Mrs Harris. Who are your people?"

"Lord Ashburton has all my credentials and letters of recommendation. I'm sure he can tell you all you wish to know," she said hurriedly. "If you'll excuse me, Tilly is about to stroke that dog, and I do not know if it's the kind to bite."

Knowing she had likely done herself no favours, Regina hurried away before Montagu could question her further.

6th June 1850, Wick, Caithness, Scotland.

"Morning, Angus. I'm sorry to call on ye on yer day off, but I plain forgot to give ye the papers ye asked me for yesterday. If I dinnae do it now, ye winnae have them for a week or more," Hamilton said, smiling at Angus and eyeing him up and down, for he was dressed in his best. "Well, ye are fine as fivepence, man. What's the occasion?"

"Mary and I are taking a walk up to the Old Man of Wick," Angus replied, looking a trifle uneasy.

"Ah, romantic. I didnae ken ye had it in ye," Hamilton teased.

"It's a walking party. A picnic, actually," Angus replied, a trifle defensively. "Malcolm arranged it."

"Oh, aye?"

"I know ye will not like it, but I couldn't say no, and… and it was all arranged, so I figured the best we could do was to go."

"What are ye blethering on about?" Hamilton said in confusion. "Why would I care if ye go walking with yer brother?"

"My brother and Mr Fraser, Miss Fleming, and Miss Halliday," Angus amended, wincing as Hamilton's gaze darkened.

"He's nae business trifling with that lassie."

"Well, I don't know that taking her for a walk in company constitutes trifling," Angus said with a frown.

Hamilton returned a stony look. "Do ye trust yer brother with Miss Halliday, Angus?"

Angus sighed. "Not entirely. That's why I'm going. Though he did ask me, and surely that shows he intends to treat her with respect. Perhaps he means to turn over a new leaf."

"Hmph," was all Hamilton could find to say on that point. He thrust the papers at Angus. "Here. Mind ye keep yer eye on her or ye will have me to answer to."

"Yes, of course," Angus said as Hamilton stalked off.

6th June 1850, The Old Man of Wick, Caithness, Scotland.

The weather had been kind, a thing Clara suspected was not often said of the region, but today the sky was as clear a blue as she had ever seen, the sun sparkling so brightly on the water it almost hurt her eyes. The Old Man of Wick was a little underwhelming in truth, the ruins of a castle that had once been mighty but now was little more than the base of a square tower. The jut of land on which the castle stood, and the narrow gully into which the sea seethed and thrashed below, however, were spectacular. Every way she turned, the views were dramatic and glorious and made her wish she had even a little skill with a paintbrush for such a scene must call to the artist in everyone. Her heart lifted at the beauty of the scene, and it made her think unexpectedly of Mr Anderson, and his advice to hold on to such moments of happiness and keep them with you. She smiled, thinking she would tell him about it the next time she saw him, and then remembered she was cross with him for being a shocking flirt and her happiness dimmed.

"Are you glad you came?"

Clara turned to discover Mr Stewart beside her. She smiled at him.

"Very," she said truthfully. "It was a lovely walk and I'm looking forward to the picnic. We've been so fortunate with the weather, too," she added, turning her face up to the sun to enjoy the warmth. It was windy on the cliff's edge, but she had taken the precaution of tying her hair securely and fastening her bonnet on with extra hat pins just in case, so that she could appreciate the buffeting of the wind with no fears.

"I'm glad you came," Mr Stewart said, lowering his voice. "So glad. You can have no notion of how beautiful you look with your face turned up to the sun. Like a rose turning towards the warmth of a new day."

Clara looked away, feeling a little awkward. She knew she ought to be flattered by such a poetic turn of phrase. That had been the sort of thing she had hoped for, hadn't it? Yet the reality of it felt different, and she wondered if she was being fickle, if perhaps she was merely a shallow girl whose head had been turned by the handsome Mr Anderson. Unease stirred in her belly. "We should join the others," she said, sending him a cheerful smile. "Miss Fleming will want help with the picnic."

"Miss Fleming has never lifted a finger in her life before. Mary is seeing to the picnic," he said wryly. "Don't be such a goose. Come along with me, just for a little walk to the castle, we'll be in plain view all the way. By the time we return, it will all be ready."

Clara hesitated. It seemed churlish to refuse when he had arranged this day entirely for her pleasure. He had also taken pains to be agreeable and had entertained them all with stories of what his boys had been up to. Malcolm Stewart was everything she had believed she had wanted, so ought she not give him a chance? They would be in plain view, as he said.

"Just a short walk then," she agreed, taking his arm.

"That's the girl," he approved. "Now, tell me how you like Wick. I'm afraid it must seem rather rough and ready after Cambridgeshire."

"A little," Clara admitted. "But I like it. I love being by the sea, and the people have been friendly, though I still don't know many of them well. I was so glad to get to know Miss Fleming, and Mr Frazer seems an amiable man. Thank you for inviting him. I'm so pleased to have been introduced."

"Yes, he's decent enough. A bit stodgy, in more ways than one," he added with a laugh, which Clara thought rather unkind. She had very much liked Mr Frazer, who seemed a kind and jovial young man. He was rather plump, and the walk had made him perspire dreadfully and become very red in the face.

"Do you intend to go home often?" he asked with interest.

"No, I don't think so. It isn't home any longer, after all," she added with a smile. "We had a few friends there, but in all honesty there's not much to return for."

"But your family is there, your grandfather?"

"My grandfather?" Clara repeated in confusion.

"Your grandfather, Baron Marsham?" he said, smiling.

"Oh," Clara said in surprise. "Well, yes, he is still there, I believe. Not that I've ever met him."

"Never met him?" he repeated, sounding shocked. "Why not?"

Clara frowned, a little put out by the bold enquiry which was none of his business. "My father does not see eye to eye with him, I believe. They have not spoken in many years."

Mr Stewart considered this as they walked. "But that sounds like exactly the sort of situation which a doting daughter would take the trouble to remedy. Surely you wish to know the rest of your family? Would you not like to meet your grandfather before he goes to his eternal rest?"

Slanting him a curious glance, Clara considered the question. "I would be curious, I suppose, but everything I have heard of the man from my father and my aunt leads me to believe he has far less interest in me than I have in him. Indeed, he appears to be a cold man who was content to cut my father off."

"Cut him off?" Mr Stewart said in surprise.

Clara nodded, rather wishing she'd not said anything. This was family business and not his affair. "Many years ago."

"Good heavens, but the man is worth a fortune, is he not? Surely your father tried to remedy the situation?"

Feeling a sudden thread of anger, Clara fought to keep her tone calm. "No, sir. Their falling out was of such a nature that my father did not feel comfortable in taking anything from my grandfather again."

And whilst her father had many faults, she could not deny that he had never wavered from that standpoint, when to do so would have greatly increased his own wealth and comfort. From what she knew, her grandfather had been a bully, and her father had stood up to him. For all his shortcomings, she could only admire him for that.

Mr Stewart stood looking out to sea, a pensive expression in his eyes.

"Who told you about my grandfather?" she asked, wondering how he'd gained such knowledge.

"I think Miss Fleming mentioned it. Her father wished to know if you were from a good family before she called on you, so he asked around."

"I see." Though the information was a little irksome, she could not blame Miss Fleming's father for his caution, which was quite normal. Mr Stewart's interest was more difficult to dismiss. She supposed she could not blame him for wanting a wealthy wife, any more than she could Miss Fleming for desiring a rich husband. Still, it was hardly flattering. "I think we ought to return now," Clara said, feeling suddenly uneasy.

"Not yet," Mr Stewart said as she went to turn away. He grasped her hand, giving her a swift smile. "You've not seen the castle, and we've come all this way."

"There's little to see, sir," she replied calmly, though his hand was holding hers too tightly. It sent an odd sensation rippling through her and she wondered if she was being foolish. If Mr Anderson held her hand so, would she feel such a surge of disquiet? Was she being unfair? "I would prefer to return, if you would be so kind as to escort me."

"Oh, but I insist, Miss Halliday. Just think how much blood may have been spilled in such a place. Is it not a romantic setting? Can you not hear the moans of ghosts of the men that lived here?"

"I don't believe I can, I'm afraid, but I'm not a poet," Clara said apologetically, trying for a rueful smile and tugging her hand free. "If you will excuse me, Mr Stewart. I would prefer to return to the others but do continue your walk if you wish to do so."

"Miss Halliday, the picnic is ready. Malcolm, are you coming?"

Clara walked away, relieved to see Mr Angus Stewart had come after them. Leaving Malcolm Stewart to follow in her wake, she hurried to meet his brother. She felt oddly breathless and strangely unwilling to be alone in the man's company any longer.

The picnic, provided in part by Mrs Macready and in part by Miss Fleming's father's cook, and in part from Mary Stewart's fair hand, was excellent and did much to restore Clara's equilibrium. Whatever maggot had got into Mr Malcolm Stewart's head seemed to have been put aside too, for he exerted himself to be charming and entertaining for the rest of the afternoon.

Still, even though she had enjoyed much of the day, Clara was not displeased when they reached the road to the school on their way home.

"Well, we'll leave you here, then, Malcolm. Mary and I will see Miss Halliday home, for it's out of your way," Angus said cheerfully, as his brother shot him a glare of annoyance.

"But I should be pleased to come too," Malcolm protested.

"Oh, of course you would, but there's no need," Angus said, clapping his brother on the shoulder. "We'll see you at church tomorrow, I expect. Goodbye, laddie."

"Tomorrow, then," Malcolm said sourly, though he bid good day to Clara prettily enough.

The moment he was gone, Miss Fleming hurried to Clara and took her arm, leaving Mr Fraser to fall in step with Mary and Angus.

"Thank goodness," she whispered in a dramatic whisper. "If I had to hold that revolting man's arm for a moment longer, I would have swooned," she said with a shudder.

"Miss Fleming!" Clara said, glancing around in concern. "He'll hear you."

"I don't care," Miss Fleming replied, sounding mutinous. "He's disgusting, and I don't care if his father is wealthy. There's no amount of money in the world that could make that match acceptable to me."

"Who is proposing such a match?" Clara asked at once.

"My father suggested it," she replied morosely. "I've told him I'd rather die, and I believe that has put paid to the notion, but all the same. It made me feel sick."

"He's a very nice man," Clara said carefully, for she could not deny that the idea of embracing Mr Fraser was not a terribly appealing one. He'd found the walk rather taxing and was wilting now in his heavy tweed suit, sweat beading on his face. "And there's much to be said for a kind husband, one who would be gentle and sweet to you."

Miss Fleming shot her a scathing glance. "So, you'd marry him over Mr Anderson, would you?"

Clara gaped, momentarily struck dumb. "As I have been asked by neither of them, I don't see any relevance in the question," she replied once she'd gathered her wits. Not for the first time she worried over some of things Miss Fleming said, and wondered if perhaps they were destined to be friends after all. Eventually Clara would have to stop biting her tongue if she kept saying such dreadful things aloud. The idea was a depressing one as there were no other young ladies beating down her door and wishing to become acquainted with her.

"Oh, come now. I saw how you looked at Mr Anderson. Not that I blame you. He's a handsome devil, and the son of an earl too, not to mention wealthy. Everything he touches turns to gold, they say. I think I could forgive him for being in trade for such a life," she added thoughtfully.

Clara stared straight ahead, wondering what on earth Miss Fleming meant by that. Had she been looking at Mr Anderson? How had she been looking? Not that it mattered; he hadn't the slightest interest in Clara, nor she in him. Miss Fleming was welcome to him, she decided, and walked on, determined not to encourage the conversation any further.

Miss Fleming's house was next and, as Mr Fraser was her close neighbour, she could not refuse him the pleasure of escorting her the final stretch as they parted company with the others. Miss Fleming's face was a picture of discontent, however, and Clara fretted over it until Mr Fraser caught her gaze. He grinned and winked at her, such a look of mischief in his eyes that she realised he was well aware of Miss Fleming's opinion of him and clearly did not give a snap of his fingers for it.

Relieved, Clara carried on with the Stewarts until they came to their front door. Stopping, she turned to them, for they clearly expected to escort her the rest of the way.

"I can walk home by myself, please don't trouble yourself. I know you are desperate to check on your little boy and the vicarage is just a step around the corner."

Angus Stewart hesitated, but Mary had already opened the front door. She gave a delighted exclamation as their nurse appeared with their baby son in her arms. Angus clearly wished to make a fuss over his son, too, and so Clara reassured him once more.

"It's barely a five-minute walk and in broad daylight. Thank you for a most enjoyable day, but I am quite content to walk the last little way by myself."

"If you are sure, then," he said, smiling. "And may I say what a delightful companion you've been, Miss Halliday. Mary is a little preoccupied now, I'm afraid, but I know she has so enjoyed meeting you."

"And I her. I beg you will remind her to call on me at the vicarage whenever she pleases, for I promise, I shall be a frequent visitor now I have seen how adorable your little boy is."

"He is a handsome fellow, isn't he?" Angus said proudly. "Well, good day then, Miss Halliday. We shall see you at church tomorrow."

Clara waved at them and carried on her way. She turned the corner, taking the street that led to the vicarage and then stopped in her tracks as she saw Malcolm Stewart ahead of her. What on earth was he doing? He must have taken a different route to get ahead of them.

“Surprise!” he called out cheerfully. “I felt sure you’d walk the last bit by yourself. Angus and Mary are so daft over that boy of theirs they can’t bear to be parted from him for five minutes at a time.”

“That’s very perceptive of you, but I do not understand why you felt the need to do so. I have bid you a good afternoon already and I’m almost home. It was quite unnecessary.”

“But I’m not yet ready to be dismissed. My brother is a pain in the neck, treating me like a child just because he’s older than me. You have no such excuse, though, my innocent dove. Why do you insist on being so cruel to me?” he asked her, and whilst there was amusement behind the words, there was a hint of something Clara did not like. Not to mention the way he called her *my innocent dove* made her feel slightly ill.

“Cruel? Whatever do you mean?”

“I’m only teasing, lass,” he said with a laugh. “Come now, take my arm and I’ll see you home.”

“I thank you for your solicitude, sir,” Clara said carefully, for she was not at all certain it was solicitude at work. “But I am quite capable of walking home alone.”

“Capable, yes, but it’s not the done thing, you know, and you can’t leave me standing in the street and walk off. Everyone will think we’ve had a lovers’ tiff.”

“Indeed, they will not,” Clara said crossly.

“They will, though. Do you not think everyone expects the vicar’s daughter and the schoolteacher to make a match?”

Clara bridled at the comment, determined now that the man would not walk her home. "I do not, unless someone were foolish enough to put such thoughts into their head."

"Is it foolish, Clara?" he asked, gentling his voice, his eyes soft behind his spectacles. There was that sweet boyish smile, his demeanour one of rueful amusement.

Clara hesitated, wondering if she had misjudged him. Was she being churlish by refusing to allow him to walk her home? She had liked him at first, and he had arranged this outing for her pleasure. Yet there was something about him that made her nerves leap. Her hesitation seemed justified when he took her arm, dragging her down narrow passage between two houses.

"Stop being so missish," he said crossly. "Neither of us is a fool, and it's clear we're meant for each other, so I see no reason to take an age about admitting it. There's no one else in this God forsaken town that's your equal, Miss Halliday and your father is not about to let you have a season, that much is obvious. So, let's stop the games and pretending and get to the nitty gritty."

"The nitty—" Clara gasped, reeling from the sudden change in demeanour. There was a cold, calculating look in the eyes that had appeared so soft only moments before, and she realised that not only had Mr Anderson been right to warn her, but she had not paid heed to her own instincts.

"I'm the best chance you have to get a husband," he said coldly, "And whilst I'd prefer someone a bit warmer in my bed than a vicar's daughter, I reckon we can get along well enough once we understand each other."

Clara stared at him, so shocked it took her a moment to react. "I think I understand perfectly well," she said, wishing she did not sound so breathless.

"We'll see," he replied with a smirk, and put his hand to her waist. Clara stamped on his foot, ignoring the obscene oath he uttered as he let her go. She exited the passage, walking quickly away, very aware of Mr Stewart following close behind.

"Not so fast, Clara," he muttered under his breath, as Clara quickened her pace.

"Good day to you, Miss Halliday."

Clara looked across the street, feeling a wash of relief at the sight of Mr Anderson. Her previous irritation with him for flirting with her—and every other girl in Wick—vanished, and she greeted him like an old friend.

"Mr Anderson, a good day to you too, sir. I hope you are well. Are you enjoying the sunshine? It's been a beautiful day. We've just returned from a walk to the Old Man of Wick, you know, with Mr Angus Stewart and his wife, and Miss Fleming and Mr Fraser. Do you know Mr Fraser? He's a very nice man," Clara said, horribly aware she was babbling but unable to stop herself.

Mr Anderson looked from her to Mr Stewart and Clara knew at once he understood. Mr Stewart stared stonily back, regarding the new arrival with far less enthusiasm.

"Aye, Fraser is a decent fellow," Mr Anderson said, not taking his eyes from Malcolm Stewart. "He's clever too. Reckon he'll do great things before he's done."

"Well, he's invested in one of your businesses so that's inevitable, is it not?" Mr Stewart replied, with every appearance of giving a compliment, yet Clara thought there was a sour note to the remark. Mr Anderson must have thought the same, for his eyes glittered and he grinned, a not quite nice smile that suggested Mr Stewart mind his step.

"Aye, laddie. Reckon it is, at that."

Mr Stewart's face darkened, and he stood taller, the two men eyeing each other. Stewart was as tall as Mr Anderson, but fine-boned in comparison. "I'll thank you not to refer to me in such a manner."

Mr Anderson laughed. “But ye are Angus’ wee brother, the one he’s always pulling out of some misadventure or other. I always think of ye as laddie. I’ll do my best to mend my ways, however, if it vexes ye.”

“It does,” Mr Stewart replied evenly.

“Ah, well, I meant nae offense,” Mr Anderson said with patent falsity before turning to Clara. “Miss Halliday, I was on my way to call on Mrs Macready. Would ye mind if I walked with ye? I need yer advice about something.”

“Oh, well, of course, Mr Anderson, if I can help, I should be glad to.”

“Excellent. *Oh,* I’ll bid ye a good afternoon, Mr Stewart,” Mr Anderson said, as if he’d suddenly remembered the man was still standing there.

“Good afternoon, Mr Anderson, Miss Halliday,” Mr Stewart replied, the words gritted out as he turned on his heel and stalked off.

Clara let out a slow breath, only now realising how tense she’d been as Mr Anderson walked beside her and she could finally allow herself to relax.

“It’s all right, Miss Halliday. I’ll nae let the likes of Malcolm Stewart bother ye.”

Clara swallowed, wondering why she was so unwilling to tell him what had happened. Perhaps because she felt so very foolish after he had warned her about Mr Stewart, and she had been arrogant enough to believe he was jealous. “There was no problem, really,” she said, aware the words were unconvincing.

“Aye, that was why yer face lit up when ye saw me,” he said wryly. “I ken well enough ye were nae pleased with me the last time we met, yet ye looked like ye had missed me something dreadful. I’m an arrogant devil, Miss Halliday, but I’m nae a fool.”

"No, but you must think I am," she admitted, for she could not deny it even though she wanted to. "For I well remember why I was not pleased with you, even if you are too polite to say, 'I told you so.'"

He shook his head, frowning. "I'd nae be so daft as that. Maybe I was out of line warning ye off the fellow, but perhaps now ye can forgive me and believe I only had your interests at heart. He's nae the man his brother is, I'm afraid, and he's nae to be relied upon."

Clara glanced up at him, struck by the uncompromising line of his jaw, the shadow of his beard already visible, everything about him was hard, muscular, *male.* He may have called Mr Stewart laddie merely to incense him, but the fellow looked like a mere boy compared to this fine example of sheer masculinity. He turned to look at her, a quizzical look in his eyes, and Clara turned hurriedly away, fighting a blush at having been caught staring so brazenly. For a moment she wondered if this was why she preferred Mr Anderson, was she really so shallow as to be won over by a handsome face? With relief, she set this accusation aside. Mr Anderson's manners might not be what she was used to, but he was honest, blunt in fact, and he said what he meant which she found reassuring. She had always felt uneasy in Mr Stewart's presence, as if there was something else going on behind his eyes that she did not understand. Looking into Mr Anderson's eyes might sometimes be uncomfortable and make her blush, but his admiration was bold and to the point and he did not make declarations of love and devotion when he clearly felt none. That might be a disappointing fact, but she could not accuse him of leading her on and making her believe he meant to court her.

"I do forgive you," she said, wishing he were not so easy to like. She could well understand why all the girls in Wick were pining for the fellow. His looks were one thing, but he was also kind, and the sort of man who made you feel safe, even though he was not safe in the least. Indeed, Clara could not help but wonder if Mr Anderson was far more of a danger to her heart than Malcolm Stewart could ever be.

"I'm glad," he said, his voice soft. "I dislike speaking ill of folk, but Malcolm Stewart is unreliable. I'd hold my tongue, for I have nae the least right to give you orders so I'll stop myself right now, but…"

"But?" Clara repeated, amused despite herself.

He laughed and ran a hand through his hair, turning to her with a sheepish smile. "I wish ye would steer clear of him."

"I'll do my best, Mr Anderson."

"That's grand, then," he replied as they arrived at the back gate to the vicarage.

He stared at her, not saying anything and Clara hesitated. There was an arrested look in his eyes, as though he'd suddenly realised something and was unsure whether to mention it or not.

"You wanted to see Mrs Macready?" she suggested, wondering if he'd forgotten why he came.

"Eh? Oh," he said, giving himself a little shake like he'd been a long way away. "Ah, nae. I just made that up to give me a reason to walk with ye," he said with a shrug.

"Well, perhaps you ought to come in and see her, for verisimilitude," she said gravely.

He laughed at that, his eyes twinkling merrily and making Clara's heart give a pleased little thud at having amused him. "Verisimilitude, eh?" he said, rubbing his chin thoughtfully.

"Yes, it means to give authenticity and—"

"I ken what it means, ye wee yin," he said, shaking his head at her. "I'm nae as daft as I look, aye? Despite what ye may think of me, I had a university education, like a proper gentleman," he added wryly.

Clara flushed scarlet. “Please, forgive me, Mr Anderson, I never meant to imply that—”

“Dinnae fash,” he said with a smile, reaching out and taking hold of a lock of hair that had finally escaped her ruthless pinning. “I ken ye meant nae insult.”

Clara held her breath as he tucked the errant curl behind her ear and then dropped his hand like she’d scalded him, looking as shocked as she was.

“Well, are ye coming in, or are ye nae?” demanded a tart voice from the kitchen door.

“Mrs Macready,” Mr Anderson said, regaining his wits quicker than Clara, who was feeling ridiculously flustered for reasons she did not care to dwell upon. “Good afternoon to ye. I just walked yer lassie home.”

“Aye, I see that,” Mrs Macready said wryly, looking from Clara’s flushed cheeks to Mr Anderson. “Ye had best come in before the neighbours start flapping their gums. Kettle’s on,” she added, turning away from the door and going back inside.

To her surprise, Mr Anderson looked at Clara, a question in his eyes. “I’ll go if ye prefer,” he said, somewhat gruffly.

Clara looked up at him, and knew she was a fool for wishing him to stay, but she did. “You had best not refuse an invitation from Mrs Macready, you never know when you’ll get another,” she told him sternly.

He grinned, a lopsided smile that did the most peculiar thing to her stomach, making her wonder if perhaps she had eaten too much at lunchtime.

He leaned closer to her, bending his head to her ear and lowering his voice. “Is that the only reason I should stay?”

Clara’s breath caught, and she looked up at him, suddenly caught in the amber of his gaze like some poor, unsuspecting creature trapped for all eternity in a beautiful orange bead.

"I…" she began, only to forget what she'd been about to say as she stared up at him. Heat rose in a wave, surging up her chest, her neck, to her cheeks as she saw his gaze travel from her eyes to her mouth and linger there. His eyes darkened, and he seemed quite unable to look away as she licked her lips.

He's thinking about kissing me, her dazed brain screamed whilst her heart performed a complicated little dance behind her ribs. The moment stretched out, all her nerves leaping, her skin feeling like it was not her own but too tight and ill fitting. Before she could even wonder if she would allow him such a liberty or not, he put distance between them, straightening and turning a little away from her. He let out a breath, frowning, before glancing back.

"I'd best nae linger," he said gruffly. "But I thank ye kindly for the invite. Give my apologies to Mrs Macready but… but I have things to attend to. Good day to ye, Miss Halliday."

With that he strode off, leaving Clara feeling bewildered and foolish and not a little bit cross.

Chapter 10

Dearest Tilly,

My poor little monster. How dreadful, and I do not blame you in the least for dropping your ice in her lap. I should have done just the same, I'm afraid, but I was a terrible little girl and not at all the kind you should try to emulate. Luckily for you, your Pops adores terrible little girls, so we all get away with murder.

I shall come to town next week, and we shall be perfectly dreadful together.

—Excerpt of a letter from The Most Hon'ble Lady Catherine 'Cat' St Just, Marchioness of Kilbane to her niece Miss Ottilie Barrington.

6th June 1850, Wick, Caithness, Scotland.

"Ye great numpty, what the devil are ye playing at?" Hamilton muttered crossly to himself as he strode away from the vicarage. He knew the rules. You didn't mess around with innocent girls unless you meant to marry them. You certainly didn't flirt and act like a great gowk with a vicar's daughter. *A vicar's daughter!* He slapped a hand to his forehead and rubbed it over his face, groaning inwardly. "Yer brains are all in yer nether regions, Hamilton Anderson, and that's a fact."

But he had wanted to kiss her so badly it had overridden good sense, and teasing her a little, getting her to admit that she had wanted him to stay had been too easy, too natural. She liked him, despite herself. Arrogant he might be, but he knew when a woman fancied him and, whilst she might disapprove of a good deal about him, the proper Miss Halliday had wanted him to kiss her. The knowledge only made him growl inwardly for now he was all riled up and bothered by a tormenting itch there was no possible way of scratching. He ought to be visiting Moyra, not getting himself in a lather over Miss Halliday. He thought he'd left his pocket watch when he was there last and it would be a chance to retrieve it, but knowing he was going to her with another woman in his mind would be an appalling thing to do and she deserved better than that. He would have to end things with her, and the truth of that only made him even more irritable.

Instead, he turned into the next street and headed towards Macrae's, pushing inside the tavern and responding to the calls of greeting and offers to buy him a drink. In his opinion, the very best thing he could do was put Miss Halliday far out of his mind, and he intended to do it.

♡♧◇♤

Clara was relieved to have the house to herself that evening, giving her time to settle her nerves and scold herself for the fiftieth time for acting like such a nitwit. Honestly, it served her right. What she had been thinking, she could not imagine. Well, she hadn't been thinking, and that was a fact. Mr Anderson's handsome face and winning smile had addled her brain like she was the veriest ninny, and she had not only allowed him to do it but had made a complete fool of herself in the process. Then there was the terrible scene with Mr Stewart, her stomach lurched as she wondered what might have happened if she had not got away from him. She had been a fool on too many counts today. Clara realised now that she was far from the sensible, mature woman she had believed herself to be. Indeed, she had shown herself up to be naïve and inexperience where men were concerned. Her pride was smarting, and she felt irritable and out of sorts and quite unfit company for anyone. She had been relieved to say goodbye to Mrs Macready when she took herself off to her own home, for the lady's gaze was far too knowing and full of sympathy and only made Clara feel a great deal worse.

With her thoughts full of reproaches and resolutions to behave better in the future, she made her way up the stairs to bed, though it was far too early. She was too fidgety to read or sew, however, and the sooner this day was over, the better. She had made it barely halfway up the stairs, candle in hand, when someone began hammering on the front door. Startled, Clara stilled and called out.

"Who's there?"

Her father still had not returned from yet another demonstration in the town, with his temperance army barricading the doors of Galbraith's tavern a few streets away, and her first thought was that something had happened to him.

"It's Tommy Brodie, Miss Halliday. I'm sorry for disturbing ye, but me mam said to fetch the reverend. Grandpa is breathing his last, so he is, and he wants to make peace afore he goes."

"Lud," Clara said in dismay, relieved her father was in no difficulty but wishing he was at home to receive his caller. She opened the door to see Tommy's usually cheerful face, wan and serious in the candlelight. He was a gawky lad a year or two older than Jimmy, though Jimmy said he was not terribly bright. "I'm so sorry to hear that. I'm afraid my father is not here, Tommy. I believe he's at Galbraith's and—"

"And would ye fetch him then, miss?" the boy said anxiously. "I dinnae want to leave me mam all alone if Grandpa goes, ye see."

"No, no, of course you must not do so. I'll find my father and fetch him to you at once."

"Oh, thank ye, miss," the lad said in relief, and ran off again before she could reply.

As fast as she could, Clara put on her coat and bonnet, and went out of the front door, hoping she could remember the way to Galbraith's. By the time she had gone three streets, she knew she had made an error. Everything looked so different in the dark, though. Turning to retrace her footsteps, Clara gasped as a slender figure barged into her.

"Ooof! Blimey, what did you do that for? You nearly broke me nose," Jimmy complained, rubbing that appendage fiercely.

"Jimmy? Are you following me?" Clara demanded.

"Of course I am," Jimmy said indignantly. "Can't have you gallivanting about at night on yer ownsome, can I? Not with you as innocent as a lamb and not knowing what's lurking in the darkness."

"As far as I can see," Clara said tartly. "The only thing lurking is you."

"I ain't lurking, I was guarding," Jimmy replied, looking offended.

Clara softened, aware that he had sought to protect her as best he could. "I know that, Jimmy, and it was thoughtful of you. The truth is, you're right, for I'm lost. I'm trying to find Galbraith's. Papa is there tonight, and old Mr Brodie is dying. He wishes to see Papa at once."

"Thought I heard Tommy's voice at the door," Jimmy said, nodding. "All right. Well, it's this way, then."

Obediently, Clara followed Jimmy through the darkness, crossing the street as he led her on the opposite side of the road from Macrae's tavern. The sound of masculine laughter came from within, the windows fogged up as light blazed from them. Clara looked over at the building as the sound grew suddenly louder, the door opening as two figures stepped out. The second and largest man paused for a moment, drawing in a deep breath before their eyes met across the street.

Clara stiffened. Well, of all the ill luck.

"Hurry up," she instructed Jimmy.

"'Ere, don't push," he grumbled. "Where's the fire? I'm going as fast as I can."

"Jimmy!" bellowed a deep voice, making Jimmy start with surprise and then stop in his tracks.

Muttering under her breath, Clara scowled as Mr Anderson, with Mr Angus Stewart on his heels, crossed the road in a few long strides and looked from her to the boy.

"What this? Why are ye walking about at night with just the lad for a chaperone?"

"Good evening, Mr Anderson," Clara said coolly. "Mr Stewart, a good evening to you. How is your wife?"

"She's well, thank you, miss."

"And little Callum?"

"He's grand too—"

"Never mind the social chitchat," Mr Anderson growled.

"Not that it's any of your business. My father is required to attend to Mr Brodie," Clara said, her voice frigid with annoyance. "As I was at home by myself, and he is outside Galbraith's—"

Mr Anderson waved this information away as if it were an annoying gnat. "Aye, aye. Angus, see to it, will ye? There's a good fellow. I'll see Miss Halliday home."

"Indeed, you will not," Clara objected. "Jimmy will escort—"

But as she looked around, she discovered Jimmy had disappeared.

"I think he's seen some of his mates," Angus Stewart said with a rueful smile, nodding to the end of the road to where Jimmy was messing about with three other boys.

"Why, it's too late for the boys to be out in the streets," Clara said, setting out after him.

"I'll see to Jimmy, don't worry," Angus said swiftly, looking between Clara and Mr Anderson. "You'll see Miss Halliday home safely, won't you?" he added, looking at Mr Anderson with a searching expression.

Mr Anderson shot him a volcanic glare, which made Angus blanch. "Aye, well, I'll be off on my errand, then. Don't worry, Miss Halliday, I'll tell Jimmy to pop in on Mary and she'll feed him cake until I get back. Then I'll bring him home to you."

"Thank you, Mr Stewart," Clara said, though she rather wished him to the devil for interfering and leaving her with Hamilton Anderson. Sending her unwanted chaperone a look of icy annoyance, she stalked off in the direction of home.

"Ye are vexed with me," he observed, keeping stride with ease, though she was walking at as fast a pace as she could manage.

"Not in the least," she said briskly. "I am only fearful of my reputation, which will be done no good at all for being seen walking with you after dark."

"Better than ye walking alone when anyone could accost ye. The streets are full of men bevied to their eyeballs after dark, ye ken."

"Like you?" she suggested, raising an eyebrow at him.

"I'm nae bevied," he replied indignantly.

"But you *have* been drinking," she said smugly, knowing he could not deny it. She could smell the scent of whisky on him and was dismayed to discover it was not an entirely unpleasant odour.

"Aye," he admitted gruffly.

"Hmph," she said, sticking her nose in the air as if this was enough to damn him. She didn't mean it in the slightest, having no axe to grind with a man enjoying a drink with his friends, but it was nice to have a means of treating him like a pariah when he had made her feel so… so very… Well, it didn't matter what he'd made her feel. She'd had no business feeling it in the first place.

"Ach, dinnae be crabbit with me because I didnae kiss ye. Ye ken as well as I do, it was a bad idea."

Clara choked, appalled that he had said such a thing out loud. Her cheeks blazed, her heart thudding as humiliation washed over her. She had at least believed he was gentleman enough not to *refer* to those dreadful moments.

"I am not the least bit *crabbit*, and I have not the slightest idea what you are referring to," she said furiously, walking so fast she was almost running. Blind with embarrassment and indignation, she took a wrong turn and found herself in a narrow alley. Muttering, she spun around, annoyed to find his broad figure blocking the way.

"You ken very well what I'm referring to," he said, his voice firm. His eyes glittered in the near darkness but despite the situation, Clara did not feel the slightest bit threatened by the looming figure. Furious, yes, but not threatened. He might be an arrogant, ill-mannered lummox, but she trusted him to behave as he ought. That, as it turned out, was a mistake.

"I do not!" she said stubbornly, letting out a squeak of alarm as he grasped her by the waist and pushed her up against the wall.

"Oh, but ye do," he insisted. "And despite all yer blethering, ye want me to kiss ye still."

"You are without a doubt the most egotistical, rude, thick-headed—" The words were silenced, her breath catching as he pressed his mouth to hers. For a moment, she could not think of anything past the fact that his lips were warm and far softer than she had imagined, and she *had* imagined, drat her disorderly thoughts. The scratch of his beard rasped against her cheek as he brushed his lips back and forth over hers, such a gentle touch from such a large man that everything inside her seemed to melt like warm treacle in response.

He drew back, regarding her with satisfaction and Clara could do nothing but stare at him with wide eyes, breathing so hard she felt somewhat light-headed.

“There, are ye happy now?” he asked, a wicked glint lighting his eyes.

Immediately furious with herself for giving him the opportunity to make such a provoking comment, she shoved at his chest, startled to find that it was akin to pushing a brick wall. Still, he straightened, putting a little distance between them, though it did not help as much as she might have hoped. He was still there, looming, all rugged handsomeness and smug, arrogant, insufferable… oh, lord, but she wanted him to kiss her again. The knowledge was beyond mortifying, and she could not bring herself to look at him.

“I am not in the least bit happy,” she ground out, frustrated by the breathless quality of the words.

“Well, I can do it again if ye want more,” he offered, apparently in all sincerity.

Clara made a high-pitched sound of pure vexation which was ridiculous and unbecoming, but it was that or stamp on his foot and she would not allow herself to sink to such childish behaviour. Instead, she pushed past him and would have practically run from the alley had he not caught a hold of her.

“Wait, make certain ye are nae seen,” he told her, which was sensible advice, sadly, so she waited as he suggested, and then gave a muffled shriek as pulled her back into the shadows.

“What on earth—” she demanded, only to find his large hand covering her mouth. It was warm and calloused against her lips, his touch firm but gentle.

"Hush a moment," he whispered in her ear, his breath warm against the side of her neck as he released her. She shivered, and he must have felt the tremor run through her. "Ye are cold," he observed, sounding annoyed by the information.

Before she could deny it, which on reflection was just as well as the truth would not have helped her cause, he pulled her close. The sensation was akin to being enveloped by a bear in a blanket. He seemed to surround her, the smell of whisky and musk and earthy male fragrances invading her senses. She was aware of the warmth of his body, like a furnace beneath his clothes, and her cheek lay against his broad chest as if of its own accord. In short, Hamilton Anderson up close was thoroughly overwhelming, and Clara did not have the will to pull away from his embrace, though she knew she ought.

Raucous voices sounded on the street, and he stiffened, the muscles that surrounded her growing taut until the ribald chatter faded away and the drunken party of men had disappeared into the next street.

Silence reigned for a long moment, and Clara was horribly aware of her own heart thudding in her ears, and worse, the fact she ought to protest at being so manhandled. Unfortunately, she could not bring herself to do so. He let out a long, somewhat unsteady sigh, and let her go, moving once more to the mouth of the alley.

"Come, lassie," he said, his deep voice a growl in the darkness. "We must nae linger here, much as I would like to."

"Certainly not," she replied, wishing she could infuse some of her usual steel into the words and frustrated to discover they sounded instead wistful and full of regret.

Still, she walked from the alley, though her legs wobbled rather oddly. Indeed, she felt rather odd all over, a restless sensation of frustration and… and *something*, simmering beneath her skin that was quite unaccountable.

They walked in silence until the vicarage came into sight.

"I'd best leave ye here," he said, sounding gruff and rather irritable himself.

"Very well. I thank you for your chaperonage. Only think who might have accosted me and taken liberties had I been all alone," she added tartly, relieved to discover she had regained some shred of dignity along the way. She turned, intending to stalk off with her nose in the air, but he caught hold of her hand, staying her.

"Did ye nae like my kisses, then?" he asked, his eyes bright as the clouds parted and a thin sliver of moonlight appeared. "Tell the truth and shame the devil," he added, daring her to lie to him.

Clara glowered at him, for the truth would certainly shame someone, but she was fairly certain it wouldn't be the devil. Trapped, she refused to reply at all and tugged her hand free, running the short distance to the house and closing the door rather harder than was necessary.

Chapter 11

Dear Miss Halliday,

I am unwell. My head pounds and I am hot one moment, cold the next. I feel utterly wretched but most of all I am bored beyond bearing. Please do come and visit me. I look a positive fright, but I beg you will not judge me too harshly, for I suffer dreadfully. We ought to have gone to London for the season, for Papa promised me I might, and now this. I am so wretched I want to die.

My maid, Abigail, is a horrible nurse and is trying to kill me by opening the windows and letting cold air into my room and feeding me noxious tinctures. I shall scream if she brings me another posset, I do declare.

—Excerpt of a letter from Miss Jessie Fleming to Miss Clara Halliday.

10th June 1850, Wick, Caithness, Scotland.

It was several days before Hamilton had to face Miss Halliday again, for which he was grateful. Though he'd been quite honest in telling her he was not bevied, he *had* drunk a good deal, and it had certainly made him reckless, a fact that was coming home to him with some force.

Though Miss Halliday would be well within her rights to cut him dead and never speak to him again, he suspected she wouldn't. Oh, she'd be cross as crabs, and she'd likely ring a peal over him the first opportunity she got, but she wouldn't ignore him. She couldn't, and that was the devil of it. She'd liked his kisses very well. He knew it and so did she, and what's more, she knew he knew it and that's why she was furious with him. Hamilton didn't blame her. He was furious with himself too, because now he knew what she tasted like, what she felt like in his arms, and damn him but he wanted more. Much more.

Try as he might to put the woman out of his mind, she crept back in. He told himself he had no intention of trifling with an innocent girl, he certainly had no intention of marrying her, and even if he were to consider such a daft thing, her father would shoot him before he let him anywhere near his daughter. All of which amounted to one conclusion, the same conclusion he'd come to from the start and was having the devil's own job remembering. Clara Halliday was off limits, and he needed to stay away from her.

After he'd apologised.

He knew he owed her that much, but the idea of it still rankled. He did not wish to apologise. Kissing her had been a rare treat, and not just for him. Though he knew he was a conceited arse, he could not help but suspect she had daydreamed about those moments in his arms regularly ever since it had happened. Not that she'd ever admit as much to a living soul. Certainly not to him, devil take her. Nonetheless, he had to apologise for taking liberties and, damn his eyes, promise it would never happen again. It couldn't. Not unless he wanted to walk headfirst into a world of trouble, and he was not that stupid.

So, he left the Fisherman's Retreat after checking in on progress and walked the short distance to call in at the back door of the vicarage.

"She's not here," Mrs Macready said sourly, regarding him with a baleful expression. "And if ye had the sense ye were born with, ye would leave her be, unless ye mean to walk out with her."

Hamilton opened his mouth to protest but found he couldn't. He was in the wrong and he damn well knew it. He rubbed the back of his neck, wishing Mrs Macready didn't make him feel like a grubby boy. "Aye, I mean to do so… leave her be, that is. I just… I need to speak with her before—"

"Before ye leave her be," Mrs Macready said with a snort.

"Aye," Hamilton replied irritably. "If I have yer permission?" he retorted, glowering.

"I'm nae yer mam, nor yer conscience. Ye will do as ye please, ye always do, but she's still nae here. She went to visit that silly chit, Miss Fleming, who's acting as though she's dying, though she's only got a nasty cold. I told the lass to stay away. It's the fourth time this week with that wretched child running her ragged like she's some kind of nursemaid. She'll make herself ill, she will, and that's a fact."

"Well, why did ye nae stop her, then!" Hamilton demanded, though he knew it was unfair.

Mrs Macready shot him an unloving look. "I tried, did I nae? I just told ye. If ye are so worrit for her, fetch her back yerself, aye?"

"Aye, I will," Hamilton shot back, riled. "See if I don't," he snapped, turning on his heel and striding back through the town. He'd gone three streets before he recollected that he could do no such thing. Hammering at Miss Fleming's door and demanding she send Miss Halliday home would do none of them any good. Still, he was too restless and annoyed with both himself, Mrs Macready *and* Miss Halliday to turn around, so he carried on in the direction of Miss Fleming's house and found himself unaccountably relieved when he spied Miss Halliday walking towards him.

Her steps were slow, her head bent, which struck him as unusual. Clara Halliday usually walked briskly and with purpose, her head up, a quick and friendly smile ready for anyone who greeted her politely and the poise of an ice queen towards anyone with the temerity to be impertinent. The thought made him smile, and he realised he admired her a good deal. His smile fell as he crossed the street towards her and saw her stiffen.

"Miss Halliday," he said, before she could tell him to go to the devil. "I beg yer pardon, but I must speak with ye."

"Oh, do go away," she said wearily, but there was no heat behind the words, only exhaustion.

"Lassie? What's wrong?" Hamilton asked, laying a hand on her arm.

"Nothing. Only I do not have the energy to scold you as you deserve, my head is aching dreadfully, and I cannot deal with you right now."

"Ye dinnae need to do a thing. I'll nae vex ye, my word on it. Only let me see ye home, aye? Ye have caught Miss Fleming's cold, just as Mrs Macready feared, I reckon."

"Oh, don't you say 'I told you so,' too," she said, sounding utterly wretched. "I couldn't leave the poor girl by herself. Miss Fleming is my friend, and she hasn't the least bit of patience or idea of how to entertain herself, and she was utterly wretched."

"Ye ken very well, that I never say I told ye so," Hamilton replied with a smile.

She gave a soft huff of laughter at that before adding, "I must say, if she felt like this, I… I quite understand how…" She paused, swaying and put a hand upon the wall beside her.

"Miss Halliday?" Hamilton said in alarm, worried now, for her cheeks were blazing, her eyes too bright.

"I'm… I'm perfectly fine," she said stubbornly. "I only need to get home."

"Take my arm," Hamilton told her. "Lean on me and just put one foot in front of another. I'd carry ye and with pleasure, but the town will be gabbing about it before sun sets if I do."

"You will do no such thing," she retorted, with a glimmer of her usual fire and Hamilton had to smile.

"Ach, dinnae pretend ye would nae enjoy it," he told her, before holding up a hand and shaking his head when she glared at him. "Nae, dinnae say it. I ken very well. I promised I widnae vex ye. I take it back, aye. I'm sorry."

She let out a sigh and took his proffered arm, leaning heavily on him. "If you want the truth, I should dearly love to let you carry me, you odious creature, for it seems a very long way."

"It's nae far now, lassie," he said gently, simmering with frustration for he wanted to carry her, wanted to sweep her up and take her home and see she was tucked up in bed and that she was warm and comfortable and taking her medicines as she ought. The sudden urge to do something so cosy and domestic as taking care of a woman who looked a shocking sight and was suffering from a disgusting cold, startled Hamilton into silence and he held his tongue the rest of the way lest he say something appallingly stupid.

They had turned onto the street where the vicarage stood when Clara stopped, closing her eyes and simply leaning against him. Hamilton caught her as her legs gave out, sweeping her up into his arms.

"Oh, but…" she protested weakly as he carried her swiftly along the road.

"There's nae a soul about, dinnae fash," he told her soothingly, kicking open the back gate and then using the toe of his boot to knock on the kitchen door. Mrs Macready snatched it open a moment later, her mouth open to reprimand him for making such a racket, and then she saw Clara.

"Holy mother!" she exclaimed in shock, pulling open the kitchen door so he could carry her in.

"Is the reverend in?" Hamilton asked, relieved when Mrs Macready shook her head.

"Nae, it's old Mr Brodie's funeral today and—and just where do ye think ye are going?" she demanded, as Hamilton carried Clara out of the kitchen and headed for the stairs.

"I'm taking her to her bedroom, unless ye reckon ye can carry her up yerself?" Hamilton replied. "And dinnae start making a fuss, for I'm doing it, so ye had best lead the way and see propriety is served, aye?"

"Good heavens!" the lady said in outrage, bustling by him. "Ye are the most—"

"Aye, aye, I ken it well enough, stop yer blethering and show me to her room."

"You are a dreadful man," Clara told him, her head resting against his shoulder, yet her arms had curved about his neck, and he could feel her fingers toying with his hair, tickling the back of his neck. "An unrepentant rogue."

"Aye, lassie, ye have that right," he told her, feeling an odd sensation kicking about in his chest.

"How dare you set foot in my bedroom," she added weakly, though he felt she said it because she ought, not because she gave a damn. He suspected she didn't care about much past the fact she was utterly wretched, and that made him feel anxious and irritable and so out of sorts he didn't know what to do. Instead, he stood in her bedroom like a lummox, holding her in his arms and quite unwilling to let go.

"Well, don't stand there like a numpty, put her down on the bed, ye great gowk," Mrs Macready scolded him, forcing him to relinquish his hold on her and settle her gently on the mattress.

She sank into the eiderdown with a soft moan, turning her blazing cheek so it rested upon the cool cotton of the pillow.

"She's burning up," Hamilton said in alarm.

"Aye, she's caught herself a lovely fever and she'll be sick as a dog for a day or two, but it's just a nasty cold, same as Miss Fleming," Mrs Macready said, her voice soothing this time, and Hamilton looked around at her, surprised to see her expression had softened.

She was looking at him rather oddly and it made him at once defensive for reasons he was uncertain he wished to consider. He opened his mouth to make some scathing remark, found he couldn't and looked helplessly back at Clara, who had closed her eyes.

"Is there anything I can do?" he asked, knowing he was only adding fuel to Mrs Macready's obvious speculation but too worried to care.

"Nae, laddie. I'll take good care of her, dinnae fash. She'll be right as a trivet in no time, I promise."

Hamilton frowned, feeling too big and out of place in Clara's bedroom. Not that it was a pretty room or contained any feminine accoutrements of the kind he might expect. Moyra's bedchamber was stuffed full of luxurious fabrics and pretty pillows and silk wall hangings, but then she had the money to indulge in such things and no husband to tell her she couldn't. Hamilton supposed the vicar must disapprove of anything that smacked of vanity and indulgence, and that made him suddenly wretched. Clara was a beautiful young woman, and she ought to be cosseted and spoiled and surrounded with pretty things that made her smile and gave her pleasure to look upon. But that was not something he could do, not without causing speculation from more quarters than just Mrs Macready. What's more, it would lead Clara to have expectations of him of the kind he could not allow.

Why?

The question popped into his brain, startling him. For all the reasons he knew very well, was the immediate answer, and he forced any further speculation away, telling himself not to be such an eejit.

"Right, well, I'll be off, then," he said briskly, though his feet seemed rooted to the floor. "You'll let me know if ye need anything, aye?"

"Aye," Mrs Macready replied, a knowing glint in her eyes as she smiled at him, which made him unaccountably irritated. She glanced at Clara, saw she had fallen asleep and lowered her voice as she turned back to Hamilton, looking far too pleased with herself. "Ye can stop by in the morning if ye like and I'll tell ye how she goes on. Flowers always make a lass feel better too, when she kens a fellow is thinking of her. Missing her, even," she added, quirking an eyebrow at him.

"Ye can stop that right now," Hamilton muttered and stalked out of the room, not allowing himself to glance back at Clara, though the effort it took not to take one last look at her was disturbing.

He was just worried about the lass, that was all, he told himself reasonably. It wasn't anything more than that. He was simply the kind of person who cared for his friends and would help anyone who needed it. All of which was entirely true, and didn't help a bit.

♡♧◇♤

Clara woke the next morning and profoundly wished she had not. Her head pounded, her throat was of the opinion she'd swallowed broken glass, and everything hurt.

"Aye, I ken ye are wishing ye died in the night, but it will pass, lassie," Mrs Macready said comfortingly as she plumped Clara's pillows. She'd sat and watched while Clara had painstakingly swallowed a small bowl of porridge she hadn't wanted and refused to budge until it was all gone.

"Are you quite certain I didn't?" Clara asked grimly, her voice rasping.

Mrs Macready chuckled and picked up the earthenware mug she'd placed beside the bed, settling it in Clara's hands. "That's what ye get for playing nursemaid to a spoiled little chit who's no better than she ought to be. Drink that up now, every drop, and then ye will sleep for a bit."

"I've only just woken up," Clara protested, peering into the glass with interest.

"Ye need to rest and so ye shall sleep." Mrs Macready noticed her dubious expression and gave a snort of laughter. "It's a hot toddy, good for what ails ye."

Clara looked up, interested despite her miserable mood. "What's a hot toddy?"

"Whisky and hot water with honey and spices," Mrs Macready told her.

"Whisky?" Clara said in alarm. "Oh, but I can't. Papa—"

"Papa can speak to me if he disnae like it, though in my opinion he disnae need to be informed about it," Mrs Macready said sternly. "Ye will drink it, and it will do ye good. It's medicinal, aye?"

Clara investigated the mug uncertainly before lifting it to her nose and sniffing. Even though her sinuses were hardly working as they ought, it smelled wonderful. She took a tentative sip, her eyebrows flying up in surprise when she discovered it didn't taste like vile medicine.

"Good, aye?" Mrs Macready said in amusement.

Clara licked her lips and took another sip, which was answer enough for Mrs Macready, who looked pleased.

A knock at the door sounded before her father poked his head in, concern in his eyes.

"My poor dear. You do look dreadful," he said anxiously, which was not exactly what Clara wanted to hear, but it was nice that he was worried for her. "You're sure it's just a cold?" he asked Mrs Macready.

"Aye, Reverend. Dinnae worry yerself. I'll take good care of her."

Papa regarded her, his greying brows pinched together. "It's just that Clara is never sick," he added fretfully. "I don't like to see you looking so frail and out of sorts, my dear. Perhaps I shall pop into the apothecary and see if he can recommend something. Or perhaps Mrs Cameron will have a remedy, she's a wonderfully sensible woman, you know."

Clara admitted herself surprised by such solicitude. Though it wasn't entirely true that she was never sick, there was never anyone to nurse her, and she had never considered her father the sort to fuss around a sick bed, so she'd got used to seeing to herself and carrying on. She'd certainly never felt this ill before, though, so perhaps her father had never had the chance to show concern for her.

All the same, to take time out of his day to see to her needs was something she had not expected. She smiled at him gratefully, wondering if perhaps she had been too hard on him, and he was not so thoroughly selfish as she believed.

"Thank you, Papa, that is a kind thought, but there's no need. Mrs Macready is taking good care of me."

Her father nodded, looking somewhat reassured. "I'll bring you a book, then. Something frivolous," he said suddenly, apparently relieved to have thought of something she might like. "A novel," he said satisfaction, before leaving the room.

"Good heavens," Clara said, once he'd gone. "Papa disapproves of my novels."

Mrs Macready smiled and nodded. "Many men take women for granted. They talk about us like we're the weaker sex, when we're the ones that keep going no matter what. It's only when we're so sick we must take to our beds that they suddenly realise we're not invincible. I reckon it does them good," she added with a wink.

Clara smiled, hearing the truth behind the words. "Thank you, Mrs Macready. You are quite marvellous and I'm so grateful to you for looking after me."

"It's a pleasure, lassie. Now you rest up and get well," she added, and left Clara to finish her hot toddy in peace.

Chapter 12

Dear Miss Fleming,

I'm so sorry to hear you are still poorly and I apologise for not visiting for so long. I hope you will forgive me, for I'm afraid I am too unwell myself to do so now. Get well soon and please let Abigail take care of you. She's really very competent and has your best interests at heart.

—Excerpt of a letter from Miss Clara Halliday to Miss Jessie Fleming.

14th June 1850, Wick, Caithness, Scotland.

Hamilton stopped by the vicarage every morning to hear from Mrs Macready how Clara was doing, but it was not until the fourth day when she was still in bed that he caved in.

"Well, aren't they just the prettiest sight," Mrs Macready said with satisfaction as Hamilton thrust the small posy of daisies at her.

He'd tied himself into a knot, trying to decide whether to bring flowers at all, and if he did, what sort. Treading the line between solicitude and not making overtures that could be misread gave him a headache and now, handing the sweet and simple bunch of flowers over, he felt like a proper twit. If he was going to bring flowers, perhaps it ought to have been something a bit more expensive than a daft bunch of daisies.

"It's nothing," he said gruffly, rubbing the back of his neck. "I just… well, ye said it would cheer the lassie, aye? So… So I did as ye asked," he added, knowing full well that Mrs Macready had done no such thing.

"It will," she said. "The reverend is in his study. Ye could have a word with him while ye are here. Try to make peace, perhaps?"

"Ach, devil take ye! Freya Macready, I have told ye once, dinnae try to manipulate me into taking a wife. It winnae work," he warned her, giving her a fierce look that had made men five times her size think twice about trying his patience.

Mrs Macready simply shrugged, the glimmer of a smile at her lips. "I hear ye."

"Hmph," Hamilton replied, and was about to leave before he realised he couldn't yet. Glowering, he turned back to her. "The lassie is getting better?"

"Aye," Mrs Macready replied, her tone reassuring. "She's tired still, but I winnae be able to make her keep to her room another day. She's sitting in a chair by the window this morning and I reckon she'll be up and about tomorrow."

Hamilton let out a breath as a weight seemed to lift from his shoulders. "That's good. I'm glad to hear such tidings. Well, I'll bid ye a good morning, then."

"I'll tell her ye asked after her," Mrs Macready called after him.

Hamilton sighed but could not deny the realisation that he wanted her to do it, wanted Clara to know he was thinking of her, even though he ought not.

Why?

The question rose its head again, and Hamilton pushed it away. He wasn't ready to look at it closely. Not yet. Maybe not ever, but certainly not right now.

"For me?" Clara gasped, staring at the posy of flowers.

She told herself it was only because of the cold that she was breathless, only because she was tired that her heart was clattering about behind her ribs. Sadly, she wasn't that stupid. It might be nice to think she wasn't as daft as every other girl in Wick and hadn't a soft spot in her imprudent heart for a flirtatious rogue who stole kisses from girls in dark alleyways. She wondered how many other kisses he had stolen, how many other girls had felt the press of his lips against theirs and spent the next days dreaming foolish dreams even though they knew it was pointless.

Too many was the certain answer that returned to her.

She, however, would not add to the numbers. Not publicly, at least. In the most secret corner of her heart, she might allow herself to think of those kisses and wonder at the way he had made her feel, both safe and in the most peril of her life at the same time. Those moments had been exciting and passionate and yet tender and sweet and, like Mr Anderson himself, there were too many contradictions to make her feel anything but dizzy with confusion.

"Of course they are for ye," Mrs Macready said impatiently, setting the little posy in its vase on the windowsill for Clara to look at. "And I tell ye this much, I never knew Hamilton Anderson to bring any lass flowers afore now. Reckon he's sweet on ye."

"Mrs Macready!" Clara said in shock, too aware that the least encouragement would tempt her down a path she could not afford to take. "You cannot believe *that*… that unrepentant rogue has anything serious in mind. I beg you will not say such things."

Besides which, Clara knew why he had really sent her flowers. It did not take vast intelligence to work out his motives. He felt guilty for kissing her. He knew right from wrong, after all, and despite her jealous musings, she suspected he did not make a habit of taking advantage of innocent girls. No doubt the day he had carried her home, he'd been looking for her so he could apologise.

The flowers were merely that, the apology he'd not been able to give her in person.

"As ye like," Mrs Macready said with a shrug. "But I stand by what I said."

Mrs Macready went out, leaving Clara staring at the daisies. In the language of flowers, daisies represented innocence and purity, she reminded herself. Yet stubbornly, her mind refused to latch on to that meaning, preferring instead to consider the other connotation attached to them—the sender's promise to keep a secret.

23rd June 1850, Wick, Caithness, Scotland.

"It looks very well," Angus said, looking around the Fishermen's Retreat with interest. Work was coming on apace and the building looked less like it was about to fall down and more like it might one day be habitable.

"Aye," Hamilton said as they stood in what would one day be the best room. It was the largest and looked out over the town with the faint glimmer of the sea visible behind the rooflines before them. It also looked towards the vicarage. Clara Halliday was standing on the front doorstep speaking to Miss Fiona Grant and Arran Ross. Fiona was only eighteen and Arran not yet twenty, but they had grown up together and the entire world of Wick knew they would marry the moment her da gave his consent. It looked like the happy day had come at last, for the two of them were holding hands and beaming at each other with daft expressions on their faces.

"Ah, Mr Grant finally gave in, I see," Angus said with a chuckle, coming to stand beside Hamilton.

"Aye," Hamilton replied, aware that his gaze had not lingered on the happy couple for above a moment, unwillingly drawn instead to watch Clara Halliday. He drank in the sight of her, noting the pink tinge to her porcelain skin that showed she had recovered her health. Her hair shone even in the overcast daylight, pulled back from her beautiful face in a simple knot, the colour of deep mahogany with flecks of bronze. He knew her eyes were as grey as the sky overhead and could flash like lightning when she was vexed by him. Despite knowing better, he focused on the outline of her lovely figure as Fiona and Arran walked away and she waved them off. Her tiny waist seemed narrower than before, he thought, and instead of admiring how slender she was, could only feel a stab of anxiety that she might have lost weight.

"I hear Miss Halliday has made an excellent recovery," Angus said, a little too nonchalantly.

Hamilton glanced at him, suspicion stirring, but Angus was inspecting the newly fitted ironmongery on the bedroom door, all handmade by a local blacksmith. He'd ensured all the trades and supplies were local, giving the work to those who lived in Wick or its environs being important to him.

"Have ye decided if ye are coming to dinner with us tonight?" Angus went on, before Hamilton could think of a suitable reply.

Hamilton frowned, reaching for his pocket watch and irritated as he remembered that Moyra still had it. He'd not seen her in an age and guilt stirred as he remembered why. He really ought to visit her, to explain that things were over between them, but work had been so busy, and his mind so preoccupied, that somehow it never happened.

The dinner party would by no means be a grand affair. Angus and Mary entertained friends once or twice a month, just a handful of people and it was always good craic and good food. Usually, Hamilton would not think twice about accepting. This time he'd hesitated, uncertain if he could bring himself to be entertaining, for people expected him to be the life and soul, which he usually was. Just at the moment, however, he was feeling a little out of sorts for reasons he could not put his finger on. Perhaps it was simply guilt over not visiting Moyra and telling her the truth of why he'd been avoiding her, a situation she had remarked when he had seen her out and about in Wick the day before. She had even suggested, in her blunt and rather forthright manner, that he'd lost interest in her because he had other fish to fry.

Hamilton had rejected the accusation before he'd really considered it, and it had only been later that he'd fretted about it, wondering if Moyra had seen something in him he had not wanted to face.

"My brother will be there, I'm afraid," Angus went on, which was reason enough to give it a miss. "Though he's under no illusion that it will be the last time if he misbehaves. Mr Fraser and Miss Fleming are also invited, as well as Harold Barker and Mrs Scott."

Christ. Moyra was going too? Then he definitely wouldn't go. At least it meant no one outside of Mrs Macready had guessed about his affair with her, or else Mary would have heard it from her mother, who was the biggest nashgab in the town and couldn't keep a secret if her life depended on it.

"I dinnae think—" he began, just as Angus added,

"And Miss Halliday."

Hamilton froze. "Clara Halliday?" he said stupidly, as if there were another such in Wick. Clara Halliday in the same room as Malcolm Stewart *and* Moyra Scott. His blood chilled in his veins.

"Aye, her and Mary have become great friends, and Mary promised to introduce her to people. What with Mrs Scott knowing everyone and being at the centre of much of the social scene in Wick, she thought she'd introduce them. Mind, it took a vast amount of persuading with her father, what with me working for ye and the reverend not liking that one bit. But I'll give Mary her due, she's a hard woman to say no to. I hear she got Mrs Cameron on to the fellow as well, telling him a young woman needed to get out and about in society. It seems Mrs Cameron has a fair bit of influence with our reverend these days," he added with a grin. "Ye ought to encourage that, I reckon."

Hamilton paid little heed to this, too consumed with worries about Clara and Angus' vile brother. "I thought ye had more sense than to have Malcolm and Miss Halliday in the same room," Hamilton growled, trying to keep a lid on something that felt very much like panic. "And I cannae believe her da would let her attend if he knew I was there."

"It wasn't my doing," Angus said with a shrug. "Mary invited Miss Halliday without telling me, and so when Malcolm asked if he could come, I said yes. Lord, Mary was furious with me, for it means we've odd numbers now as she cannot find another single lady, but I could hardly uninvite him, and even my brother won't be an idiot in company. It's not like there will be an opportunity for him to be alone with her. I'll make sure she gets home safe too, so don't worry. At least if you don't come, the numbers will be even again and I need not fear the reverend finding out," Angus mused thoughtfully, blithely unaware he'd pitched Hamilton into a nightmare.

Don't worry? Holy God. As if her getting home safe was the only thing to fret about. Hamilton's heart gave an uneven thud, and he told himself to calm down. Moyra would say nothing about their affair at a dinner party. The idea was ludicrous, and no one had the slightest idea of his interest in Clara. He *had* no interest in Clara past the fact he was a healthy male with the usual appreciation such a creature had for a beautiful woman. Yet there was a fizzing sensation under his skin, tension thrumming through him as something like foreboding clouded his brain.

He couldn't go, he decided. If he went, he'd be on alert and one or the other of them would think it odd. His mother and his sister seemed to have some God-given instinct that told them when he or one of his brothers was hiding something, and he saw no reason this feminine attribute ought to have missed Clara Halliday.

Moyra certainly had it, for she knew his attention was waning and suspected him of hiding his interest in another.

Well, he needed to put her straight in any case. Whether or not she believed there was nothing between him and Clara she deserved to hear from him that their affair was over. Perhaps he could do it later tonight, after the dinner. He let out a breath of relief at having made the decision, and then considered the question from the other direction. What if Clara found out about his affair with Moyra?

"Aye, I'll come," he blurted, before he could think better of it.

"Excellent," Angus replied, slapping him on the back. "We'll see you at seven-thirty, then. Don't be late." Hamilton swallowed, suddenly viewing the coming evening with all the pleasure of a man climbing the scaffold where a noose awaited him.

"Thank you so much for inviting me," Clara said as Angus Stewart took her cloak. "And thank you, Mr Fraser, for escorting me here. It was so kind of you and you were so patient with Papa, too. I'm sorry he lectured you so sternly when it was barely a few minutes' walk."

"My pleasure, my dear. Think nothing of it," Mr Fraser said cheerfully, his kind face growing round as he grinned at them. "Oh, something smells good! Mary, what are we having?" he asked, sniffing with appreciation as he walked further into the house.

"Wait and see," Mary said cheerfully, hurrying past him to greet Clara. She was a petite woman with comfortable curves, jet-black hair, and an apparently boundless energy for friends and family. "Clara! Oh, love… you look perfectly stunning."

Clara laughed at the extravagant praise, quite certain it was merely her friend's good nature that saw beauty in all things.

"Mary, if you pour the butter boat over me, I'll have no room for your marvellous dinner."

"Mary's right," Angus said frankly as he handed her cloak to their maid. "I'll not say ye are the loveliest sight I ever saw, for my Mary has that privilege, but ye look as fine as fivepence. Far too lovely for such an informal affair. You should be attending some grand dinner in town somewhere."

"Hush, both of you," Clara protested. "You will put me to the blush, and this is my very best dress, so it's only that you are unused to seeing me in such finery," she added, certain that the deep blue silk gown, which *was* rather fine and beautifully, if simply, tailored, ought to take the credit.

"Well, we shall see what our guests make of you, and then you may eat your words," Mary said firmly, taking her by the arm and guiding her into the parlour where the guests were chatting, drinks in hand. "Now then, of course, Mr Fraser, you have already greeted this evening, and you know Angus's brother."

Clara smiled at Mr Fraser and gave Malcolm Stewart a coolly polite nod, ignoring the way his gaze travelled over her and determined to stay as far out of his way as was possible in a small room.

"This gentleman is Harold Barker, our bank manager in Wick."

Harold was a broad-shouldered man of medium height and ruddy good looks. He did not look like a man who spent all his days in an office and gave Clara the impression of an outdoorsy, virile fellow who disliked sitting still. At Mary's introduction, he pulled a face.

"Ach, Mary, love. Don't be giving a poor fellow such a dull introduction, the poor lassie will run a mile."

Mary laughed and patted his arm. "Not if she has any sense, she won't. Clara, don't let this naughty man tease you and don't go thinking he's dull and stuffy, for you'll be sadly mistaken."

Mr Barker grinned at this sally, making Clara smile too as Mary carried on around the room.

"Of course, Miss Fleming needs no introduction," Mary added, as Miss Fleming gave a coquettish curtsey, which made Clara smile.

"How lovely you look, Miss Fleming," she said truthfully, thinking that the young woman's rather dashing and fashionable gown of bright green trimmed with black lace quite outshone her own sedate outfit. "You make me feel perfectly dowdy in comparison."

"Oh, I think not."

Clara turned to see a beautiful woman of perhaps thirty years of age, with rich guinea-gold hair arranged in a stylish coiffure and wearing a magnificent gown of deep burgundy red. She regarded Clara with obvious interest. Her voice was warm and melodious and her manner friendly as Mary introduced them.

"Moyra, my dear, this is Miss Clara Halliday, whom I've told you so much about. Now tell me, isn't she every bit as beautiful as I said she was?"

"You hardly did her justice, Mary," the woman replied, with apparent sincerity.

"Clara, please meet my dear friend, Mrs Moyra Scott," Mary said with obvious pride as she made the introductions. "Moyra knows everybody and everything and is just the person to guide you, for she is far too sophisticated for our little town, so we all look to her."

"Stuff," Moyra said frankly, making Clara smile. "You are a deal too generous with your praise, love, though I appreciate the sentiment. Miss Halliday, I should be delighted if you wish to call on me so I might make some appropriate introductions. Society in Wick is rather limited, I'm afraid, but there are one or two families who will be excellent connections for you."

"You're very kind, Mrs Scott. I should be pleased—"

"Sorry I'm late." The deep voice cut through the murmur of voices and made all the tiny hairs on the back of Clara's neck stand on end. She turned, watching in mute dismay as Hamilton Anderson strode into the room. *Lud.* If her father found out he was here, there would be the most terrible scene. What had Mary been thinking of inviting him when she was here, too? Oh, if she had only known he was coming, she would never have accepted the invitation, she thought crossly, becoming increasingly vexed as she realised that was a blatant lie. Of course she would have come.

His arrival seemed in some subtle way to galvanise everyone. Angus and Mr Fraser beamed, clearly delighted to see him. Mr Barker regarded him with something that looked like amused resignation, and Malcolm Stewart did little to hide his obvious animosity. The effect on the women was no less marked. Miss Fleming exclaimed with delight, going at once to greet him with a proprietary air which made Clara want to blush for the girl. Mary's greeting was warm and full of genuine affection, and Mrs Scott… Clara studied her with interest, noting the way she did not look at Mr Anderson at all. That seemed a little odd. Clara envied her the ability to ignore him, however, for she could not do so. Her eyes drank in the sight of him, her heart lifting, because her heart was an idiot who didn't know what was good for it.

Mr Anderson looked around the room and their eyes met. Clara felt the connection like a jolt of electricity, a shock that made her skin prickle with awareness. It lasted barely a moment, for he looked away again, and Clara gathered herself, smiling warmly at Mr Barker as he came to stand beside her. He was older than her, perhaps forty years of age, but with such an air of vitality about him that he seemed younger.

"You have not been here long, I think, Miss Halliday. How are you finding our little town?"

"Not very long, no. Since the beginning of May, so not quite two months, I suppose, and I like it very well indeed."

"You surprise me. Most English ladies find the weather a trial and the lack of amusements tedious, I fear."

"Then they were poor-spirited creatures to be sure, for it is most invigorating to live so close to the sea. When the sun shines upon Wick, it seems brighter than I have ever seen it before, especially the way it glitters on the sea, like diamonds."

"Why, Miss Halliday, that is most poetic, though I confess it pleases me to discover such an elegant young woman so enchanted by the landscape, which one must allow is dramatic rather than pretty."

"Certainly it is," Clara said, happy to agree with this description. "Quite breathtaking, in fact."

"And you are not repining for the amusements of a grand town like London?" he pressed with a smile.

Clara shook her head, accepting a glass of lemonade from the maid who brought it to her. "I have never been to London, sir, so it would be foolish to languish over something I have never known."

"Never been to London?" Mrs Scott cut in, having overheard their conversation, a glass of champagne held delicately in her gloved hand. "My dear girl, but you must go. A beauty of your quality would be a tremendous success. Do you not think so, Mr Anderson?"

Clara felt a betraying rush of heat to her cheeks as Mr Anderson joined their circle and she studied the patterned Turkey carpet beneath her feet with apparent fascination.

"I beg your pardon, Mrs Scott, what was the question?" he asked politely.

"I said that Miss Halliday ought to go to London. It is a crime, surely, for such a beautiful creature not to be given a season."

Mr Barker cut in before Mr Anderson could give his opinion. "How cruel you are, Mrs Scott, when I hear rumours that both you and Miss Fleming intend to leave us again in a few weeks. Would you deprive us of all our feminine companionship? Poor Mary will be besieged."

Mrs Scott laughed at this sally, but turned to Mr Anderson once more, apparently determined to have an answer.

"I'm sure Miss Halliday will do as her father bids her," he said, neatly avoiding the question. "Does the reverend have such plans for you?" he asked her.

"No, sir. My father has made no plans," Clara replied, wishing she could say otherwise. It must be nice for Miss Fleming to know she had options. Likely these men gathered here were the most eligible in Wick, for she knew Mary had made it her mission to find Clara a husband. The thought was rather unsettling. Mr Fraser, Harold Barker, Malcolm Stewart, and Hamilton Anderson. One of them might one day call her wife. The thought made colour rush to her face once more.

"Lord, but she's such an innocent child. Look at that blush," Mrs Scott murmured in an undertone to Mary as she gazed at Clara.

There was something in her eyes that made Clara feel horribly gauche.

"Mrs Macready told me you have been unwell," Mr Anderson said quickly, diverting attention and directing the conversation elsewhere.

Clara looked at him gratefully, knowing he was well aware of her illness.

"Only a cold, sir, but I thank you for your concern. I am quite recovered, I assure you."

"I had it too," Miss Fleming cut in, sliding her arm through Clara's. "It was quite dreadful. I thought I would die of it, and indeed the doctor was most concerned, for I have a delicate constitution, you see. He fretted that my lungs would be damaged, and the cough was so fatiguing I feared I should fall asleep and never wake again," she added with a sigh. "As it was, I've missed weeks of the season, which is so unfair I could weep."

Clara noted both Mr Anderson and Mr Fraser looking at Miss Fleming with undisguised amusement, and quickly cut in.

"Indeed, you were most poorly, far more than I," Clara said soothingly. "My constitution is more akin to that of an ox, so I was never in any danger."

"Ye would have been in less if ye had nae been waiting on Miss Fleming when ye knew she was ailing," Mr Andersons said sharply, making Clara start, for there was a distinct note of censure behind the words. She saw the moment when he realised too late what he'd said, but quickly recovered himself. "So Mrs Macready tells me."

"You call on Mrs Macready with surprising regularity," Malcolm Stewart remarked casually. "Is she a relation of yours?"

"Nae directly, but she is cousin to Mrs Baillie, who was like a second mother to me when I was a bairn at Wildsyde," Mr Anderson replied, holding Mr Stewart's gaze.

"Ah, I see," Mr Stewart said, a thin smile at his lips. "That must be why you were so often at the vicarage. I wondered if perhaps you had found God."

"God kens where I am well enough without me looking for him," Mr Anderson replied sharply. "And I look in on Mrs Macready as a favour to a woman who is dear to me."

"Indeed, and it shows what a kind heart you have, Mr Anderson," Miss Fleming said with approval. "And I do not know what business it is of yours, Mr Stewart," she added, glaring at the man.

"Oh, none at all," Mr Stewart replied easily, his eyes glinting with malice. "Only one makes connections and sometimes wonders at them."

Clara stared at him in mute horror, desperately aware that he was trying to make trouble for Mr Anderson, and apparently not caring in the least that he might ruin Clara if anyone picked up on his implications. Happily, Miss Fleming seemed oblivious, and Mr Fraser and Mr Barker were regarding Mr Stewart with expressions that were carefully blank, though their contempt was obvious.

Only Mrs Scott was silent, studying Mr Hamilton with a thoughtful gaze. Mr Hamilton regarded her steadily as he asked, “Is it true you are leaving for London, Mrs Scott?”

“Miss Fleming’s father was kind enough to invite me to accompany her when she goes,” Mrs Scott replied, taking a sip of her champagne. “I had not quite decided if I ought, but now I think I shall accept his kind offer.”

“You will?” Miss Fleming said with a crow of pleasure. “How lovely! What a merry party we shall be! Oh, if only you could come too, Clara. Poor you being left behind when we go to have such an exciting time.”

“I shall be quite content, I’m afraid I am not at all used to grand parties and society and would only embarrass myself,” Clara said with a reassuring smile, hoping to avoid some scheme where Miss Fleming tried to invite her too. Her father would never allow it and would likely offend Mr Fleming with the force of his refusal.

“Yes, I suppose that’s true,” Miss Fleming replied, and with such candour, Clara struggled to hide her amusement, especially when she saw the glint in Mr Anderson’s eyes. His lips quirked as their gazes met and Clara forced herself to look away.

“Don’t pretend you do not know how to comport yourself as a lady, Miss Halliday, when we can all see such a delightful creature before our eyes,” Mr Barker said with a smile. “I for one am relieved you are not to leave us poor gentlemen to sink into despondency with all our beauties lured away by the delights of town. You must keep our spirits up, you know, but there is no doubt that you would set that great city on its ear.”

"And that, my dears, is why I shall leave," Mrs Scott said with a short laugh. "A widow grows terribly tired of her own company, but with such competition here, I see I would be quite overlooked, and I would do better to seek companionship in a larger pool."

"But I'm coming with you," Miss Fleming said with alarming naivety.

"So you are, my dear, forgive me," Mrs Scott said kindly. "Ah, and there is the dinner gong. Mr Anderson, would you be a dear and escort an elderly widow lady to her seat, please?"

Mr Anderson agreed, and Mr Barker was quick to offer his arm to Clara, and so the party filed into the dining room, with Mr Fraser escorting Miss Fleming, and Malcolm Stewart following alone.

Chapter 13

Pip,

Don't you dare scold that poor child for her mischief yesterday. I know she behaved very badly, but you deserved nothing less. What on earth were you thinking? Honestly, do you really wish to marry such an insipid dimwit? If Tilly hadn't had created a scene to make the point, I would have done so myself, and it would have been far more embarrassing to you than her little performance, I promise.

—Excerpt of a letter from the Most Hon'ble Catherine 'Cat' St Just, Marchioness of Kilbane to her brother, The Right Hon'ble Philip Barrington, The Earl of Ashburton (children of the Most Hon'ble Lord and Lady Lucian and Matilda Barrington, The Marquess and Marchioness of Montagu).

23rd June 1850, Wick, Caithness, Scotland.

"Well, now all becomes clear," Moyra murmured dryly as Hamilton escorted her into dinner.

"Don't make mountains out of molehills," he replied in an undertone.

"Oh, I'm not. I'm making sense out of your sudden lack of interest and the way you hovered defensively around that glorious child. Not that I blame you," she added with a sigh.

"I was not hovering," Hamilton shot back, indignant at the implication.

Moyra slanted him a pitying glance and sighed. "Men. Fools every one of them."

"What's that supposed to mean?" he demanded.

"It means you had better pull your finger out and marry that girl before Harold Barker does."

"Harold?" Hamilton said with a snort, for he liked the fellow well enough, but he did not consider him competition.

"Harold is a man of taste and knows how to treat a lady. I considered catching him myself," she added with a smile, before winking at Hamilton and adding. "I still might. But don't underestimate him, or Malcolm Stewart, for he'll queer the pitch if he gets the chance. That man does not like you, my dear."

"That wee clipe can—"

"He means to cause trouble," she told him, squeezing his arm. "I mean it. Act, before you are sorry for not doing so. I always knew you'd find yourself a nice girl and settle down. I had no illusions, and you gave me none, but that is the nicest girl you will ever see in all your days if I'm not mistaken. If you don't secure your interest with her at once, you are a fool, and I never took you for a fool, love."

Hamilton brooded over this, hearing the truth in Moyra's words. He had not liked seeing Clara smiling up at Mr Barker. He hadn't liked it one bit. The truth was, he felt sick with jealousy at the idea she might prefer speaking with any of the men here more than to him because he'd behaved like an ignorant arse when he ought to have treated her like the lady she so obviously was. She deserved better.

Hamilton waited for Mary to guide them to their seats before seeing Moyra settled and finding his own. To his relief, he discovered he was sitting beside Clara on her left, with Mr Barker on her right. Unfortunately, Miss Fleming sat on Hamilton's left and seemed determined to monopolise his attention. The moment the vexing girl paused and took a breath, he turned to Clara.

"I am pleased to see ye looking so well, Miss Halliday," he said, finding himself gazing at her profile. The candlelight shone on her lovely face, casting her fine skin with a soft, golden glow that gave him the oddest sensation. He'd been watching her all night in truth, listening to her, to the way she drew people out, genuinely interested in learning about them, about their thoughts and opinions. Everything about her was graceful, her voice soothing, her laugh a warm, rich sound that slid over his skin like silk, quite unlike Miss Fleming's practised laughter that set his teeth on edge. It hit him then, square in the chest, making him strangely breathless and tense, as if he stood on a precipice as he realised Moyra was right. Clara Halliday was something special, a woman that did not come along more than once in a lifetime. If he lost her, he'd regret it for the rest of his days.

"Thank you, I am well," she replied serenely, though she did not turn to look at him.

"I was worried for ye," he added, which was no more than the truth.

"You are very kind, but I'm sure there was no need. Mrs Macready took good care of me."

She still hadn't turned to look at him and the need to have her meet his eyes was suddenly the only thing he cared about. If she looked directly at him, perhaps he'd be able to tell if she still thought about their kiss, about him, or if he had buggered everything up as he feared.

All the reasons he ought not to get involved with her suddenly seemed frail and insubstantial. Even her father's obvious animosity could be handled. He was Hamilton Anderson, for God's sake, not some witless fool. He could charm the birds from the trees if he cared to do so. Everyone said it. One crabbit old clergyman would not keep him from his goal.

He wasn't entirely certain when the change had come over him, but he thought perhaps it was the moment he'd walked in the room tonight and seen Clara in that dark blue gown. He'd always known she was lovely, not just beautiful, but with the light of goodness and compassion that shone from within her. She was a woman who was gentle, sweet, and strong as a lioness. The kind who would put him in his place if the need arose and not submit to him just because he said so. He suddenly had the desperate desire to know everything about her, what music she liked, what books she had read, what it felt like to dance with her.... Did she wish to live forever in Wick? It occurred to him then how much of his time he'd spent of late thinking about her or trying not to think about her and failing. She was the perfect mix of sweet and tart, at once strong and fragile, and the thought of kissing her again made his entire body prickle with a restless energy that he doubted would leave him until he knew she was his.

"Did ye like the flowers?"

As he had hoped, she glanced around. "Hush," she scolded him, her lovely eyes flashing. "Have we not enough trouble with Malcolm Stewart trying to stir the pot?"

"Dinnae fash yerself about him," Hamilton advised her. "I can deal with his kind."

"What does that mean?" she asked in alarm. "I will not have you fighting and causing trouble."

"Are ye gonnae stop me, hen?" he asked in amusement.

"I dislike being referred to as poultry," she told him, making him chuckle.

"How about *mo leannan?"* he asked, lowering his voice.

She shot him a suspicious glance. “What does that mean?”

“Ye are a clever lassie, ye can figure it out,” Hamilton teased her, wishing fervently they were alone so he could tell her just what it meant in private.

She huffed and looked away from him, and they were silent as the soup course was served. Conversation rippled up and down the table, though Hamilton paid it no mind. He was only interested in the woman beside him now. The scent of her reached his nose, something delicately floral and entirely feminine. Roses, perhaps? It was too faint to be certain, and the desire to trace it back to its source was tantalising.

“I did like them. Very much.”

Hamilton glanced around at her in surprise, smiling with pleasure as he realised she had finally answered his question.

“I am glad. I wished after that I had sent ye roses, or lilies, but—”

“Oh, no. I should not have liked those half so much,” she admitted. Hamilton held his breath as she turned her face to his. “They were perfect.”

“Like yerself,” he said with a smile.

To his dismay, she frowned and looked away. “Please don’t do that.”

Hamilton was about to ask what she meant by that but the conversation at the table swelled to encompass her, and she was lost to him for the next quarter hour as Mr Barker monopolised her conversation. Hamilton shifted restlessly, condemned to converse with Miss Fleming, which was a simple enough exercise if one turned the conversation so she could speak about herself. Still, listening, usually something he did with ease, was a challenge as he tried to eavesdrop on Clara’s conversation with Mr Barker at the same time. The fellow had certainly set his sights on her, that much was clear. Hamilton felt a sudden kick of anxiety behind his ribs and told himself not to be daft. Just because Mr Barker was a respectable banker did not mean he was a better prospect.

He considered this with a sinking sensation as he realised her father might view the match in a different light altogether. Moyra was right. He'd been a fool, and he'd be a bigger one to drag his heels.

"I lived in Thorney," Clara was saying to Harold Barker, the next words muffled until she exclaimed with delight. "You don't mean it! Not really. But when were you there? Do you mean to say you know Mrs Kershaw?"

"She's my aunt," Mr Barker said, sounding triumphant at the discovery. "There, I knew we had things in common. We are destined to be great friends, Miss Halliday, for fate has tied its ribbons about us."

Hamilton made a sound of disgust that had Miss Fleming looking at him oddly.

"A bone," he said hastily, pointing at his throat as the fish course was removed.

"Yes, I know Mr Ludlow too. Of course, of course, a dear old fellow. Always losing his spectacles."

"Yes!" Clara replied, laughing, such a genuinely merry sound that everyone at the table turned towards her. "But how is this? How can you have visited, and Papa and I never have known of you?"

"Ah, but your father does know me," Mr Barker said with obvious satisfaction. "And I believe I had the misfortune of calling upon him once when you were away visiting your aunt."

"Oh! That's how it happened," she said, shaking her head before adding ruefully. "And of course, Papa would never think to inform me that anyone interesting had called upon us."

"I am flattered in the extreme to be considered worthy of noting, Miss Halliday, and I can only curse my rotten luck that I did not get to meet you sooner. But fate has decided to smile upon me, at last."

"Perhaps fate was being kind in keeping you *out* of my company," Clara replied, rallying. "You do not know me well yet. Perhaps I will turn out to be a dreadful trial."

"That, I cannot allow. Not under any circumstances," Mr Barker said, his voice soft now, and Hamilton noted the blush rising to her cheeks with increasing irritation.

"How is Jimmy?" he asked her, determined to steal her attention back again.

Clara turned away from Mr Barker to regard Hamilton. The blush had faded but her eyes still sparkled with merriment and the sight pleased him more than he could credit despite the jealousy that nagged at him. It was wonderful to see her happy, to watch her shining in company rather than hidden away in the vicarage where no one could see how very special she was. She ought to preside over a grand dinner table, her fortunate husband, the envy of every man present. The desire to have her attention entirely for himself was suddenly paramount in his mind and he determined to keep it.

"He's well, I thank you."

"Your father—"

Clara shook her head. "No, he doesn't know, though I'm feeling horribly guilty about that."

"Nae, lassie. Ye did a wonderful thing. I am proud of ye for it."

She gave him a searching look. "You are?"

He nodded. "Ye were brave and ye did right by the laddie, despite knowing it might bring ye trouble. Ye acted when so many others would have flapped their gums and wrung their hands but not actually lifted a finger."

“Thank you,” she said, and somehow the compliment had lit her up from the inside.

Hamilton thought she glowed with pleasure and the knowledge that he had done that made him feel quite ridiculously pleased with himself. Wanting to mend bridges and encourage her to think well of him, he carried on.

“Jimmy will need to learn a trade, though. He cannae live in the kitchen all his days.”

“I know,” she said, and the pleasure in her eyes dimmed, replaced by worry for the future. “But I do not know how to find such a place for him, or even if someone would take such a boy. I would speak for him, of course, but…”

“But that might look a little odd when yer father is ignorant of his existence,” he suggested.

She nodded, and he smiled, knowing he could take the anxious look from her eyes. “I’ll see to it.”

Clara blinked at him. “You will? You would do that for Jimmy?” she asked in wonder, gazing at him with an expression that made him feel he had won something quite extraordinary.

Hamilton held her gaze, his voice soft as he replied. “Of course I would, and if ye gave me the opportunity, there’s not much I widnae do for ye either, lassie. Ye need only name it.”

She looked away from him, but he heard the sharp intake of breath, noted the way her gloved fingers fidgeted in her lap. He had flustered her, and the sight of her confusion was at once endearing and wonderful.

“I cannot think why,” she replied after a long pause.

“Can ye nae?” he asked, careful to keep the words gentle and with no edge of amusement that she might misread. “Then ye are nae half so clever as I imagined.”

She glanced around at him, a searching look in her eyes but the main course arrived, and Mr Barker had been given the challenge of carving the lamb. Hamilton noted the care the man took to select the most succulent pieces for Clara and wished the fellow to the devil.

The food was excellent as it always was, and Angus was careful to ensure the wine flowed steadily. It was clear everyone was having a marvellous time, all except Malcolm Stewart, who had the look of a sulky boy condemned to finish his sprouts. He was drinking heavily and taking no trouble to disguise the fact, either. Now and then Hamilton would be on the receiving end of a look of venomous dislike, which he found no difficulty in ignoring. The nagging worry that the fellow might cause trouble for Clara, however, was one that he could not dismiss. He might need to have words with the little rat.

Hamilton was careful with Clara for the rest of the evening, keeping the conversation light and doing his best to make her laugh. Though she was obviously still wary, he kept her attention for most of the night, and knew he'd given her something to think about.

After a wonderful meal and an enjoyable time lingering over port and then tea with the ladies, the evening was finally over. Mr Fraser, Miss Fleming, and Mrs Scott all lived on the same side of town, so Mr Fraser took it upon himself to escort them home. Moyra whispered in Hamilton's ear before she left, reminding him to come and fetch his watch.

"I'll leave the back door open, but I'll not have you visiting me again if you mean to court Miss Halliday. Fetch it tonight and we'll have a drink to wish you happiness."

Hamilton said nothing but nodded. Whatever happened with Clara, he needed to end things with Moyra, and he was only relieved she seemed so reasonable about it.

He was just wondering how to dispose of Mr Barker so he could escort Clara the short distance to the vicarage when Angus came to his rescue.

"Harold," he said in an undertone, so the ladies could not hear. "I need help to get Malcolm upstairs. He'll have to sleep here tonight."

"Ah," the fellow said with immediate understanding. "Yes, he appeared to be dipping rather deep."

"And not for the first time," Angus replied with obvious frustration.

"Ah, well, these young men will push their luck at times, I suppose. I'll give you a hand, of course," Mr Barker said with a smile, and headed back to the parlour.

Angus turned to Hamilton, a serious glint in her eyes. "You will see Miss Halliday *safely* home, I know. If her father finds out, I'll be in the basket and—"

"Aye, Angus. Of course, I hear ye," Hamilton said at once, not about to give him a reason to think better of it and make other arrangements. "Don't fret, and I thank ye for ye thoughtfulness."

"I'll see ye married yet," Angus replied with a wink.

Hamilton snorted and turned to see Mary's maid handing Clara her cloak.

"Allow me," he said, taking it from her and settling it around her shoulders.

Clara avoided his gaze, staring instead at a button on his waistcoat as if it held the answer to everything as he did up the fastenings under her chin.

"Would ye do me the honour of allowing me to walk ye home, Miss Halliday?"

Clara glanced up at him, a look of sheer panic in her eyes. "Oh, but Mr Stewart—"

"Angus is having the devil of a time getting his brother up the stairs, for he's had a skinful," Hamilton said gently, steering her to the door. "I'll make sure ye get there safely. My word upon it. Goodnight, Mary, thank ye for a lovely evening."

"You're welcome, and you, Clara. I'm so glad you came."

"It was a wonderful evening," Clara agreed. "Goodbye. I'll see you in church."

Before Hamilton had the chance to close the door behind them, Clara strode off, at such a pace it was clear she intended to leave him behind.

"Are ye that eager to be rid of me?" he asked, catching her up with ease.

She refused to look at him. "Walking home with you is fraught with danger, as I'm certain you recall."

"Aye, I recall. I've recalled it a deal too often, if ye want the truth."

"Don't say such things," she said sharply, and even in the moonlight he could see the flush of colour upon her fair skin.

"Why not? Does it nae please ye to hear that thoughts of yer kisses are driving me distracted?"

"Indeed, it does not," she said, though the words were breathless.

"Slow down," he said impatiently, taking hold of her arm. "Ye will give yerself indigestion by walking at such a pace."

"My digestion is of no concern of yours," she retorted indignantly.

Hamilton chuckled. "Aye, maybe, but I want to talk to ye and I cannae do so with ye rushing about like a wee mouse with a cat on its tail."

"How apt a description," she said with a short laugh.

Hamilton stopped in the street, and it must have surprised her, for she stopped too, turning to face him with confusion in her eyes.

"Is that what ye think of me? That I'm a predator, out to hurt ye?"

She considered this before she answered. "I do not believe you intend me any harm, Mr Anderson. I fear, however, that your little games will end in pain all the same."

"Games?" he repeated as she walked off once more. "What games?"

She sent him a look of sheer exasperation. "Please do not insult my intelligence by pretending you don't know what I mean."

"Well, I don't!" he exclaimed testily. "Explain yerself."

"I mean," she said through her teeth. "That it may seem like an amusing jest to flirt with every girl in Wick and have them all pining over you, but you will not add me to their ranks."

"I dinnae flirt with all the girls in Wick!"

She stopped in her tracks and stared at him, arms folded.

Hamilton cleared his throat. "I never lead anyone on!" he protested. "A wee bit of flirtation is harmless. Making a lassie feel pretty and making her smile is nae a crime, is it?"

Her expression softened, and she shook her head. "No, of course not, but… but giving the impression it means more than that… well, that is very bad of you."

"I never did such a thing," he said gruffly.

She gave a soft laugh and walked on, taking the lane that led to the back of the vicarage. "Yes, you did."

"When?"

The back gate opened without a squeak as she entered the backyard and Hamilton followed her in.

"When you kissed a foolish vicar's daughter just to prove a point, and then sent her flowers when all you really wished to do was apologise for behaving badly," she said, and his heart clenched as he heard the hurt in her voice.

"Clara," he said, reaching to take her hand, but she danced backwards, out of reach.

"I did not give you leave to use my name," she said, chin up, eyes blazing defiantly, trying too hard to act as though she didn't give a damn when he could see he had wounded her pride.

Damn him to hell. He went after her, catching her before she could reach the back door and pulling her into his arms.

"Little fool," he said roughly. "If ye think I kissed ye to prove any point past that I am losing my wits over ye, ye are much mistaken."

"Fool, am I?" she said, and he could see the storm clouds gathering in her eyes now. Cursing himself for an idiot, he shook his head and took a step backwards, letting her go.

"Nae," he said, when his every instinct was to gather her in his arms again and kiss her until she realised he was the one in danger here. "Nae, Clara, I am the fool. Ye must forgive me though, for I have never… ach, ye are right. I flirt with all the lassies and make them smile but I never pretend an interest I dinnae have. But I do this time, and… and I'm making a proper mess of this, am I nae?" he added in frustration.

Her lips quirked a little, the anger in her expression dissipating at his obvious confusion. "You are, rather," she said, and he heard the amusement there with relief.

"Clara," he said, his voice low. "I think of ye. I think of ye when I try like the devil to think of anything else. I tell myself I am a fool to get involved when yer father despises me, and I have nae desire to take a wife but… but there ye are. The moment I wake up, there ye are, and when I sleep…"

"Oh."

The sound she made was soft and full of wonder and did terrible things to his equilibrium. Knowing she would likely slap him, and rightly so, he pressed his mouth to hers and she grasped his arms as he wondered whether she would push him away. For a moment she was rigid in his embrace and then everything softened, and she let out another soft sigh, this time of capitulation that he knew would live in his memory until the day he died.

She could not deny the way she felt for him, not now. She might not like her desire for him, but she could not pretend it away. The knowledge sang through his blood, triumphant male pride burning with satisfaction as she returned his kisses, inexpertly but with obvious desire.

"Clara," he murmured, gathering her closer, nuzzling into her neck and breathing in the sweet scent of her. "Roses. I could smell roses all night and it was driving me mad."

"M-Mr Anderson, we really ought not—" she said hesitantly, but Hamilton caught her mouth again, desperate to taste her, to ingrain the delicious flavour of her kisses in his mind so he could recall every detail when he was forced to say goodnight.

He ought to do that now, of course, but he could not. He did not want to let her go. Not yet. He dragged his mouth from hers just long enough to growl, "My name is Hamilton, I give ye leave to use it whenever ye like."

"I ought not… I ought not be here at all," she said, yet she gripped his arms still, not letting go as he pressed ardent kisses down her lovely neck.

"But here ye are," he murmured, his hands spanning her narrow waist, wanting to demand the right to call her his own but knowing he could not, not yet. "Such a good girl doing such a wicked thing, kissing a man in the dark. What does that tell ye?"

"That I'm not half so good as I thought I was," she said, sounding so wretched his heart seemed to squeeze in his chest.

"Nae," he said softly, gentling his lips on her skin, kissing her forehead tenderly. "Dinnae be daft. It means ye feel something for me, more than ye want to let on, or else I could never have persuaded ye to kiss me. Dinnae deny me, lassie, not when I want ye so fiercely."

He nipped at her plush lower lip, making her gasp and lost no time in sliding his tongue into the warmth of her mouth. She made a startled sound and pulled away, gazing at him in astonishment.

Hamilton grinned at her. "Let me teach ye how to take my kisses," he murmured, aware that his voice had grown low and husky. God but she was delicious. He could not remember ever wanting anything as much as he wanted her. His body was rock hard with longing, thoughts of all the ways he wanted to love her dancing in his mind's eye.

Somehow, he had backed her up against the wall in the dark of the yard, though he did not remember doing so. At least they were out of sight here, hidden from the vicarage windows and from the street. He brushed his lips over hers, hearing her sharp intake of breath as he did so.

"Part yer lips as I kiss ye," he told her, heat surging beneath his skin as she obeyed him, and he slid his tongue inside once more.

She was still at first, obviously puzzled until she tentatively slid her tongue against his. Desire lanced through him, and he growled low in his throat, deepening the kiss, taking more and more as his hands moved restlessly over her.

"Ye are the most delicious thing I ever tasted," he told her, before taking her mouth again, harder still, like a man starved who had finally found sustenance.

She was the air he breathed, she was necessary, and he could not get enough. One hand drifted from her waist, sliding up and up until it cupped the firm, round breast that filled his palm. She started in surprise, one hand lifting to curve around the wrist of the hand that caressed her, but she did not pull it away. He groaned, maddened by too many layers that kept his touch from her skin, squeezing the softness that lay beneath and wishing he could take it in his mouth. Imagining the taut little nub under his tongue was enough to unravel what little remained of his brains.

"What's that? Who's out 'ere?"

A door to their right pushed open and Clara gave a muffled squeal, pushing at his chest as Hamilton stepped back, fighting to regain his wits, which seemed to have been scattered all over Wick, damn him to hell.

"Oh, J-Jimmy!" she said, her voice trembling. "I'm so sorry if we woke you. Mr Anderson was just… he was just—"

"I'm just seeing her home, Jimmy," Hamilton said gruffly.

Jimmy, who was obviously indignant at having been woken up, rubbed his eyes and then glared at him suspiciously. "Oh, aye?" he said, with exactly the same inflection that Hamilton might have given the unconvinced reply. "That's what you're calling it, eh?"

"Jimmy!" Clara said sharply. "Mind your manners."

"Far as I can see, I'm the only one who *is* minding 'em," he said sourly. "But you'll be running along now, won't you, Mr Anderson, seeing as Miss Clara is home safe now?"

"Aye," Hamilton said in frustration, having no other option now Jimmy had poked his oar in. "But I'll be calling on ye, Clara. Ye hear me?"

Clara nodded but did not meet his eyes and he hoped Jimmy's interference had not undone all his good work.

"Goodnight, lassie," he told her softly, unable to help himself from adding, "Sweet dreams."

Chapter 14

Cat,

I had no intention of marrying the girl, for heaven's sake! However, I'd like to know how I'm supposed to find a wife if I do not converse and dance and spend time with women in order to discover if there is one I like. I will thank you to keep your nose out of my affairs and leave Tilly to me and to Mrs Harris. Neither of us need your advice.

—Excerpt of a letter from The Right Hon'ble Philip Barrington, The Earl of Ashburton to his younger sister, the Most Hon'ble Catherine 'Cat' St Just, Marchioness of Kilbane (children of the Most Hon'ble Lord and Lady Lucian and Matilda Barrington, The Marquess and Marchioness of Montagu).

24th June 1850, Wick, Caithness, Scotland.

"'Ere, I wanna word with you."

Hamilton turned as the sharp voice cut through the bustle of the harbour and saw Jimmy pushing his way past fisherman big enough to lift him with one hand and toss him out to sea. They let him through, though, and Hamilton realised he'd become a familiar figure down here of late. That wouldn't do. The life of a fisherman was a hard one and Clara would fret over the laddie. He'd have to find him something better than that.

"Well, I'm waiting, was there any word in particular ye were wanting to share?" Hamilton asked dryly as the lad stood before him, arms folded, his narrow face screwed up into something fierce and battle ready.

"I want to know what your intentions are," the boy said, holding Hamilton's gaze unblinking.

"My intentions?" Hamilton repeated, startled into a bark of laughter that he would have smothered if he'd not been so surprised.

Jimmy's small fist shot out and punched him in a spot that made Hamilton double over as pain exploded in his privates.

"Ye wee bawbag," he said breathlessly, grasping Jimmy by the scruff and towing him behind a fishing boat in dry dock for repairs. Blinking away tears as his eyes watered, Hamilton gave the lad a shake. "What the hell did ye do that for?"

"For taking advantage of Miss Clara," Jimmy said defiantly, though his face was white now, fear in his eyes as he regarded Hamilton with trepidation. "She's a good girl, she is, not some doxy to be messing about with in the dark."

"Ach!" Hamilton said impatiently, feeling like a proper brute now. "Wee yin, ye have nae need to fret. I mean to court her, but I'm sorry I dinnae speak to ye first, aye? I ken very well that ye try to keep her safe, and I thank ye for it."

"You've asked her to marry you?" Jimmy said, his eyes lighting up at this information.

"Give a fellow a chance," Hamilton said, trying to get his breath back. "Nae, I have nae done so yet, but I mean to court her, like I said."

"And that was courting, was it?" Jimmy said, a sarcastic edge to the question, clearly still sceptical of his intentions.

Hamilton sighed. “I ken very well, I didnae behave as I ought,” he said defensively. “A fellow… well, even a gentleman can get carried away, aye, when his blood’s up, but I meant her nae insult and I would nae dishonour her, my word upon it.”

“Swear it,” Jimmy said, spitting in his hand and holding it out to Hamilton.

Eyeing him resignedly, Hamilton did likewise, and they shook upon it.

“You mind you treat her proper from now on, like a lady,” Jimmy told him sternly.

“I will,” Hamilton growled, losing patience with the little devil. “And ye winnae use that dirty trick on me again if ye are wishing to keep yer hands attached to yer arms. If I wed the lassie, she will be wanting bairns at some point, and that winnae help my cause, aye?”

Jimmy sniggered at that. “I got you good, didn’t I?” he said in satisfaction.

“Aye,” Hamilton said sourly. “But I’m wise now, so dinnae try it again.”

“I won’t. I got other moves, though, so don’t you go thinking I can’t get ye good if you misbehave. And I taught Clara a couple of ‘em too,” Jimmy retorted, and then darted off as Hamilton offered him a clip round the ear.

♡♧◇♤

“I dinnae ken what that porridge ever did to ye, but I reckon it disnae deserve such treatment,” Mrs Macready said dryly, regarding Clara as she sat at the table in the kitchen, stabbing her spoon distractedly into the rapidly cooling bowl.

“I beg your pardon,” Clara said, straightening and looking sheepish.

Though her father disapproved of her eating in the kitchen with Mrs Macready, he had gone to the church hall early that morning and was not around to scold her.

"Is it nae to yer liking?"

"Oh, yes! Yes, it's very good, I'm just wool gathering is all," Clara said, fighting a blush as she remembered exactly what she'd been thinking about. Her mind was in turmoil, her entire being upside down and inside out and it was all Hamilton Anderson's fault.

She still could not believe she had allowed him such liberties. What had she been thinking? What might she have allowed if Jimmy had not appeared to rescue her from her own lack of moral fibre? The boy had believed she'd been taken advantage of, bless him, and had even run her through a few moves that would get her out of trouble if ever the need arose. But she hadn't *wanted* to be out of trouble last night. Clara let out a low groan and then chided herself as Mrs Macready turned back to her.

"Are ye ailing, lassie?" she demanded, narrowing her eyes at Clara. "Ye have nae gone and caught another fever, I hope? Ye *are* looking a wee bit flushed."

Oh, good heavens!

"No! Nothing of the sort, I promise," Clara said in a rush.

"Eat yer porridge, then," Mrs Macready said, watching her closely as she poured them both a cup of tea. Once she'd prepared the brew to both their likings, she sat down opposite Clara, her intelligent blue eyes sharper than usual.

"I'm nae a gossip," she said, her tone firm. "And if *somebody* was to confide a secret to me, I'd keep it close, aye, and take it to my eternal rest. So, if *somebody* had something on their minds that perhaps they couldnae speak to anyone else about, I'd be a good person to talk to, aye?"

"I'm sure," Clara said faintly, her heart beating very hard.

"Ye went out to dinner last night, then? How was it?"

"Oh, lovely. A wonderful meal and good company. I met Mrs Scott, do you know her? She was very kind to me, and I also met a Mr Harold Barker."

"Mrs Scott, aye?" Mrs Macready said thoughtfully, her eyebrows tugging together. "And Harold is a gentleman, an excellent sort. He'd make a good husband, aye."

"Oh, well, I had not thought of—" Clara began, laughing unsteadily.

"Nae, ye are too caught up with Hamilton Anderson to think of anyone else," Mrs Macready said with a wry smile.

Clara stared at her and then let out a groan, putting her head in her hands. "I'm such a fool," she said wretchedly. "You warned me and… and *I knew!* I knew he was dangerous. I mean, any fool can see it. He's handsome and charming and funny and—"

"And ye are thinking ye will never meet anyone better than him so long as ye live."

"Yes," Clara said in despair. "I'm to spend my life here where there are few eligible men, and he's one of them, and… and…"

"What happened?" Mrs Macready said, folding her arms. "Come, lassie, out with it. I'll have the whole, for I cannae judge if ye dinnae tell me all of it."

"Oh, I couldn't!" Clara said, horrified by the idea.

"Aye, I reckoned it was like that," Mrs Macready said with a snort, shaking her head. "Nae that I blame ye. If such a bonnie laddie was to make up to me, I'd reckon I'd be a puddle at his feet too. Some men just have a knack for melting our brains, that's all there is to it."

"Yes!" Clara exclaimed in frustration. "That's exactly it. I knew… *I knew* what he was about and yet…"

"And yet," Mrs Macready said, laughing softly. "The lament of many a lassie. Still, I'll say this: he's a gentleman despite his wicked ways. He'd nae trifle with a girl of your sort if he had nae serious intentions."

"You really think so?" Clara said dubiously.

"I do. What was the last thing he said to ye before he took himself off last night? I'm assuming he walked ye home, ye see," she added with a smirk.

Clara blushed and then blushed harder as she remembered the wretched man wishing her sweet dreams. The horrid creature must have known her dreams would be quite indecent and filled with his wicked voice, tempting her in the darkness. "He said… *oh!* He said he would be calling on me," Clara said, her hopes lifting as the memory returned to her.

How dreadful of her to have forgotten such an important bit of information because she'd been consumed with thoughts of everything else he'd said and done.

"Ah, there ye are then. He'll be wanting to walk out with ye."

"Oh, but Papa—" Clara said helplessly.

"If ye want my advice, lassie, ye will leave yer da to Hamilton. He's the kind who can charm the birds from the trees. Well, ye ken that well enough by now, I reckon," she added with a wicked chuckle.

Clara sighed. "I do," she said wistfully as her eyes drifted to the clock over the mantelpiece. "Oh, lud! Look at the time. I promised Papa to help him this morning. I was supposed to be there before nine and it's ten past already. Excuse me, Mrs Macready, I must dash."

Clara pushed open the doors to the church hall and admitted herself surprised as she was enveloped in the sound of feminine laughter and chatter. Her surprise only deepened as she viewed her father, standing in the middle of a group of ladies, beaming with pleasure.

"Mrs Aitken, you are teasing me," he said reproachfully, but with obvious good humour.

"Ach, reverend, I widnae do such a thing, but it's true, there's nae herring in the biscuits. We eat them morning, noon and night, but they dinnae taste good with sugar, ye ken."

"Well, the biscuits are delicious, though I'm relieved there's no fish in them after all," he said, brushing crumbs from his cassock. "Ah, Clara, my dear, how good to see you," he said, spying her as she came into the hall.

"I'm sorry, I'm late," she said, looking around her at the welcoming faces and then starting with surprise as she spied Malcolm Stewart among their ranks.

"Good morning, Miss Halliday," he said cheerfully. His eyes were shadowed and dark ringed after last night's indulgence, but he seemed in excellent spirits. "And may I say how bonnie you are looking this morning?"

"Good morning, Mr Stewart," Clara replied, icily civil, before turning back to her father with a questioning expression.

"Mr Stewart has joined our cause," he said confidentially. "As a young man in Wick, he has been exposed to the very worst the town has to offer and realises that something must be done. A convert, in fact! Isn't that marvellous?"

"Marvellous," Clara said, not feeling half so convinced that such a transformation had taken place. She eyed Malcolm dubiously and looked away as he winked at her. Lord, but he was a dreadful man. How she could have thought otherwise, she did not now know. Hamilton had been right to warn her about him.

"What do ye think of this, Rev?" one of the ladies asked her father, holding up a freshly painted placard. It bore a simple yet well executed painting of a mother and child hugging each other whilst the father sprawled in the gutter with a bottle in his hand.

"Oh! Mrs Munro, that… that is splendid!" her father said, making the woman blush with pleasure.

"I think ye are easily pleased, Reverend Halliday, but thank ye all the same."

"Mrs Munro, you work so tirelessly for our cause, I can be nothing but grateful for all your hard work, but you have real talent. You know, I was thinking of creating a theatre group for the children, perhaps to put on a nativity performance at Christmas. Would you be interested in painting some scenery, do you think? I would provide the materials, of course."

Clara blinked, astonished by what she was seeing. Her father was thinking of putting on a nativity? He was providing paints and materials? Whilst she had noticed his increasing ease with the women of the town as he got to know them, such a suggestion was startling. She remembered too his solicitude when she'd been ill, that he had taken the time to consider what she might enjoy most during her illness. What on earth was happening?

Mrs Munro and the other women exclaimed over the marvellous idea, which was just the thing to teach the little ones about the good book and give them some fun at the same time.

Her father chuckled and chattered good naturedly and it occurred to Clara that he had finally found something in his temperance group that he had never had before. His cause was their cause, and they were working together to do good in the community. He had never connected with his congregation before, never been amongst them and spoken to them directly, only stood as a figurehead who lectured from the pulpit. Yet so many evenings stood outside the pubs and taverns of Wick, could not be spent in silence, the women certainly would not have been silent. At some point he must have begun to listen, and to interact with them, and to understand their lives in a way he had refused to do before now. Perhaps too, he was gaining a sense of compassion for others that he had always been sadly lacking.

“A nativity, Papa?” Clara said, once she could gain his attention.

“Yes,” he said, whilst sorting through a stack of prayer books. “Dear me, some of these are in a sorry state. I think we may need to order some replacements. Not that I can take the credit for the idea of the nativity, as it was Mrs Cameron’s suggestion. A very wise woman is Mrs Cameron,” he added, pausing with a book in his hand as he glanced across the hall.

A plump, rather pretty woman in her early fifties caught him watching her and blushed, smiling back at him before carrying on with arranging flowers obviously meant for the church.

“Is that Mrs Cameron?” Clara asked with interest.

“What’s that?” her father said distractedly. “Oh! Oh, yes, indeed. The very same. A most capable woman, well, she’s brought up five children single-handedly, for her husband drank himself to death years ago. Poor fool,” he added sadly, shaking his head.

Clara looked once more at Mrs Cameron, who was laughing good-naturedly with the other women, and smiled. She looked like a kind woman, and Clara decided she would do well to get to know her. Before she could do so, a hand on her arm stayed her.

“Miss Halliday, might you assist me for a moment?”

Malcolm Stewart smiled at her, and Clara stiffened as she looked up at him, noting that the smile did not reach his eyes. Tugging her arm free, she returned an expression just as insincere.

“I beg your pardon, Mr Stewart, but I was about to lend a hand to Mrs Cameron.”

“Oh, no need, no need,” her father said easily, setting the prayer books aside. “I’ll go. You help Mr Stewart, my dear.”

Cursing her father's newfound joviality, Clara turned back to Mr Stewart. "What was it you needed, sir?"

"Come, and I'll show you," he said, leading her to the far side of the room where a door led into a small storeroom. Clara hesitated on the threshold, and he smirked at her.

"You can keep the door open if you are afraid," he said with a mocking tone.

Clara folded her arms, remaining where she was. "I shall," she said coldly. "For you are no gentleman, and not to be trusted."

He merely shrugged, leaning against a shelf stacked with cleaning supplies. There, he stopped, chewing on his lip and staring at her insolently.

"Well? What do you require assistance with?" Clara asked rather impatiently.

"With a conundrum," he said, watching her too closely for her comfort. "What to do when someone I care about is making a fool of themselves."

Clara stiffened. "Unless that person is a family member, I should proceed with extreme caution," she said coolly.

"But it would surely be a sin to say nothing when an innocent girl is being lured into a situation she does not comprehend? Are you certain you don't wish to close the door, Clara? Someone might overhear us?" he said gently, with a blatantly false show of solicitude.

Clara glared at him, certain now that he meant to continue making trouble for Mr Anderson and herself. "No, I thank you, I shall keep it open. In the first place, I am Miss Halliday to you, sir. In the second, you seem determined to have your say, so pray, do so and speak plain rather than making disgusting insinuations."

His face hardened at her forthright reply and, when he spoke, there was obvious satisfaction in the words. "I was not, as my brother believed, entirely out of my senses last night. It was simply a ruse so your devoted Mr Anderson would not trouble himself about my whereabouts. Once Angus and that old woman Barker had left me, I climbed out the window, and I followed you, *Clara.*"

Clara felt the blood drain from her face as she considered what he might have seen.

"Ah, yes, I see that your holier-than-thou attitude has suffered a blow. Well, you had best be prepared for another, my dear, for your lover is not only vile enough to take advantage of an innocent girl, but he went straight from you to his mistress."

"You are the most reprehensible man I have ever had the misfortune to come across," Clara exclaimed, too appalled and shocked to modify her words or to think clearly. "How dare you spread such vile gossip?"

He simply shrugged, looking disgustingly smug. *"I'm* reprehensible? When Hamilton Anderson held you in his arms one moment, and then went directly to Mrs Scott and bedded her."

Clara gasped, disbelieving that he could say such a thing out loud, or that he could implicate a woman who had been kind to her just last night. "I don't believe you," she said furiously. "And I will not listen to any further slander. Shame on you, Malcolm Stewart. Your brother and Mary would be deeply ashamed if they knew how far you have sunk because of your jealousy towards Mr Anderson."

Clara turned on her heel, wanting nothing more than to be out of his company as quickly as possible but he reached for her, grasping her arm and tugging her into the room, closing the door behind them. Clara sucked in a breath of shock, her heart pounding too fast.

"I wonder what the reverend would say if he knew what liberties you allowed that man last night?" he demanded, his voice harsh, his breath on her face a hot rush of stale wine fumes that filled her senses and made her want to wretch.

Clara faced him defiantly. "If you think to blackmail me, sir, you may think again. Tell my father if it pleases you, and you'll see me married to Mr Anderson before the end of the week. A situation which would suit me very well," she added, satisfied to see the flash of anger in his eyes that told her she had aimed well.

"Why, you little..." Grasping her by the arms, he pushed her up against the wall, pressing his body against hers, and for a moment Clara's brain froze with terror. His mouth pressed against hers and she made a sound of disgust, turning her head away as she suddenly remembered Jimmy's advice for unwanted male attention. Steeling her resolve, she raised her knee with a sharp jerk. Rather to her surprise, it worked just as Jimmy had promised it would, and Mr Stewart stumbled back, clutching his privates, his mouth open in a silent scream as tears sprang to his eyes.

Clara lunged for the door, but it opened just as she reached it, and she stared in horror as she saw Mrs Cameron on the other side. The lady's face darkened as she stared at Mr Stewart.

"Are ye all right, lassie?" she asked Clara gently, her expression one of concern.

"Y-yes," Clara said breathlessly, relieved that Mrs Cameron had guessed correctly, though she did not feel at all well.

"Run along then. I'll keep an eye on this one and make sure he disnae follow ye," she added, standing back to let Clara pass. "And dinnae fret. I'll say nothing about it to anyone. I'll make sure ye are nae left alone with him again."

"Thank you, Mrs Cameron." Holding her head up, Clara stalked out of the church hall, caring nothing for the fact she had not told her father where she was going or what she was about. She walked blindly, her heart crashing in her chest as the awful suspicion that Mr Stewart might know something she didn't ran wild in her mind. The scene with Malcolm Stewart had been vile and frightening, but it was hardly a surprise to discover he was a filthy lecher and would take advantage of a woman by force if the opportunity arose. Hamilton Anderson, however, she had come to trust, to care for, more than care for, and her heart broke at the idea she might have misjudged him yet again. Images of Hamilton holding Mrs Scott's voluptuous form in his arms tortured her. Why wouldn't he prefer a woman like that, one who was experienced and sophisticated? She'd been married and was clearly a woman of the world. She would know how to kiss, how to please a man. Had they laughed over Clara's ineptitude, her clumsy kisses and ignorance?

Tears pricked at her eyes, and she told herself she was getting herself in a sorry state for no reason. Malcolm Stewart was a disgusting excuse for a man and had done everything in his power to hurt her and drive a wedge between her and Mr Anderson. She would not allow him to do so. Yet the pain in her heart would not ease, the horrid seed of misgiving he had sown taking root despite her best efforts.

Too distracted to look where she was going, Clara turned a corner and collided with someone before she could avoid it. The scent of ambergris surrounded her, gentle hands gripped her arms, steadying her, and with an appalling sense of inevitability, Clara found herself staring into Mrs Scott's deep brown eyes.

"Why, Miss Halliday, whatever is the matter? You are as white as a sheet. Are you unwell?" Her rich voice was gentle and filled with concern and Clara was momentarily overcome with the terrible desire to scratch her eyes out. She steadied herself, shaking her head.

"No, not unwell," she managed, wishing her voice didn't sound so unsteady.

"Well, something is the matter," Mrs Scott said, narrowing her eyes. "I think you need a stiff drink, my dear."

"Is Hamilton Anderson your lover?" Clara clapped a hand over her mouth, realising too late she had said the awful words out loud. Her cheeks blazed with mortification as Mrs Scott stared at her, eyes wide. "Forgive me," Clara said, and would have turned and fled, but Mrs Scott grabbed hold of her hand.

"Not so fast," she said, her grasp surprisingly strong. "I think someone has been causing trouble. I suspect I could take a guess who it is, but I'd rather you told me. Come along, Miss Halliday. I think it's time you and I got better acquainted."

Born along by a will stronger than her own, Clara submitted, following Mrs Scott meekly back to her home, an elegant and modern affair with high ceilings. There, they were greeted by a discreet butler who settled them both in a beautifully decorated parlour and left them alone.

Clara looked around the room with interest, taking in the luxurious fabrics and the many artworks decorating the walls. This was a woman of taste and one who was used to making her own decisions, dealing with her own money, and making her own way in the world. In comparison, Clara felt gauche and silly, and she wished she had not come.

"Here," Mrs Scott said, handing her a glass with a small measure of amber liquid in it. "I ought to give you whisky, I suppose, but I confess I can't stand the stuff. Don't tell anyone. It's sacrilege in these parts. Give me a good cognac any day, however. Much better for the digestion, too," she added, smiling at Clara.

Mrs Scott sat down on a settee covered in a rich green damask fabric and patted the space beside her. "Come here, pet."

Clara did as she asked, too curious and too bewildered not to.

"Who told you I was Hamilton's lover?" Mrs Scott asked bluntly.

"Is it true?" Clara demanded, feeling this was far more pertinent a question for the moment.

"First things first," Mrs Scott said with some force, "I take it I am to thank that rat, Malcolm Stewart, for your distress?"

Clara nodded unsteadily as Mrs Scott said some very vulgar things under her breath. "Fellow ought to be horsewhipped," she added savagely. "It was obvious last night he meant to cause trouble. Still, Hamilton will deal with him, I have no doubt."

"Is it true?" Clara pressed. "Did he… Did he kiss me last night and come straight to you?"

"Ah, he kissed you!" Mrs Scott said, apparently delighted by this information. "I worried he might not act as swiftly as he ought, but the fellow had sense enough to act. That's good."

"Mrs Scott!" Clara said, her temper fraying.

"Hush, pet, drink your cognac," Mrs Scott said, patting her hand. "I do hope you're not going to be silly. You cannot have believed that Hamilton was a man with no experience? Of course, he has had lovers, and in a town like this it is difficult to be discreet, but he has always managed it. Yes, he was my lover, to answer your question, but no longer."

"Since when?" Clara asked, her heart thudding very hard.

"Since the moment he laid eyes on you," Mrs Scott said with a wry smile. "You silly girl, don't you realise it ought to me sobbing and carrying on? I'm the one he cast aside. I'm older than you, and it's been a long time since I was half so sweet and innocent. I knew I could never hold such a man, and so I shall not break my heart over him. You, though, you are the kind who could be the love of his life if you don't mess it up."

Clara stared at her, a little stunned by her words. "M-Me?"

Mrs Scott laughed, shaking her head. "Oh, youth really is wasted on the young. Yes, you, love. You've got him on a string, did you but know it. If you crook your little finger, that man will come running."

"That's ridiculous," Clara said frankly.

"Is it?" Mrs Scott sipped her cognac and regarded Clara for a moment. "Try it," she suggested, winking at her.

Clara stared at her. This woman had been Hamilton's lover, surely they ought to despise each other, and yet she found she could not. Jealousy gnawed at her heart at the idea of Hamilton kissing her, taking her in his arms and… and she would *not* think about that. But he'd ended things between them, for her, because he wanted Clara, not Mrs Scott.

"Mr Stewart said he came here last night," she pressed, needing to understand this.

Mrs Scott nodded. "He did. You'll have to manage him, Clara, for he's forever forgetting his hat or his watch or something. It was his watch on the last occasion, which I have had for some weeks as I've not seen him," she added with a smile. "He came last night to fetch it, and we had a drink together to say goodbye, and I wished him luck with his beautiful Miss Halliday."

"Truly?" Clara said, wanting so much to believe it, she hardly dared.

Mrs Scott put down her glass and took Clara's hand, holding it between both of hers. "Truly," she said, staring into Clara's eyes. There was a wistful tone to her voice that told Clara she was not quite so sanguine about Hamilton leaving her as she let on and Clara wondered at it. Could she really believe everything the woman said about Hamilton. Yet she believed *in him*, and she felt in her heart that he would not do such a reprehensible thing. "That man is falling hard, Clara, so don't be a fool for the sake of a little hurt pride. There aren't many like him in the world, and you'd be an idiot to let him go. Don't let the likes of Malcolm Stewart ruin everything for you both."

Clara let out a shaky breath and nodded. "I won't, and… and thank you, for speaking to me so candidly."

"Candid is the only kind of speech I approve of," Mrs Scott said with a laugh and reached for her glass again, holding it up towards Clara. "Here's to you and Hamilton, may you fall madly in love and have the kind of romance the rest of us only dream about."

"And may you find someone who loves and admires you as you deserve, which is a good deal, I think," Clara said boldly.

Mrs Scott laughed, delighted by the toast. "I'll drink to that," she said, so Clara chinked her glass against Mrs Scott's and the two of them drank to a wonderful future.

Chapter 15

Clara,

I must see you. Come to me tonight, at the Fisherman's Retreat at 8pm, for there is something I wish to say to you in private. Please come, sweetheart.

—signed Hamilton Anderson.

23rd June 1850, Wick, Caithness, Scotland.

"You're in a sunnier mood than ye were this morning," Mrs Macready observed as Clara arranged her father's dinner tray.

"Yes, I am. Do you know, I think Papa has made friends with the women of the town. You should have seen him at the church hall, laughing and chatting with them. I never thought to see it."

"Aye, they think the world of him," Mrs Macready admitted. "And credit where credit is due, he's been helping them in practical ways too, though I reckon Mrs Cameron's influence had a deal to do with it," she added, giving Clara a sideways glance.

"So I gather," Clara replied with a smile. "What's she like, Mrs Macready? Should I be concerned?"

"Well, she's nae of the same class as yer da, so if that troubles ye, ye may wish to step in. A word in her ear and she'll back off, I reckon. But she's a good sort, calm and no nonsense. She comes across as being a bit of a silly creature, but she's not in the least. She'll manage your da with her hands tied behind her back, that I will say," she added with a laugh. "And he'll love every minute of it, too."

"That's rather the impression I got, though I didn't really speak to her," Clara admitted, remembering Mrs Cameron's kindness when she had helped Clara escape. "And I don't care in the least if she's of the same class, only that they are happy. Do you really think it's serious? How strange to think Papa might get married again."

"Mrs Cameron had a look in her eye that tells me she means to catch yer da, and he's been too oblivious to notice until recently. I hear her words in some of the things he's said of late, though. He's softening under her influence I reckon, more thoughtful, aye. Ye ought to encourage him," Mrs Macready said firmly. "Invite the lady to take tea with ye. If yer da is married, he'll nae be so eager to keep ye at his side."

Clara smiled. "Everyone is giving me good advice today," she said with a laugh.

"Oh? Who else?" Mrs Macready asked, spooning the rich beef stew she'd made onto a plate.

"Mrs Scott."

The spoon clattered to the table, and Clara looked around in surprise. "Don't look so appalled. She was very kind. I know all about her and Mr Anderson too, so don't stand there with your mouth open. It's all over now, and I cannot blame either of them in the least for enjoying each other's company."

"Well," Mrs Macready said, clearly too shocked to say more. She wiped her hands on her apron and reached for the spoon, shaking her head as she carried on dishing up the meal. "Well, I never did. What did this paragon have to say to ye?" she demanded, gathering her wits at last.

"She said I ought to try crooking my finger, for Mr Anderson would come running," Clara said a little smugly.

Mrs Macready gave a snort of amusement. “Aye, well, Mrs Scott always did ken the best way to keep a fellow on a string. Reckon ye ought to listen to her.”

“Reckon I shall,” Clara said with a laugh, hefting the tray.

Mrs Macready laughed, setting the lid back on the saucepan. “Well, if ye are nae yet ready to eat I’ll set the saucepan by the range to keep warm. There’s plenty there for yer supper, and for Jimmy too, though where that laddie has got to, I dinnae ken. Up to mischief, I dinnae doubt.”

“Playing with his friends, most likely,” Clara said soothingly, for she had come to trust Jimmy and believed he was a good boy at heart. “Goodnight, then, Mrs Macready, and thank you for everything, as always.”

Mrs Macready fastened her cloak and nodded as she reached for her bonnet. “Ye are welcome, lassie. I’ll see ye on the morrow, bright and early.”

“Well, early anyway,” Clara replied with a laugh as she carried the tray up to her father.

He was in his study, working on his sermon and humming softly under his breath.

“Papa, your dinner is ready.”

He looked up, then began hurriedly clearing space on his desk. She waited until there was room enough to set the tray down.

“My, my, that smells wonderful,” he said with anticipation, reaching for the napkin.

“Are you going out tonight?” Clara asked, watching with amusement as he dug into his dinner and nodded absently. Once he’d swallowed the mouthful, he spoke with enthusiasm.

“Yes, indeed. We have something special planned for this evening,” he added, winking at her.

“Special?” Clara asked with trepidation. “In what way?”

He tapped the edge of his nose and grinned. “You’ll see.”

“Papa, you will be careful, won’t you?” Clara said, for as much as he seemed to have gained some valuable insight into the lives of the people of Wick, she didn’t believe he had entirely changed his spots. Rubbing people up the wrong way was something he did with far too much ease to be dismissed as a possibility.

“Yes, yes, of course. Don’t you worry,” he said, waving her away. Considering herself dismissed, Clara left the room and was about to return to the kitchen when she saw an envelope on the doormat in the hallway. Hurrying over, she picked it up, saw with surprise it was addressed to her, and broke the seal.

Her heart skipped as she read the short message from Hamilton. He wanted to see her, something he must say to her…

Clara’s breath caught. Of course, it was very wrong of her to meet him in secret, *alone.* But unlike Malcolm Stewart, she trusted him, and Mrs Scott had told her his intentions were all that they should be. Besides which, she wanted to see him very badly, and she did not know when that might next be, as tomorrow was Sunday, and her father would want her help.

She glanced at the note once more. 8pm? It was almost that now. Deciding she would be brave, she stuffed the note in her pocket, put on her cloak and drew the hood up over her hair, shielding her face. It was the work of a moment to slip out of the front door. Since the street was deserted, Clara quickly made her way up the steep incline to Hamilton's tavern. It was looking very handsome now, and she thought perhaps it would not be too long before it opened. She only hoped she could keep her father from causing him trouble when it did.

Finding the door unlocked, Clara turned the handle and pushed it open, darting inside and closing the door behind her. The place was in darkness, but a glimmer of light shone from upstairs, so she followed it, tiptoeing up the stairs. When she got to the top, the light was brighter, and she saw it came from one of the bedrooms. Hurrying to the doorway, she felt her heart lift as she saw Hamilton. He was frowning over a dozen fabric samples laid out on a table in front of him. She didn't know if he heard or sensed her watching him, but his head turned.

"Clara!"

"I couldn't not come," she exclaimed, running up to him. "Did you think I wouldn't?"

He stared down at her as if he was completely stunned by her appearance. "I hardly ken what to think? But I'm glad… Clara, lord but I have missed ye, and I dinnae care if that's a daft thing to say when I saw ye last night, but it's too long, lassie."

"It is," she agreed, smiling and wondering if he could see everything she felt, for she was too foolishly infatuated with him to hide it.

"Ye are nae vexed with me?" he asked, reaching out and stroking her cheek. "I'm afraid I behaved very badly."

Clara shook her head. "I let you behave badly, didn't I?" she added, her smile dimming a little as she considered that. "You… You don't think the worse of me—"

"Little fool," he said fondly, and took her hand. "It pleases me more than ye can comprehend when ye show that ye want me. Come away from the windows though, love. I dinnae want anyone to see ye here. Will ye nae be missed?"

"Not for a little while," she said, gazing up into his handsome face, his amber eyes warm in the lamplight. Did this man really care for her? It seemed an impossible dream. He could have anyone he wanted; surely a vicar's daughter was not aiming high enough when his father was an earl. Perhaps, even if he did want her, his parents would not approve.

"What are ye fretting about?" he asked softly, caressing her cheek with the backs of his fingers. He touched the place between her eyebrows and stroked softly. "Ye are frowning, lassie. I dinnae like to see ye troubled."

"Oh, nothing," she said, not wanting to confess such concerns when he'd not even declared his interest in her yet.

His hand dropped to her chin, and he raised it up, forcing her to meet his eyes. "Ye are a little liar. Are ye worried I'm toying with ye? That I mean to dishonour ye and leave?"

Clara blushed, surprised he put it into such stark words, but then he was not the kind to prevaricate. "I would not have said it quite that way, for I believe you are a gentleman, that you would not treat me so ill, but… but all the same…"

"But all the same, I've nae told ye my intentions," he said, his voice low. As he spoke, he moved her, guiding her gently until her back rested against the wall. His body pressed against her, hard and so very vital. There was so much energy in his frame, still as he was, like seeing the smooth surface of a deep river and knowing there were dangerous currents hidden beneath.

"N-No," Clara stammered. "You have not."

"My intention is to kiss ye, lassie," he teased, nuzzling into her neck. "And to make ye sigh and call my name."

"Hamilton," she whispered unsteadily, as he nipped at her ear. She shivered as she felt his teeth graze the tender lobe.

"Aye, just like that, but louder."

He chuckled, a wicked sound that raised all the tiny hairs on the back of her neck and made her feel too much, desire too much. She ought not be here. It was she who was wicked, behaving in a manner no decent girl should ever do. How had she got here, how had this happened, when she knew she was breaking every rule?

"What else do ye think I intend?" he asked her, his deep, rumbling voice like the purr of some great cat vibrating through her.

"I c-couldn't possibly imagine," she said desperately, pressing her palms against his waistcoat and feeling the heat of his body through the fine woollen weave. She lay her cheek on his chest, and he kissed the top of her head.

"Are ye sure about that? What is it ye dream of, when ye are alone in your bed? Do ye think of me?"

"No, of c-course not," Clara said with a gasp, shocked he should ask her such a thing.

He only laughed, though, taking her face between his large hands and gazing down at her. "Ye are lying again. For a vicar's daughter, ye are terribly sinful, Clara Halliday. I'll have to break ye of such habits, I reckon."

Clara shoved at his chest, mortified, but he didn't budge so she buried her face against his waistcoat instead. "You are the most odiously conceited man in the world," she complained hotly.

"Aye, but I'm nae wrong," he said, and she could hear him smirking, the devil. "Tell me, Clara, tell me ye think of me."

There was a different note to his voice now, no longer smug and teasing, but closer to desperation. Clara forced herself to meet his gaze once more and her breath caught at the need in his eyes, the desire for her blazing in the wide, dark pupils that swamped the beautiful copper and gold.

"I think of you," she murmured, though the words were breathless. "I think of you all the time," she admitted, too far gone for caution.

"Clara," he said, speaking her name in a way she had never heard it said before.

It was the name of a woman who was desired beyond reason, a woman who was bold and loving and unafraid to take what she wanted. It made Clara want to be worthy of it, to be that woman. To be *his* woman. So when his mouth captured hers, she met him with equal passion, curling her arms about his neck and pulling him down to her, holding on tight. All the same, when he reached down and grasped her bottom, lifting her up, she gave a squeal of surprise. He carried her and though the indignity of it was shocking to her, Clara wrapped her legs about his hips as he crossed the room and sat her down on a tabletop. He did not move away, however, his body insinuated between her thighs, only the bunched-up fabric of petticoats and skirts keeping them apart.

"I ought not," Clara fretted, cheeks blazing now, but he stared down at her with such affection in his eyes that she could not be afraid.

"Nae, ye ought to be at home, safe with Mrs Macready, but ye came to me," he said, his voice soft, satisfaction blazing in his eyes. "I cannae pretend that I'm sorry. If I were any kind of gentleman, I would send ye away, but I cannae bring myself to do so. Not yet, at least. I shall, I promise, but… but not yet…"

He kissed her again, deeply and passionately, clouding her mind as the feel of him so close chased good sense far away. The slide of his tongue was an intimate delight of the kind she had never dreamed, and she could not get enough. With his arms supporting her, he lowered her down, his large body pressing her against the tabletop. Too late, Clara realised she was laying down with Hamilton Anderson on top of her, her thighs parted and his very male, very hard body in a position no young lady ought ever to allow.

"Hamilton?"

"Aye?" he asked, his voice husky as one hand tugged at her skirts. She gasped at the feel of his warm fingers curling about her calf and sliding higher. He tickled the tender skin behind her knees with light caresses, making her breath catch before his hand slid higher, moving over her garter to make contact with bare flesh. "I will speak to yer da, Clara. First thing in the morning. I swear it."

Clara relaxed, any reservations she'd had dissolving like warm honey with his reassuring words, along with her resolution to not behave badly.

"Ah, but ye are like the finest silk, *mo leannan."*

"You never told me what that meant," Clara said, momentarily distracted.

"It means 'my sweetheart,'" he murmured, rubbing his cheek against the swell of her breasts. *"mo chridhe, a thasgaidh, mo ghràdh,"* he continued, tugging her skirts up and out of the way and pressing his body harder between her legs until she felt the hard length of what she realised with a jolt of shock was the inescapable evidence of masculine arousal through the fine fabric of her drawers.

Clara's breath snagged in her throat as the intimate contact sent a bolt of sensation lancing through her body. Without thinking, she chased it, her hips lifting to meet his and pushing against that forcefully male part of him.

Hamilton made a choked sound and smothered a groan as he responded in kind, rubbing himself against her with rhythmic thrusts, kissing her over and over, sliding his hands over her body in slow caresses, making her dizzy as time passed in a passionate fog until she was beside herself, uncaring of what he did, of what she allowed, only that he make it stop, or make it better, or do *something!*

"Hamilton?" she said urgently, hearing the question in his name but not knowing what she was asking for. He seemed to know better than she did, however, as he pressed his mouth to hers once more, kissing her hard and deep as his hand slid between her legs, finding the slit in her drawers and sifting through the silken curls. Clara jolted, stunned by his touch in a place so secret and entirely forbidden. Her mind reeled, wondering how she dared let him, but her body wanted, aching and clamouring for more. His deft fingers sought and found the tiny bud that ached and throbbed and caressed her, his touch just firm enough, just fast enough, and he devoured her shocked cry as her body convulsed in his arms, giving itself over to him for it seemed to belong to him, anyway. She buried her face in his shoulder as the sensation faded, shocked and bewildered by what she had done.

"Ah, but ye are the sweetest thing," he crooned, kissing her tenderly, stroking her face. "Lord but I will die of wanting ye, but I have behaved badly enough for one night, devil take me. Can ye forgive me, *mo ghràdh?"*

"Forgive you?" she said unsteadily, still not quite believing what had happened, what she had allowed.

"Aye, forgive me," he said gently, pulling her upright and rearranging her skirts until she was decent again. "I am a wicked fellow, but I'll be on yer doorstep first thing, ye understand? I dinnae take such things lightly. I widnae have touched ye so if I had nae the best of intentions. I would never dishonour ye in such a way."

Clara sighed. She had believed him, trusted in him, but it was still reassuring to hear him repeat his words.

"Did ye still think I would take advantage and walk away?" he asked, frowning down at her.

She shook her head. "If I had believed that, I would never have come when I got your note," she said, smiling up at him. "But all the same, I am glad to hear it."

"My note?" he repeated, frowning at her. "What do ye mean? I never sent a note."

Clara stared at him in consternation and reached for the note she had stuffed in her pocket. "Yes, you did. It's here in black and white," she said, handing it to him.

Hamilton's frown deepened as he scanned the words. "That's nae my hand, lassie," he said, his tone suddenly grave. "Someone is playing games, I reckon, and I dinnae like it. Up ye come. I fear ye have walked into a trap and—"

As he spoke, the sound of singing reached their ears, a flickering light visible outside, reflecting on the windows. The singing got louder and louder and the familiar sound of a hymn was now unmistakable.

"What on earth…?" Hamilton muttered, crossing to the window but keeping to the side, out of sight as he looked out.

"It's my father," Clara said in dismay, realising the something special his temperance army had in mind tonight was to cause Hamilton trouble.

Hamilton didn't answer at first, a frown between his eyebrows as he watched the street below.

"Yer da is here right enough, but it's nae him leading the procession, Clara. It's Malcolm."

"What?" Clara hurried to the window, though Hamilton held her back, so she did not risk being seen. "Good heavens. Whatever is wrong with him?" she asked, for Malcolm was singing with more than simple enthusiasm, waving his arms and bellowing the words as he attempted to conduct with the flaming torch he carried. Indeed, many of the women carried such torches, singing with pride as the firelight touched their faces, lighting them up in the darkness. The hymn came to a rousing conclusion, and the reverend stepped hurriedly forward before Malcolm could launch into another song, which he seemed determined to do.

"Excellent, excellent," her father said, beaming at the ladies before giving Malcolm a slightly wary smile. "Well done, Mr Stewart. Your fervour does you credit, but we must save our voices and move on if we are to walk our procession around the entire town tonight. Must not peak too early, eh?" he added, with a rather agitated laugh.

"Oh, no!" Malcolm cried, shaking his head fervently. "No, I can't have that, for you and I both know that the devil has taken root in Wick, a serpent slithering beneath our feet, and his nest is right here, under your very nose. Did you not tell me yourself you wished to rout the demon from his lair?"

"Er…" Reverend Halliday glanced at Mrs Cameron, who raised a questioning eyebrow at him. "Yes, well… whilst I denounce the opening of yet another tavern in this town, I fear… I fear I may have reacted rather too strongly. I have had time to reflect and—"

"And has the devil crawled under your skin too? Has he wheedled his way into your life and tempted you into sin?" Malcolm demanded, thrusting the torch towards her father, who took a hasty step backwards. "The sins of the flesh are just as evil as the sin of drunkenness, Reverend Halliday. Are they not, Mrs Cameron?"

Gasps and a few startled laughs echoed down the street and Clara watched in distress as her father merely stood with his mouth open while Mrs Cameron pushed past him.

"Ye mind yer tongue, ye nasty little whelp. I know what ye are and I've warned the reverend of yer sly ways. Why, ye never were the man yer brother was, Malcolm Stewart, and ye are a bedamned hypocrite, for I can smell the whisky on yer breath from here, and here ye are singing and carrying on like ye are one of us. Ye just wish to make trouble for Mr Anderson, for ye ken very well he has won Miss Halliday's heart, and ye cannae stand it."

"Oh, he's won more than her heart, I fear," Malcolm sniggered before raising his voice and shouting up at the windows where she stood with Hamilton. "Hasn't he, Clara, dearest?"

Clara made a shocked sound, her knees suddenly weak as she realised Malcolm meant to ruin her, and was doing an excellent job as everyone was looking up at the building. Hamilton pushed her back.

"Ye will stay here," he told her firmly. "Dinnae budge until I come for ye, nae matter what happens. Do ye promise me?"

Clara nodded, dazed and afraid of what this meant for her.

"Don't fret, lassie," Hamilton said, squeezing her hands. "I'll nae let ye down, and we can be married before morning if it comes to it. They'll be nae disgrace for ye, ye have my word."

With those bracing words, he left her and hurried down the stairs.

Chapter 16

Mrs M,

I fink something is wrong. Plese come.

— signed Jimmy.

24th June 1850, Wick, Caithness, Scotland.

Hamilton pushed open the front door of his property to discover Malcolm Stewart still shouting up at the bedroom windows, calling Clara's name. The reverend had finally roused himself to action and was red in the face, shaking his fist at Malcolm and demanding he stop his slanderous comments. All to no avail. Hamilton's tactic was rather more brutal and certainly more effective. He walked up to Malcolm, grabbed him by his coat lapel, and punched him in the face.

Malcolm sprawled on the ground, the flaming torch knocked from his hand as blood flowed from his nose. He grinned up at Hamilton as his mouth filled with blood, giving him the look of a man who was not quite sane. Hamilton suspected he wasn't in that moment, for the drink was upon him and he'd seen reasonable men do and say terrible things when in their cups. Not for the first time, he wondered if perhaps the reverend had a point, and if perhaps he had been standing on the wrong side of the argument. Whilst he would never agree with banning whisky—the idea was a horrifying one—he could not deny it caused a good deal of desperation in the town.

"Mr Anderson!" Reverend Halliday exclaimed, staring down at Malcolm sprawled in the gutter.

"Aye, I ken it was nae very Christian of me," Hamilton said gruffly, very aware that he would need to ask this man for Clara's hand the next day. "But I cannae have the fellow slandering an innocent girl, for Clara is nae with me," he added, raising his voice for the benefit of the crowd.

"No, indeed!" the reverend said. "I meant only to thank you for doing what I could not."

Hamilton glanced around in surprise and nodded as he saw the reverend's gratitude writ large upon his face. "I'm afraid Mrs Cameron has the right of it," he told the reverend. "Malcolm Stewart is sly, sneaking blackguard and always has been. He's out to make trouble and disnae believe in yer cause any more than he believes in anything but his own pleasure. He's also off his heid with the drink."

"I feared as much this evening, but I confess I did not wish to believe it when he has been such a lively addition to our numbers," the reverend said mournfully. "But the poor young man needs our help, then," he added, turning to where Malcolm had been lying and frowning to discover him gone.

Hamilton turned too, just in time to see Malcolm pick up the torch he had dropped and throw it through the downstairs window of the inn. Hamilton did not know if he had planned to do it or had simply taken leave of his senses, but if he really intended to set a blaze, he could not have aimed better. The decorators had been working downstairs, and all their paints were stacked neatly in the middle of the room with their brushes and cleaning cloths and ropes for hauling paint tins. The paints were oil based, and highly flammable. In the time it took for Hamilton to run for the door and snatch it open, an inferno had erupted inside, blocking his path to the stairs.

♡♧◇♤

Clara smothered her mouth with her hand as she watched Hamilton punch Malcolm Stewart in the nose. Though she despised violence, she could not deny a brief surge of satisfaction at the horrid man getting his comeuppance. It was the least he deserved.

"Clara!"

Clara turned in surprise as she saw Jimmy at the bedroom door.

"Jimmy! What on earth are you doing here?"

"When I got home and ye weren't here, I had a bad feeling in me belly," he said grimly. "I didn't know why, but I heard that rat Malcolm at the church hall, egging yer da on to come here, with lit torches and… I just knew he were gonna cause trouble. I sent Tommy Brodie with a note for Mrs Macready, but then I thought to come and warn Hamilton, but when Malcolm started calling yer name, I just knew."

"Oh, Jimmy," Clara said, blushing and feeling quite appalled that he should have guessed where she was.

"Aye, well. Me and Hamilton will be havin' words," he said darkly, which might have been funny coming from such a young boy if he had not been so entirely sincere.

"There's no need, Jimmy. He's going to speak to my father," Clara said, going to him and resting her hand on his shoulder.

"Said so, did he?" Jimmy asked sceptically. "And you believed him?"

"Yes!" Clara said, smiling at him. "He did, and I do. He's an honourable man, a good man, and I trust him."

"You've changed your tune," he observed, still looking unconvinced.

"I love him," she said simply.

Jimmy looked faintly disgusted by this admission and shook his head. “Well, I suppose if he marries you, it’s all right, but he’d best pull his finger out and ask the rev. I’ll not have him dragging his feet and—”

The sound of breaking glass, screaming, and a loud whoosh of sound that made Clara’s heart skip with fear interrupted his indignant speech.

Jimmy clutched at her hand, his eyes wide, suddenly very much a little boy when he had seemed so grown up just moments before. “What was that?”

Clara shook her head and hurried to the door. She snatched it open, ran to the stairs and peered down, only to see smoke billowing up towards her.

“Oh, my!” she exclaimed, pulling Jimmy back.

“Is there another way out?” he asked. “Servants’ stairs?”

Clara turned around on the landing. A corridor stretched on either side of them with doors off it leading to bedrooms, and another staircase ran up to the servants' quarters, but there was no visible route down other than this one. All the same, they ran along the corridor, snatching open doors in case a hidden staircase lay behind one.

“What do we do?” Jimmy asked, panic in his voice. “I don’t want to burn, Clara.”

“We’re not going to burn,” she told him firmly, though her heart was thrashing madly in her chest. *Keep calm, keep calm*, she told herself. If they couldn’t take the stairs, then it was out the window they must go. “Come along now, my brave lad. You must keep your head and make sure we both get out safely. Yes?”

Mutely, Jimmy nodded, but his shoulders firmed, a determined look in his eyes. “Right ho, Clara. Out the window then?” he guessed.

"That's the way," Clara said, and then gave a shriek as something crashed against the wall beneath them, and then careened up the stairs.

It was a shapeless lump, smoking and steaming, and Clara gave a shout of surprise as the scorched, sodden blanket was thrown to one side and Hamilton revealed himself. He was black with smoke and soot, his hands burned, and his hair singed on one side. He carried a small axe, and grinned at Clara, breathing hard.

"Hamilton!" she cried, throwing herself at him. "Oh, you foolish man, you could have been killed," she exclaimed, hugging him with both relief and terror.

Hamilton coughed, wiping his eyes, which were streaming. "Scold me later, eh? Jimmy, ye wee devil. I might have known it. Come on, the pair of ye. We are in the proper fix, I'm afraid, but we'll right it all before morning, if we can get out of here."

Ushering them all back into the bedroom, Hamilton closed the door behind them to keep the worst of the smoke out and flung open the windows. Clara now saw he carried a big coil of rope over his shoulder which he dropped to floor, taking one end and grimacing with pain as he tied it tightly around Jimmy's waist.

'Jimmy, hold the axe a moment," Clara said, handing it to him and reaching for her petticoats. Using the sharp edge she tore the fabric, ripping long strips off. "Give me your hands," she said to Hamilton, and quickly wrapped the makeshift bandage about his palms.

"Thank ye, love," he said, smiling at her before turning back to a white faced but resolute Jimmy. "I've sent someone to fetch a ladder but I dinnae ken how long that will take. So, I'll lower ye down, laddie, Just hold on to the rope and dinnae look down."

"Clara!"

Clara saw her father's face, wreathed in horror as he looked up at her. He held a bucket of water, a chain having been formed to put out the fire. Clara froze, knowing that her father would be ashamed of her for what she had done. Perhaps he would never forgive her and throw her out of doors.

"Don't fret now, lassie," Hamilton told her firmly, giving her hand a quick squeeze. "Keep yer heid. I'll make everything right, just trust me. Right, Jimmy, out ye go."

"Oh, but… I don't reckon—" Jimmy protested, looking deathly pale as Hamilton picked him up and set him on the ledge.

"I've got ye and I winnae let ye fall," he promised the boy, giving Jimmy a push before he could object and bracing himself as he took the boy's weight. "Halliday, help the lad," he called down, and Clara watched with relief as her father ran forward, his arms held aloft as he waited for Jimmy to come low enough to get hold of. Clara viewed the scene with her heart in her mouth as her father took Jimmy in his arms and lowered him carefully to the floor.

"The rope! Hurry!" Hamilton called, as her father fumbled with the knot and released Jimmy so Hamilton could pull the rope back up.

"Jimmy, oh, Jimmy!"

Clara saw Mrs Macready running across the street as Jimmy staggered to his feet and ran to meet her, throwing his arms about her and holding on tight. With a sigh of relief that Jimmy was safe, Clara turned back to Hamilton, whose face was impassive.

"Thank you for coming for me," she said as he tied the rope securely about her. "I admit I was rather frightened and—"

The words died as Hamilton hauled her into his arms and kissed her hard, much to the appreciation of the crowd beneath who whooped and added encouraging words.

Muttering curses, Hamilton broke off, his voice almost angry as he checked the knots he'd tied.

"Clara Halliday, if ye think I have gone to the trouble of falling in love with ye only to let ye go up in smoke, ye dinnae ken the least thing about me. Now get out the damned window and tell yer father I'll be marrying ye before the month is out, whether he likes it or no."

"Yes, Hamilton," Clara said obediently, gazing at him in wonder as he helped her onto the ledge.

Hamilton Anderson had fallen in love with her! Suddenly she was not as terribly afraid as she might have been with this marvellous piece of information to hold close to her heart.

"Don't look down, lassie. Keep yer feet against the wall as I lower ye, like ye are walking," he told her, his tone gentler now. "I'll nae let ye fall. Not now, not ever."

"I know," she whispered, smiling at him as she braced her feet as he instructed, watching his powerful frame bear her weight as he lowered her, hand over hand. The strain on his face was obvious, and she winced inwardly as she understood the pain he endured despite her bindings as he held her steady.

"No! I was the one! I was going to save her! You've ruined everything, you bloody brute!"

The enraged voice came from inside the building and Hamilton's head whipped around as someone else came into the room. Clara screamed as she saw Malcolm, blackened and enraged, shove Hamilton aside. Clara fell two feet before Hamilton steadied himself again, lowering her quicker but no less carefully as Malcolm put his arm about Hamilton's neck and began to squeeze.

Clara felt her father's hands pulling her to safety, saw Hamilton register the fact she was safe, and then the two men disappeared.

"Hamilton!" Clara screamed, attempting to run for the front door, but her father and Mrs Cameron held her back.

"Nae lassie, dinnae be a fool. Hamilton can handle that bampot with one arm tied behind his back. Ye just wait with me and yer da, he'll be down presently."

The sound of fighting and furniture breaking was almost drowned out by the sound of the fire and those trying to douse the flames had to fall back as the smoke and heat grew in intensity.

"Hamilton!" Clara cried, increasingly afraid as he failed to appear.

"I'm here," he said, his voice hoarse as he appeared at the window. "Reverend, I have another parcel for ye," he added, hauling a battered Malcolm Stewart upright. He'd already tied the rope in place and now lifted the half-conscious man onto the ledge.

"Ye would do better to leave him there," shouted a woman Clara recognised as Mrs Macdonald.

Hamilton gave a weary huff of laughter. "Tempting though that may be, Janet, Angus would never forgive me." With that, he gave Malcolm a slap to rouse him. "Wake up, ye wee clipe. Ye will help or I'll drop ye and have done," he warned.

Malcolm blinked hazily and then woke fully as he saw he was being hung out of the window.

"Argh!" he exclaimed, panic in his eyes.

"There ye go," Hamilton said with a snort, and began lowering the fellow with a deal less care than he'd shown Jimmy or Clara, but he got the man to the ground safely.

"Hamilton, *hurry up!"* Clara shouted, hugging her arms about herself with terror as she saw the way the smoke billowed around him. Hamilton whipped his head round at the sound of a crash close to him in the room, and whatever it was, it seemed to galvanise him into action. There was no one to lower him on a rope, however, and his burned hands felt as if they were on fire as he climbed out onto the ledge.

"Oh!" Clara exclaimed, unable to take her eyes from him as he tried to find a foothold to make his way down.

There were none, and the flames licked faster from the lower windows now, the heat appalling. Those throwing water at the fire moved faster, but it only made the choking smoke worse. Unable to do a thing to help him, Clara watched helplessly as the fumes momentarily hid him from view, and then Hamilton let go of the ledge, falling heavily to the ground with a thud.

"Hamilton! Hamilton!" she cried, uncaring of who saw as she ran to him, throwing herself down beside him and taking his face in her hands. She wiped his filthy face with her skirts as he led out a groan of pain. He muttered a few obscenities to which Clara thought him quite entitled.

"Dammit, that stings," he grumbled irritably, looking at his hands.

Clara took them in her own hands, kissing his knuckles. "Oh, my love," she said, and Hamilton grinned as he looked around the crowd who had gathered around them.

"Ye heard that, I hope. She called me *my love*. Ye are all invited to the wedding, by the way," he added.

Clara blushed, belatedly looking around to see the women of her father's temperance army standing about them.

"Aye, laddie. We heard. Ye must marry him now, lassie, or he'll pine away. Sore in love with ye he is."

"He'll die of it!" added another woman, chortling with laughter.

"He nearly did!" said another.

"Aye, I will," Hamilton said, sounding as if he might mean it too. He took her hand between his fingers and brought it to his lips. "I dinnae care about buildings burning, or even if I lost everything I own, but I'll nae lose ye, Clara Halliday. The thought of it makes me feart more than anything else in this life. Say ye will make me the happiest of men and marry me."

Clara looked at him, the disreputable rogue, sooty and scorched, his clothes all torn, his eye swelling shut, and bleeding in more places than she could count. He looked dreadful and wonderful, and so very, very dear.

"Yes, Hamilton, I'll marry you," she said, to which whoops of laughter were swiftly accompanied by the suggestion they fall back. The men of the town had come out to help the effort to put out the fire, and one hurried up to Hamilton belatedly carrying the requested ladder.

"A wee bit late, Jock, but I appreciate the thought," he said dryly. "Just save what ye can, aye? It looks like I may have a bit more work to do."

"Ye will be doing nae work with yer hands in that state," Mrs Macready said fiercely. "Ye will come with me this minute so I can get ye patched up. You too, Jimmy. Lord, but I've had frights enough this night to send me to my grave. Ye are turning me grey, laddie, and I'm nae letting ye out of my sight again, d'ye hear me?"

"I do," Jimmy said with a sigh, though Clara thought he did not look entirely displeased about the situation.

Her father was harder to read. He was standing stock still, regarding her as though he had never seen her before.

"Come along, Clara," Mrs Macready said, her voice firm but softer now. "You must come too. Ye can speak to yer da later, when he's calmed down and returned to his senses."

Clara glanced back at him, seeing Mrs Cameron take his arm. The woman smiled at Clara, a warm, approving smile that seemed to tell her the reverend was in good hands. Too overwhelmed by the events of the evening to consider why she should believe such a thing, Clara allowed Mrs Macready to hustle them all into the vicarage kitchens.

Clara looked around the room in what felt like a daze. Everything was just as she'd left it scant hours earlier. The saucepan was still beside the range, keeping warm, waiting for her and Jimmy to have their supper. The feeling grew as Mrs

Macready swung the kettle over the range and stirred up the fire with brisk, practised movements. She settled Jimmy in a chair beside the warmth and wrapped a blanket about him, giving him a kiss on the cheek which, for once, he did not scrub away with his hand. Clara smiled, but somehow nothing seemed quite real. Nothing except Hamilton, who was large and alive and filled the room with his presence as he demanded if Mrs Macready had a drop of whisky, for he rather felt he'd earned it.

Suddenly Clara laughed. That he had the temerity to ask for whisky under her father's roof struck her as remarkably funny, and a moment later she was clutching at her sides and fighting for breath.

"It's the shock," Mrs Macready told Hamilton as he watched Clara in bemusement.

"It takes some folk oddly, and ye are a wicked fellow asking for drink in the vicarage," she scolded him, and then began rummaging in the bag she carried about everywhere with her. "Still, as ye saved my wee Jimmy and Clara, I shall let ye borrow Mr Macready's flask. I always keep it with me since he passed, purely for medicinal purposes," she added sternly, wagging a finger at him.

"Aye, I believe ye," Hamilton said, fighting to keep his expression placid as Clara sniggered beside him. "Haud yer wheesht or she'll take it away again," he muttered, shaking his head at her.

Finally, Clara subsided, and she realised it must indeed have been the shock, for she didn't think it funny now. She felt exhausted and shivery and jittery with nerves. Mrs Macready had poured the hot water onto the tea leaves, and the rest into a basin. Clara got up, intending to help Mrs Macready bathe Hamilton's hands, but the lady only pushed her back into the chair and told her to prepare the tea if she wanted to make herself useful. Clara tried but found her own hands were shaking too much as she tried to arrange the cups and saucers.

"Clara."

She turned to find Hamilton's gaze upon her, warm and full of certainty.

"It'll be all right," he told her, his voice steady, his presence everything she wanted it to be, solid and reassuring, a rock to cling to when her world turned upside down.

"Will it?".

"Aye, lassie. I'll make it so, if I must rearrange the world to suit ye."

"He would, too," Mrs Macready said with a snort before she unwrapped the filthy strips of petticoat and dipped Hamilton's hand in the water, then they all leapt from their seats as Hamilton let out a bellow of pain.

"Holy God! Are ye trying to kill me, woman?" he demanded, glaring at her.

"Ach, don't be such a wee bairn. 'Tis only a bit of iodine in the water," she told him calmly.

Hamilton gritted his teeth and endured, but did not object when Clara asked if she might bind his hands up again. Mrs Macready eyed Hamilton's set jaw and nodded, handing her the clean bandages.

"Good and tight, mind," she told her.

Clara bound them carefully, feeling Hamilton's gaze upon her as she worked. She glanced up once the first hand was done, her breath catching at the look in his eyes.

"Do ye mean to keep yer word and marry me?" he asked her.

Clara smiled and nodded, feeling suddenly shy. "Yes."

He made a sound of satisfaction and sat back to allow her to bind his other hand. "Good, for I winnae let ye go now, Clara. I think Mrs Macready had a point with wee Jimmy, and I dinnae mean to let yer out of my sight."

"Is that right?"

Even Hamilton started a little as her father's voice filled the room.

Clara turned with a gasp, her heart picking up as she wondered if they were in for an unpleasant scene. He turned to Hamilton first, narrowing his eyes.

"You, sir, are a liar. You told everyone that Clara was not in the building."

"She wasn't as far as I knew," Hamilton said brazenly as Clara kept her eyes downcast. "She went in after Jimmy, who'd come looking for me. Isn't that right, Jimmy?"

"Aye, that's right," Jimmy piped up, bless the boy, and sounding more like a little Scotsman with every day that passed. "I heard that cove, Malcolm Stewart, egging you on to go to Hamilton's place, so I figured I'd cry beef, so he didn't get caught out. I was too late for that, though, what with the time it took me sending you that note, Mrs M," he added sadly.

"You did very well, laddie," Mrs Macready said firmly, ruffling his hair.

Clara watched as her father looked at Jimmy with sudden interest. "I know you," he said slowly, suspicion glinting in his eyes.

Jimmy paled, and Mrs Macready hurried to stand in front of the boy, putting herself between him and the reverend. "Ye may at that, sir, but Jimmy is my responsibility now, and none of yers. He's coming to live with me, so long as he's a good boy and minds his manners," she added with an attempt at sternness that somehow got lost as she gazed fondly down at the lad.

"You mean it, Mrs M?" Jimmy said, wide-eyed with shock. "You really want me to?"

“Aye. I do,” Mrs Macready said fiercely, glaring at Reverend Halliday like he might deny it on her behalf. “You are a sweet laddie, Jimmy, and ye deserve a good home, and if ye would like to make yers with me, I’d be glad to have yer company. ’Tis silly me rattling about alone in that house with my bairns grown and Mr Macready gone ten years and more.”

Clara stared at her father, who seemed to be held up purely by the grip Mrs Cameron had on his arm. “I think I’d like to sit down, Flora,” he said in a somewhat plaintive tone.

“Aye, Robert, and so ye shall,” Mrs Cameron said briskly, pulling out a chair and plumping up a cushion before guiding the reverend into it.

He sat heavily and ran an unsteady hand over his forehead before gazing at Jimmy once more.

“You,” he said with reproach in his voice. “Are the boy from London, the one who came to Thorney to escape a beating from some dreadful gang. The one *you* told me you had sent back to where he had come from, as I instructed you to do,” he added, turning his accusing gaze upon Clara.

“Ye did what?” Mrs Cameron said, pausing in the act of pouring him a cup of tea.

The reverend looked at Mrs Cameron and saw, as they all did, the steely glint in her eyes. “Ye widnae do such an unchristian thing as turn yer back on a child in peril, would ye Robert?” she asked, a tone to her voice that suggested there was only one answer to this question.

“Er… well, I may have been somewhat hasty, I suppose, but I’m so glad that you have found a home with Mrs Macready, er, Jimmy, is it?” the reverend said weakly, giving Mrs Cameron a placating smile before turning to Jimmy again. “That’s good, very good. A wonderful Christian woman is Mrs Macready, so you make sure you mind her and repay her for her generosity.”

“There’ll be nae speak of Christian charity and repaying anything,” Mrs Macready said, startling them all with the force of her response. “He’ll come as my laddie, to be loved like any of my other bairns. I’ll nae have him feel he owes me for every meal or stitch of clothing on his back.”

“Oh, Mrs M!” Jimmy said in a choked voice, starting up from the chair and throwing himself at the lady with such force she staggered. He sobbed against her ample bosom and Mrs Macready blinked hard, hugging him tightly in return.

“There’s nae need for waterworks,” she said, not unkindly as she was sniffing vigorously herself. “I’m glad to have ye, dinnae be forgetting that. It gets a mite lonely with all my bairns grown and gone away.”

“It sounds like the perfect arrangement,” Clara said, finding a lump in her throat at the happiness she could see in both parties’ expressions.

“It is,” Mrs Macready said firmly. “But what of that nasty piece of work who caused all the trouble?”

“He’s being carried to his brother’s house,” Mrs Cameron said, looking pleased to divulge information they did not have. “The ladies have gone with him to explain what happened. I’ve nae doubt Angus will call upon ye in the morning to hear it from yerself, Mr Anderson,” she added.

Hamilton grimaced, clearly not looking forward to that meeting.

“There is rather a more pressing point to discuss, Clara,” her father said, his expression hard. “What is this about you marrying Mr Anderson? As far as I knew, you did not even like the fellow, let alone know him with any degree of intimacy. What has been happening behind my back? I told you she ought not to have gone to that dinner at Angus Stewart’s house, Flora. I told you it—”

“You told me a good many things, and if ye are thinking of telling me Miss Halliday should nae marry a fine fellow like our

Mr Anderson, I will be thinking ye have taken leave of yer senses," Mrs Cameron said frankly. She crossed her arms, and Clara saw with interest that as sweet and kind as she might appear, Mrs Cameron was not a woman to be bullied or put upon.

"This man is the one causing all the trouble, Flora!" the reverend objected.

"He is nae," Mrs Cameron said with a sigh. "Ye cannae make a man into the devil just to suit yerself, Robert. He's a good man, nae perfect, none of us is, aye. Are ye so unblemished in the eyes of the Lord?"

Rather fascinated, Clara watched her father consider this. "No," he admitted. "I have come to see that I have made a good many mistakes, and I've been hard on you, Clara. But that only shows that I ought to step in if my daughter is at risk of making a bad marriage."

"A bad marriage?" Flora repeated, eyes wide with incredulity. "Are ye thinking of finding her a duke? He's the son of an earl, he's wealthy and well thought of, and with your influence, perhaps ye could do great things together, aye?"

Clara held her breath as her father considered this.

"I'll think on it," he said, his tone grudging.

"Ye will think fast," Mrs Cameron said tartly. "For I tell ye now, Robert, a house can only have one mistress, so I'll nae be wedding ye if she is still in residence, for that will be misery for all concerned."

"Flora, I really don't think we ought to discuss this—"

"In front of yer daughter? When she is the one most concerned by the decision? Nae, Robert, we'll have this out now or not at all. Ye asked me to wed ye, and I said yes, but I'll nae take over a household where yer daughter is mistress and have her resent me when all she wants is to have a home of her own, and rightly so."

Clara watched, stunned, and not a little impressed by the ease with which Mrs Cameron stood up to her father, who blustered and muttered for a bit longer.

Glowering, he folded his arms. "I want more than I can say, to marry you, Flora, but I cannot in all conscience approve a match between my daughter and a man who not only owns a distillery but intends to run a tavern under my very nose!"

"Aye, well, about the tavern," Hamilton said, meeting the man's eyes. "I've been thinking about doing something else with it, seeing as how it will need starting over again anyhow, presuming there's anything left of it," he added grimly.

"Something else?" the reverend said suspiciously, clearly imagining the worst.

"Aye. I was thinking of gifting it to the church, so ye could use it for… I don't know. For charitable things," he said, rubbing the back of his neck with his hand and then wincing as he remembered they were bandaged and sore. "Like a place for the women to go when the men are violent with drink, and a place where ye can talk to those men in private. Somewhere that feels more homely than the church or an office, aye? I dinnae ken, I'm sure the ladies will have better ideas, but I'll do the work and set it up how ye think best, if ye reckon ye can do some good in the town with it."

For once in his life, Reverend Halliday was speechless, gazing at Hamilton with an open mouth. Mrs Cameron filled in the blanks.

"Well, I think that is a splendid idea, and most generous one, is it nae, Robert? I dinnae see how ye can disapprove of a man so willing to put his hand in his pocket and do good in Wick, and as Mr Anderson employs a huge number of men, between his shipping and the distillery, he's got a lot of influence in the town too. If such a man were to set a good example, I cannae see but it would do a deal of good," she added guilelessly.

Hamilton made a sound of displeasure, low enough that only Clara could hear it, but he nodded. "Aye, right enough, Mrs

Cameron. The truth is Reverend, yer words and the work ye have done in the town have made me think. Ye were right to call me a hypocrite. There is a problem in Wick that needs attention, mind I dinnae hold with telling a man what he can or cannae do, but something needs to change. I'd be happy to help with any sensible scheme. My family has been investing in the town for some years now, but perhaps we ought to do more. I'll speak to my da. Between us all, I reckon we can make a difference."

The reverend stared at him, apparently stunned into silence so Hamilton carried on.

"Though I warn ye, I'm nae intending to live in Wick all year once we are married. If ye dinnae mind it too much, Clara, that is? I meant to discuss it with ye, of course, for I ken ye like it here."

"Where would we go?" she asked, not caring much where they lived, so long as he was there, but thinking it would be wise to know all the same.

"My elder brother's estate at Wildsyde is a vast place and the middle one, Muir, has a sheep farm there too. I'd like to be close to the family. I've bought land from Lyall to build a house. I always figured I'd move back… when I had a family of my own," he added with a smile. "It's countryside, a bit wild and remote, but the family are all there. I think ye would like it," he added, though she heard a thread of anxiety behind the words and knew it was important to him.

"I'm sure I will love it. What a wonderful place to raise a family."

"Aye, it is that," Hamilton said, grinning with relief. "Me and my brothers and my sister had a grand time as bairns. Plenty of scope for adventures, ye ken."

Clara laughed and nodded.

"Could we visit? Me and Mrs M?" Jimmy piped up, clearly liking the sound of that.

"Aye, of course, and with pleasure," Hamilton said. "That is, if I have yer blessing, Reverend Halliday, to marry Clara?"

Reverend Halliday scowled and looked around the room, every face he met fiercely determined that Hamilton should marry Clara, most especially Mrs Cameron's. Having the good sense to know when he was defeated, the reverend rearranged his expression into something rather more beatific.

"Welcome to the family, Mr Anderson."

Chapter 17

Lyall,

It is horrifying to have to admit this in writing, but I took your advice.

I'm marrying the girl.

—Excerpt of a letter from The Hon'ble Mr Hamilton Anderson to his elder brother, The Right Hon'ble Lyall Anderson, Viscount Buchanan.

25th June 1850, Wick, Caithness, Scotland.

The next morning, Hamilton arrived at the vicarage front door, smartly dressed as curtains twitched the length and breadth of Wick. News of his having won not only Miss Halliday's hand, but the Reverend Halliday's approval, spread with such speed that, by midmorning, there was no one who did not know of it.

Bemused but in too good a humour to complain, Hamilton accepted the words of thanks as he walked from his offices close to the harbour and endured the good-natured ribbing from the fishermen who were full of helpful, if vulgar, advice for his wedding night.

To his surprise, Jimmy opened the door of the vicarage, and Hamilton grinned at him.

"Ye are still here, then. I thought ye would stay with Mrs Macready now?"

“I did,” he said proudly, adding in a confidential tone. “I slept in a proper bed last night, with sheets and blankets and everything. It was her son’s room, and she give it to me.”

“Ye deserve it,” Hamilton said, patting the lad’s skinny shoulder. “But as soon as we have a new schoolmaster, I expect to see ye there, ye hear me. Ye are a bright laddie, and ye must make the most of yer skills.”

“Aye, I know it. Mrs Macready said so too,” he said gloomily.

“But if ye are clever at school, I’ll be able to find a place for ye. Perhaps if ye do very well, ye could work with Angus one day, running things for me.”

“Like Angus Stewart? Him with that nice house and the pretty wife?” Jimmy said with interest.

“Aye, the same, and ye could have a nice house and a pretty wife too one day, if ye want it and dinnae mind working for it. It’s a way off, Jimmy, but it does ye nae harm to have ambition, aye?”

“Is that why you have so much money, ’cause you’re ambitious?”

Hamilton snorted. “Aye, I guess so, and I dinnae like being idle. I’m the sort that gets into mischief if I have nae something to occupy me.”

“So am I,” Jimmy admitted ruefully.

Hamilton nodded, understanding. “Well, at least ye ken it. Now, take me to Clara, is she ready?”

“She is,” Jimmy said, leading him through to the front parlour.

To his alarm, Hamilton found not only his betrothed, but her father and Mrs Cameron too, all of them dressed for an outing. Clara’s face was the picture of dismay as he met her eyes. “Papa and Mrs Cameron are going to accompany us on our walk,” she said, an apology in her voice. “For propriety’s sake.”

Hamilton swallowed a curse and merely nodded. "Aye, well, we'd best do things right. If ye are ready, then, Clara?"

She nodded, and the party headed to the front door. Mrs Cameron laid a hand on his arm as she passed, whispering, "Sorry, laddie, I tried my best. Ye had best marry her as soon as ye can."

"It had not escaped my attention," Hamilton said dryly. "I thank ye for trying, though."

Mrs Cameron winked at him as she hurried out the door and took the reverend's arm.

"I'm sorry," Clara whispered as they fell into step, with Reverend Halliday leading the way.

Hamilton patted her hand. "'Tis nae bother, *mo leannan.* We'd nae have got a moment of privacy in any case, not with the whole town flapping its gums about us. But we must do our best to set a date, aye? I dinnae want this situation to carry on long. I'm nae a fan of long engagements, ye ken."

"Tomorrow suits me," Clara said impishly, smiling up at him. Hamilton gazed down at her, realising he must have the same daft expression on his face that Muir got when he gazed at Delia. He didn't care, either. He wanted to drink in the sight of her beautiful face for hours, just to be in her company, even if the blasted reverend had to come too. His heart felt oddly light, and yet full to bursting. It was a strange sensation, not unpleasant, but it would take some getting used to. He smiled, remembering not so very long ago when he'd danced at his brother's wedding and convinced himself he wasn't green with envy. He'd told himself he was in no hurry, that he was happy enough, but he knew now he was ready for this, for Clara, for a life together that promised to be everything he could have dreamed of.

Still, for Clara, this would be another upheaval, and not long after having moved to Scotland. "Do ye mean it? It's not going too fast for ye? It will be a big change, to leave yer father's house."

Clara slanted him a wry look that made him laugh. "Aye, well, a fellow likes to be sure."

She leaned into him and Hamilton realised they had both slowed their steps, allowing her father to get farther ahead of them. "I came here because my father was sent here. I had no choice, no say, but I was glad. I wanted to come to where there were people, to find a husband. Do you think that is very bold of me?"

He snorted at that. "I think it very sensible. Living with the Reverend Halliday is nae for the faint hearted, I reckon."

"Hush, he'll hear you," Clara scolded, though when they looked ahead, the Reverend and Mrs Cameron had their heads together and were oblivious to anything except each other. "I think they'll do very well together," Clara said, smiling at the sight. "Papa needs someone to stand up to him, to keep his feet on the ground and speak sense."

"Aye, Flora Cameron is a sensible woman," Hamilton said with a twinkle in his eye.

"You think she set her cap for him," Clara asked with interest.

"I dinnae ken nor care. I dinnae blame her, either. She's worked hard and raised five bairns after her lout of a husband drank himself to death. She deserves some ease, and she can handle yer da, and that's all to the good."

"You are a wise man, Hamilton Anderson," she said, squeezing his arm.

"I am," he said, affecting a grave expression. "But it speaks well of ye that ye recognise the fact."

Clara gave him a playful smack, shaking her head sadly. "Odiously conceited, dreadful man," she said with a sigh.

"Maybe, but I am yer own dreadful man, conceited or otherwise."

"Are you?" Clara asked softly, and Hamilton looked down at her, seeing the question in her eyes. "There won't be another Mrs Scott for me to worry about, or to turn a blind eye to, then? For I've never been very good at pretending things aren't exactly how they are."

Hamilton took her hands in his bandaged ones, touching them gently as he stared into her eyes so she could see the sincerity in his. "Never, lassie. If I speak my vows, I'll mean them until my dying breath. I have sown my wild oats and enjoyed doing it, but that's over. I mean to have the kind of marriage my parents have, that my brothers and my sister seem to have achieved too. All or nothing, Clara. I'll have yer heart for my own, and ye will have mine too, all of it. Can ye stand it?" he asked, his lips quirking, yet meaning the question all the same. He knew what he was, and he knew he could be overpowering and over exuberant, too full of energy and restless spirit.

"I cannot wait, Hamilton, and you must know you have my heart. You have had it for longer than I think I knew myself."

"Aye, well, I'm irresistible," he said with a shrug, and then ducked away, laughing as she tried to clip him around the ear.

"That's right, lassie, ye start how ye mean to go on," called a woman from her upstairs window, watching them as they passed in the street. "I've a nice heavy skillet I can lend ye if ye like. He's got a heid like his da's that one, stubborn as a mule and hard as iron."

"Aileen Carson, I'll thank ye to keep yer suggestions to yerself," Hamilton called back, taking Clara's hand in his. "Come away, lassie, before she gives ye any ideas."

Tugging her down the street, Clara ran after him, laughing helplessly as Mrs Carson called further suggestions until they were out of sight.

24th July 1850, Rochford House, Just outside Wick, Caithness, Scotland.

Despite Hamilton's initial wish to marry Clara before June was out, it was a full month later before the big day. It was his own choice too, despite his impatience to set a date, for he told her he would not be enjoying his wedding night with his hands bandaged, and the burns were severe enough to need time to heal properly.

The day dawned with a fine drizzle settling over Wick and the surrounding countryside, slicking the streets and giving the summer landscape a fresh dewy look that made all the myriad shades of green sparkle. The air was warm though and Hamilton sensed that the sun would shine by mid-morning.

His sister Georgie's husband, the Duke of Rochford, nodded a greeting from his place at the head of the breakfast table. Georgie had kindly given Hamilton and Clara Rochford House to use until they found a house of their own, as his own rooms in Wick were bachelor accommodations and not suitable for a bride. The grand Palladian house was barely two miles from the centre of Wick, and the duke and duchess only used it when visiting family, Rochford's seat being Mulcaster Castle in Cumbria. Mulcaster was a vast, intimidating cavern of a place that Georgie had somehow managed to turn into a home. The place suited Rochford, who was also vast and intimidating. Even by Anderson standards, he was a big man, and badly scarred, giving him a forbidding aspect that made him appear far fiercer than he was. His heir, eight-year-old Jamie, the Marquess of Draven, sat at his elbow. He was a sturdy lad with a shock of dark hair and the whisky coloured eyes of his mother. The boy was working steadily on a plate of eggs and bacon but stopped long enough to grin as he saw Hamilton.

"Good morning, Jamie lad, Rochford," Hamilton said, helping himself to a slice of sirloin steak and fried potatoes and settling down at the table.

He tucked into the steak as Rochford grunted—his usual greeting in the morning—and lifted a coffee cup, regarding

Hamilton over the rim. "A vicar's daughter," he said, his deep voice rumbling with amusement. "The poor wee girl."

Hamilton paused, his knife and fork suspended in mid-air and scowled at him. "What's that supposed to mean?"

"She could have done better," Rochford lamented, shaking his head.

Hamilton rolled his eyes and applied himself to his breakfast, too used to such baiting from his brothers to rise to it.

"Your parents arrived half an hour ago, by the way. They said Lyall and the others ought not be far behind, but little Gordy had hidden his best shoes again and they were turning the place upside down looking for them when they left. Your mother went straight to the kitchens on arrival, of course, to ensure everything is prepared for the wedding breakfast."

Hamilton snorted. "Of course she did. She won't believe it's all in hand unless she sees it with her own eyes. Probably not until we are all sat down and listening to the toasts." He gazed down at the steak he'd been cutting into, and his stomach lurched as it hit him. He was getting married. *Today*.

He swallowed, the bite of steak feeling as if it had stuck in his throat. Married. Today. Something distinctly like panic surged through him.

Hamilton was distantly aware of movement, the scrape of a chair, and looked up a moment later as Rochford set a glass of whisky in front of him. "Took enough time for it to sink in, but I figured it would eventually," he said with a twisted grin. "Drink that, it will settle your guts."

"What if I mess it up?" Hamilton said, reaching for the glass, aware of a panicky sensation in his belly like snakes writhing.

"Oh, you will," Rochford said, sitting himself down again.

"Well, yer a great comfort," Hamilton said impatiently, downing the generous tot of whisky and glaring at him.

Rochford smirked but shook his head, relenting. "Providing you are faithful, and you learn to apologise at regular intervals, you'll do fine," he said gruffly. "I hear she's a sensible lass, so she can't be blind to the trouble she's getting into."

Hamilton laughed at that. "True," he said, feeling suddenly much better.

♡♧◇♤

"Well, lassie, ye are the bonniest bride there ever was," Mrs Macready said with satisfaction.

"That she is," the new Mrs Halliday remarked. Her father and Flora—as she had insisted Clara address her—had married a week earlier. A quiet little ceremony with only Flora's youngest daughter and Clara in attendance, they had celebrated with a fine dinner prepared by Mrs Macready, and the happy couple were taking a trip to visit Flora's eldest daughter in Somerset after Clara's wedding. Clara had been pleasantly surprised to discover Mrs Macready and Flora were making significant efforts to get along, for she had feared there might be ructions in the kitchen. Instead, the household was a well-run and industrious one with Flora at the helm and, if the Reverend Halliday was a little in awe of his new bride, Clara thought that was all to the good. She was aware, however, that the situation between the women was one that would not continue smoothly for long. Mrs Macready and Flora both had strong opinions on the way things ought to be done, and whilst they were falling over each other to be accommodating at the moment, that would wear on both their nerves in time. Deciding she would discuss the problem with Hamilton, for the moment, Clara put it out of her mind, for she had far more exciting things to consider.

Turning this way and that before the looking glass, Clara could hardly believe the picture reflected back at her. Satin ribbon and lace lavishly adorned the gown of ivory silk and, though Clara did not know how much it had cost, she knew enough to estimate it must have been a small fortune. The fabulous dressmaker had come to her, a concession from a woman who dressed the great and the good, and a gift from Georgie, who'd used her influence to make it happen.

Whilst Clara had been aware that Hamilton was a successful man, she had never considered quite how successful, or thought much of his family connections, past feeling somewhat overawed that his father was an earl. Having discovered he was not only fabulously wealthy, but also that his sister was the Duchess of Rochford, had put her into a pelter as she fretted she was marrying too far above her station. That his family might despise her, or Hamilton might come to regret marrying her, had given her awful sleepless nights until her father had stepped in. Speaking to her in the gentlest tones she could ever remember him using, he reminded her that her grandfather might be a vile bully, but he was also Baron Marsham, an ancient and revered title, and she had nothing to blush for.

"This came for you this morning," Mrs Macready said, bringing her back to the present.

She and Flora stood side-by-side as they presented Clara with a large, red leather box.

Clara took it, noting the excited glint in the two women's eyes. She had already received lovely gifts from both Mrs Scott and Miss Fleming, who had sent a very pretty note of congratulations to her and a promise to call in when she was back home again. Clara suspected the fact Miss Fleming had just become engaged to a wealthy young man herself had softened the blow, but she wished the young lady all the luck in the world and hoped she was as happy as Clara herself.

"It's from Hamilton?" Clara guessed, her heart leaping at the weight of the leather box she held.

"Nae, Father Christmas!" Flora exclaimed impatiently. "Of course it is from Hamilton, open it up! Open it up!" she protested, flapping her hands at Clara.

Clara did as she was told, almost dropping the box in alarm as the contents flashed and sparkled in the sunlight streaming through the window.

"Saints be praised," Mrs Macready whispered, putting her hand to her heart. "I never saw anything so lovely in all my days."

Clara stared at the glorious parure of diamonds. A necklace, ear bobs, bracelets, a brooch and a tiara were laid out on a bed of cream silk. "Oh, my," she said, feeling rather breathless.

"There's a note too," Flora said, shoving it at Clara, who opened it with trembling fingers.

> *To my beautiful bride,*
>
> *I know you will shine brighter than any diamond, but I wanted to give you something as a token of thanks for making me the happiest of men. I will see you soon, mo leannan.*
> *Hamilton.*

It was only when she heard their wistful sighs that Clara realised the ladies were reading over her shoulder and tucked the note away with a blush.

"Ye will have a fine wedding night, lassie," Flora teased, winking at her. "He's a braw, handsome laddie, so he is."

"Ye do ken what happens on yer wedding night, Clara?" Mrs Macready asked with a frown.

Clara blushed a deeper shade and the two ladies exchanged glances.

"Sit yerself down, lassie," Flora said, steering her to a chair. "Freya, fetch her a tot of whisky. I reckon she may need it."

"Well!" Clara's father stared at her, leaping from his chair in the parlour as she stood before him. "Well, I never did."

For once in his life, the reverend seemed quite without words, which was rather touching.

"Isn't she the prettiest thing ye ever saw, Robert?" Flora said, moving to take his arm. Papa patted his wife's hand absently and walked closer to Clara. To her surprise, his eyes glittered with emotion.

"How you remind me of your mother today. You have her eyes, you know, grey and serious, yet with that twinkle that shows your spirit."

"Thank you, Papa," Clara said, feeling suddenly quite emotional herself.

He took her hands and squeezed her fingers gently.

"The Anderson family are lucky to have you, Clara, and don't you go thinking otherwise. What's more, I… I shall miss you, my dear. You have been a better daughter to me than I deserve, and I am proud of you."

"Oh, P-Papa," Clara said, suddenly choked as she did something she had not done since she was a small girl and hugged him tightly.

He seemed quite as taken aback by this as she did, but he hugged her in return and kissed her cheek.

"Well, if we are all ready, we had best get ourselves to the church or young Mr Anderson will be fretting himself to death," Flora said, smiling fondly at them both.

"Goodness, and with a duke and duchess, and an earl and a countess in the congregation!" her father said, and she realised that despite his words, he was feeling a little overawed himself.

They walked outside where a carriage waited to drive them the short distance to the church and discovered all their neighbours standing outside, cheering Clara and wishing her joy as her father helped her up. Feeling every bit like the fairy princess she had once imagined herself to be as a child, Clara waved back, and her heart skipped with anticipation as the carriage drove away.

Chapter 18

Dear Larkin,

I'm not sure you'll get this in time, but I'm in a bit of a fix. Actually, Vi and I are in a good deal of trouble…

—Excerpt of a letter from Mr Leo Hunt (Son of Alice and Nathanial Hunt) to The Hon'ble Larkin Weston (Son of The Right Hon'ble Solomon 'Solo' and Jemima Weston, Baron and Baroness Rothborn).

24th July 1850, Wick, Caithness, Scotland.

For the rest of his days, Hamilton would remember the first sight of his bride as she walked towards him. Whilst he would do nothing so daft as to swoon on his wedding day, he had to admit that for a moment there his knees had felt decidedly odd. He had known from the start that his Clara was a beauty, despite the modest and not always entirely flattering gowns she wore and the simple knot in which she arranged her hair. Today, however, in a dress so fine it was worth every penny of the small fortune it had cost him, sparkling with the diamonds he had gifted her, and with her hair in a becoming, if complex, style that flattered her lovely face, she was simply breathtaking.

"Ye are a lucky devil, and there's nae doubt about it," Lyall murmured to him as Clara made her way down the aisle.

"If I am dreaming, dinnae wake me," he replied, shaking his head. "How the devil did I manage it?"

"Never mind that, just don't muck it up," Lyall said with a grin.

The rest of the service was a blur in his mind, his emotions and thoughts a tangle of joy and anticipation that made concentration impossible. He supposed he'd spoken his vows and given the correct responses for Lyall hadn't stepped on his foot or called him a numpty, but somehow they were back at Rochford House, sitting at the wedding breakfast, surrounded by friends and family, and he could not quite recall how it had happened.

The lavish breakfast had been extravagant and delicious, and now the guests were relaxed and the champagne—and Hamilton's best whisky—was flowing as the noise in the room rose by the minute.

Hamilton turned to his bride, who was pink with pleasure and laughing at something his father had said to her. He reached for her hand under the table, and she turned to him, her eyes sparkling.

"Have I told ye how bonnie ye look?" he asked, feeling strangely breathless, for looking upon her seemed to knock the air from his lungs each time.

"You have," she said with a laugh. "So many times I have lost count, and I shall become impossibly conceited if you keep on."

"Like me, eh?" he said with a grin.

"Worse than you!" she exclaimed, making him laugh.

He leaned closer, lowering his voice as he murmured close to her ear. "This is the best day of my life, Clara, and I cannae wait for it to be over so I can be alone with ye."

She darted him a shy smile, her cheeks pinker than ever, but she did not seem the least bit anxious or uncertain, which was reassuring.

"We can't leave yet," she said, before adding a question that lifted his heart higher still. "Can we?"

Hamilton grinned. "Aye, we can."

"Are ye needing a hasty exit?"

Hamilton looked past Clara to see his father regarding him with amusement. "Aye, can ye help?" he asked, knowing his father would understand and create a diversion if he could.

"Never say I dinnae do anything for ye," the earl said, shoving back his chair and getting to his feet. He'd made good inroads into the excellent bottle of whisky Hamilton had given him and was in high spirits, which boded ill for the guests. "Away with ye then," he added, before walking to the centre of the room.

"Quick," Hamilton said, hustling Clara towards the nearest door.

"What? Why?" she asked in confusion.

Hamilton grinned at her as he ushered her out of the room. "We've got to save ourselves, love. Da's about to sing."

Clara laughed merrily, the sound wrapping itself about Hamilton's heart as he took her hand and towed her up the stairs. Rochford House was a large place, and their bedroom was on the opposite side of the festivities, so the sound of merriment dimmed and finally faded away as Hamilton led her along the endless corridors.

"What a beautiful house," she said, staring around her with wide eyes as they walked.

"I will build ye one just as fine. Better, even," Hamilton promised. "I've already an architect working on the plans, but ye must look them over and see if everything is how ye would like it. I want it to be perfect for ye."

"You are spoiling me," she protested, gazing at him in wonder. "I had no expectation of such… such…" She threw up her hands, shaking her head, apparently lost for words and Hamilton stopped to pull her into his arms.

"I will spoil ye, I want to do so. I want ye to have the best of everything, to have the happiest, most perfect life I can give ye."

She stared up at him, reaching up to cup his cheek with her hand. "You only need to love me to do that, Hamilton," she whispered, the words sinking into his heart and making it ache with happiness.

"Aye, well, I intend to do that too," he said gruffly, desire and anticipation thrumming beneath his skin as the delicate scent of roses teased his senses. "Come, lassie, hurry. If ye keep looking at me that way, we may not make it to the bedroom."

"Hamilton!" she exclaimed, so scandalised that he roared with laughter. "You are dreadful," she scolded him, but he noticed she was laughing too, though she tried to hide it.

Finally, they arrived at the lovely guest suite his sister had prepared for them, and Hamilton led her in, watching her face with pleasure as it lit up.

"Oh, what a beautiful room," she breathed as she walked through an elegant sitting room to the bedroom, taking in the lovely pale green floral wall hangings, gold framed pictures and luxurious velvet curtains and upholstery. Though it was the middle of July, it was still Scotland, and the suite of rooms was large, so fires burned in the hearths, warming the temperature to one that would be pleasant to enjoy naked.

Georgie had filled their bedroom with roses, as Hamilton had requested, and the sweet scent drifted around them, lush and intoxicating. Clara went to one of the lavish displays and breathed in, closing her eyes and sighing.

"I'm dreaming," she said happily.

"I thought so too, when I saw ye coming up the aisle towards me," Hamilton admitted. "For a moment I was honestly terrified I might wake up."

She turned to look at him. "Truly? You're really happy?"

Hamilton went to her and took her in his arms. "How could ye think otherwise?" he asked, touching her cheek with reverent fingers. "I have wanted ye since the first moment I saw ye, when ye woke me in the schoolroom."

She smiled at him, clearly pleased by the admission. "Why were you there, when you and Malcolm have clearly always been at odds?"

He shrugged. "Malcolm was too drunk to work but I couldnae leave the boys without someone to school them. I'm nae the greatest teacher in the world, but better than none at all."

Clara stared at him and then reached up, framing his face with her hands. "You are a good man, Hamilton Anderson, the best man I have ever known, and I am so very, very proud to call you husband."

Oddly, Hamilton found his throat felt grow tight upon hearing such words and so he simply took hold of her hands and turned his face into each, kissing the palms.

"Then let me make ye my wife, Clara," he said, his voice gruff.

"Yes," she replied simply.

Hamilton swallowed, the anticipation that had been building all day threatening to drive him to distraction, but he only smiled at her and turned her around, striving to at least appear calm. He didn't want to frighten the poor girl by pouncing on her, though he was sorely tempted. His nerves were fraught. Over several months of celibacy—and the nightly dreams of his bride with which his imagination had furnished him—had his patience strung tight as a bowstring. He could only pray he would not act like an impetuous boy in his haste.

He moved to unfasten the tiny pearl buttons that marched down her spine and discovered his hands were trembling. With a soft laugh, he reached for the silver flask he'd hidden about his person, took a fortifying swallow, and tried again.

Clara looked over her shoulder, her expression perplexed.

"Is there a problem?"

"Nae, lassie, I'm only muttering curses against dressmakers who want a new husband to lose his mind."

"There are an awful lot of buttons," she admitted with a choked laugh. "It took forever to do them up."

"It winnae take forever to undo them," he promised her firmly.

It took a good deal longer than his fraying nerves liked, however, but finally the dress sagged to the ground. With more haste than skill, he undid petticoats and too many confusing layers until only her shift, corset, and drawers remained.

Clara peered over her shoulder at him again, smiling uncertainly.

"I think I'm winning," Hamilton said with a shaky laugh, never having felt so nervous about bedding a woman in his life.

Get a grip, ye numpty, he told himself. Yet unwrapping his virgin bride set him on edge, with a reverence he had not expected. He wanted everything to be perfect for her. He tugged at the corset strings, reminding himself he was a man of experience, and he'd had no complaints so far, but that didn't seem to help. Especially when the corset fell, and Clara turned to face him. The shift was still moulded to her shape where the corset had held it tight to her skin, and the fine cotton did little to hide the dark shape of her nipples, and the lush, high breasts they ornamented.

It took him a moment to recall his plans for their wedding night, but Hamilton gave himself a mental shake and took her hand.

"Come, lassie, I want to show ye something."

Clara followed him as he led her through the bedroom to a door that opened onto an opulent bathing room.

"Oh, my word!" Clara exclaimed.

He knew very well that they did not have such a thing at the vicarage. She would have made do with a jug, bowl and a flannel most of the time, a dip in the tub before the kitchen range being a good deal of work for her and Mrs Macready to prepare.

Hamilton went to the bath and put in the plug before turning the ornate gold taps and Clara gave a squeal of delight as water poured into the tub. Steam rose from the hot tap, and she gasped as she hurried forward and ran her fingers under it.

"Hot water!" she breathed, looking quite overwhelmed.

Hamilton laughed. "Aye, and an indoor water closet too," he said, which was quite indelicate, but her eyes grew round all the same. "And we'll have this in our home too, love. So ye can bathe in hot water whenever ye wish to."

"How decadent," she said, watching with interest as he poured scented oil into the bath and the room filled with the heady perfume of roses.

"My favourite," she said, smiling at him.

"Mine too, now," he replied with a swift grin. "I thought ye might enjoy a bath in hot water now, and that… well, I might help ye bathe, if ye have nae objection."

She turned pink at the question but shook her head. "You're my husband now, Hamilton, you must do as you wish."

He took her hand and squeezed it. "Nae lassie. That's not how it will be, and dinnae make out like ye would allow it to be, either.

Ye will tell me plain if ye dinnae like something, just as ye always have, and it disnae matter if that is in the kitchen, the garden or the bedroom. Ye will talk to me and tell me 'no' if something disnae suit ye."

"How stern you are," she teased him, but there was a warm light of approval in her eyes that did much to settle his nerves. She was no milk and water miss that he might accidentally crush. She was Clara, strong and fierce and ready to do battle when the need arose.

Hamilton laughed and reached for the little ribbon tie that gathered the neck of her chemise, giving it a tug. "Can I take this off ye now?"

To his surprise she shook her head, and he wondered if she was suddenly overcome with modesty. He ought to have known better as she undid the little ribbon tie at the neck herself and began slowly lifting the shift, revealing her lovely legs an inch at a time. Hamilton stood watching as his bride was revealed to him in torturously slow increments. She paused as the first hint of dark curls appeared and he made a sound of protest which made her grin broadly.

"Have mercy," he croaked, which made her laugh and tug the shift over her head, casting it aside with abandon. His mouth went dry as he looked her over, his gaze alighting on her splendid breasts.

"Heaven be praised," he whispered in awed tones.

"Hamilton," Clara protested, smothering a choked laugh. "I'm sure that's blasphemy."

"It is nae, for I am quite in earnest," he said, gazing at her in wonder. "I would fall to my knees in thanks to God for having given me such a gift, and that's the truth. In fact, I shall do just that. Let me see the rest of ye, love, before I run mad."

Hamilton knelt before her, tugging down her drawers with more haste than he intended. Forcing himself to go slowly, he took his time, running his hands up her stockings, aware of the fine material sliding beneath his palms. He paused to stroke the fine skin of her inner thigh and leaned in to press a kiss to the dark triangle of curls, hearing her swift intake of breath.

"Ye liked it when I touched ye here," he said, gazing up at her.

She nodded, biting her lip as he toyed with the soft thatch tickling his fingers back and forth. "I liked it too, I liked hearing yer pleasure, Clara. I hope to hear a good deal more of it too. Not only tonight, but for the rest of our days and nights. I intend to love ye often and well, lassie."

"I don't think I shall have anything to complain about then," she replied, making him smile as he heard the tremor of nerves in her voice.

"I promise ye shall nae, and if ye have, ye must tell me at once, aye?"

"Aye," she replied, and he chuckled, and then just gazed at her for a long, silent moment until he saw her shiver. Rousing himself from his trance, he helped her to step into the bath. Once she was settled, he bent and kissed the top of her head. "I'll be but a moment, I'll just get rid of some of this getup. I dinnae want to accidentally stab my bride with this blasted sword," he said gruffly, not wanting to leave her but thinking she might want a few minutes to herself.

"Have I told you how splendid and handsome you look in all your finery?" she said before he could leave. "I was so proud when I saw you waiting for me in the church. I thought I would burst."

Hamilton grinned at her. "Aye, ye did, but ye can tell me as much as ye like. I did think I looked well, though. The Anderson men have fine legs, ye ken," he said, twitching his kilt to give her a flash of his knees. "Dinnae pretend ye have nae noticed," he added, waggling his eyebrows.

"Dreadful, dreadful man," Clara said, laughing helplessly.

"I speak nothing but the truth," he said airily as he went into the bedroom, removing the sgian-dubh from his sock and unpinning the huge brooch on his chest. With as much speed as he could muster, he removed everything but shirt and kilt and hurried back into the bathing room, rolling his sleeves up as he went. He stopped just inside the door, committing the picture before him to memory.

Clara lay back in the bath with her eyes closed, her body and face flushed from the heat, tendrils of dark hair falling about her face and curling in the damp air. The oil scented water clung to her skin where her body broke the surface, glistening and making her appear like some beguiling water nymph, come to tempt him down into dark water. He'd go without a second thought, he decided, moving to kneel beside the bath.

Her eyes flickered open as she realised he was back, a slow smile breaking over her lovely face. "This is bliss," she said with a sigh.

"I'm glad," he said, amused by how quickly she had taken to such decadent treats. "But I'm going to make it even better," he added, aware there was a wicked note in his voice.

She regarded him sceptically but said nothing until he showed her the cake of soap in his hand.

"Oh," she said, swallowing visibly. "I… I can do that myself, you know."

Hamilton bit back a laugh at her obvious confusion. "Dinnae fash, lassie. It's my duty to care for ye now, as yer husband, ye ken. So, will ye let me do so?"

"If… If you want to, certainly," she said. "It's only Mrs Macready and Flora never mentioned that… that you would," she added hesitantly.

"Aye, well, I'm glad they gave ye the basics, I suppose, but I reckon they'll have left a good deal out that we shall explore together."

"Like washing me."

"Aye, exactly." Hamilton lathered the soap in his hands and then frowned as a thought occurred to him. "They didnae frighten ye?"

She smiled at that and shook her head. "No. They were very kind, though Flora made me blush terribly," she added with a laugh.

"Not as much as I shall," he promised her, leaning in to press his mouth to her lips.

She welcomed his kiss, far more practised now as she slid her tongue against his, welcoming him to explore further. With reluctance, Hamilton drew away, eager to touch what was so tantalisingly displayed before him.

Moving slightly behind her, he slid his soapy palms over her shoulders and arms, forcing himself to wait and revelling in the feel of her slick skin. By the time his hands coasted over her breasts, his cock was clamouring for attention, and the sound of her quick intake of breath did nothing to ease its plight. His own breathing was hardly steady either, and not for the first time he congratulated the Scot's race for wearing kilts, so his straining body did not have to suffer the confines of breaches. He sighed, caressing and squeezing the delicious swells, delighting in the feel of the hard buds of her nipples as they tightened at his touch.

"Oh, that's blissful," she said dreamily.

"Aye," Hamilton replied, in perfect accord with the statement. "Lord, but ye are perfect," he whispered, nuzzling into her ear and nipping at the lobe.

"Not in the l-least," she stammered. "I have knobbly knees," she said sadly.

Hamilton raised his head, staring at the knees before him, which looked as smooth and lovely as the rest of her. "Ye have rocks in yer heid if ye think that. I never saw such pretty knees, and I have an excellent pair of my own by which to judge," he added, for the sole purpose of making her laugh.

It worked, and she slanted a look up at him. "You really do," she admitted.

"Aye, my da says Ma married him purely on account of his knees."

She burst out laughing at that, which made his hands slip on her glistening skin and her soft parts wobble enticingly. "She did not!"

"Aye, it's true! I swear it. Ye ask her yerself," he told her, suddenly distracted by having found her belly button. He wriggled a finger inside and she squealed, doubling up.

"No! No!" she protested.

"Ah, ye are ticklish," he said with satisfaction. "That's interesting."

"I am and you are not to tickle me," she said, trying her best to sound fierce and failing utterly.

"Whatever ye say," he murmured in her ear, licking the outer shell and watching shivers race over her skin. He fell silent then as his hands coasted lower, sliding into the little thatch of curls. He cupped her with his hand, a possessive sense of delight stealing over him. "I remember that night, when I touched ye for the first time? I have thought of it every night since, much of the daytime too. Do ye think of it too?"

"I could hardly forget such a thing," she said, her voice muffled by his shirt sleeve, for she had turned her scarlet face against his arm. "And yes, of course I have thought of it."

"I remember every moment, every caress," he said, his voice growing hoarse. "I remember how ye came for me so prettily. Do it again, lassie. Show me how ye like my touch."

She did as he asked, rewarding him by spreading her legs wider and raising her hips, seeking his touch and sighing with pleasure as he happily gave her what she wanted. Hamilton groaned as he slid a finger inside her, feeling her soft flesh closing around him and imagining how it would feel to lose himself in her. The impatience to do so was a sore temptation, but he was not about to rob either of them of pleasure of anticipation, so he continued to touch her slowly, carefully, knowing they had all the time in the world. His free hand toyed with her breast, pinching her nipple gently and caressing the plump swell that fit his hand so perfectly. Clara responded to his touch without reserve, making his heart soar with the trust she put in him, with the simple pride of knowing such a woman loved him.

"That's the way," he urged, kissing her temple. "Give yerself over to pleasure, to me."

She did, taking him at his word, crying out and convulsing under his touch as the water around her rippled and sloshed against the sides and she clung to his arms, making his shirt sleeve sodden, not that he gave a damn. The sight of her taking her own pleasure was the most marvellous thing he'd ever seen in his entire life. Hamilton leaned over the bath, capturing her mouth, kissing her hard and deep, mad with joy and lust and need as the desire to pull her from the bath and take her there and then on the tiled floor was temptation beyond bearing.

He was breathing as hard as she by the time the waves of pleasure subsided, his body aching with need. "Come then, *mo leannan*. Out ye get, or I shall have to climb in with ye and it will be a bit of squeeze, I'm afraid."

He helped her up, holding her tightly, for she seemed unsteady on her feet, a fact that did nothing to hurt his masculine pride. Towelling her dry gently took a while, however, as he had to stop and kiss each beautiful part of her, especially his new favourite view of her.

Sitting on his knees behind Clara, he could do nothing but exclaim in awed tones. “Love, ye have the most perfect arse. Truly, it is close to a miracle, I reckon.”

Clara buried her face in the towel, laughing helplessly as Hamilton kissed first one cheek, then the other. “Splendid,” he said, sighing happily, stroking and squeezing the plump curves and rubbing his face against them like a cat. He reached one hand forward, stroking again the place between her thighs as her breath hitched and he touched her gently, aware she would be sensitive still. The desire to put his mouth there and lick was a fire in his blood, but he did not trust himself to do such things until she was safely in bed, and he was in no danger of taking his bride on the bathroom floor.

He took some time ensuring this part of her was quite thoroughly dried, before he could drag himself away, but he wrapped her in a heavy satin dressing gown—part of her wedding trousseau—and led her back to the bedroom.

The covers were turned down, and he watched with pleasure as she shed the robe and then turned sideways, lifting her arms to the pins in her hair.

“I think this is my favourite view,” he said, anticipation growing as her hair loosened, for he had been longing to see it undone. “I can see all the best bits at once.”

She slid him an amused glance and then his breath caught as her hair cascaded down her back, long enough to brush the curves of her splendid backside. Giving him a coquettish smile that did odd things to his heart, she slid into bed, shivering as she did so.

“I’ll be there to warm ye, lassie, in just a moment,” he promised her, heart thudding with expectancy of what was to come, undoing his kilt and casting it aside before dragging the shirt over his head. He moved towards the bed, with no thought in his mind but making love to his wife, and then paused, arrested by the look in her eyes.

Hamilton knew very well he was a handsome, well-made fellow, but never in his life had he felt so much pleasure in that fact as now. Clara's eyes glowed with delight, growing dark as her gaze travelled over him from head to foot, lingering on his arousal with obvious fascination. She stared with unashamed interest, a fact which not only pleased him but boded well for the coming night.

"How magnificent you are," she said, a breathless note to her voice that made his arousal leap with anticipation.

"Aye, I am," he said, for the sheer pleasure of watching her shake her head at him. Grinning and unabashed, he went to the bed and slid beneath the covers. Hamilton reached for her, overwhelmed by his good fortune as her cool, silken skin met his.

"Goodness, and how hot you are," she exclaimed, stroking her hand over his chest. "I shan't be cold in the winter, at least."

"Not if ye stay close," he agreed, silencing any further comments by taking her mouth, kissing her deeply, pulling her close to him as his hands explored. She was pure delight in his arms and joy sank deep in his heart as she responded eagerly to his touch, pressing closer and exploring his body in turn.

He lay still as she shifted to her knees, gazing down at him with interest before reaching out a hand and toying with the hair on his chest.

"There's a map," he said with a wry grin. "Just follow the path to the most interesting places."

She gave a little snort, which delighted him, but did as he suggested, trailing her fingers from the hair on his chest, along the line that arrowed down his belly to his arousal. It twitched and jerked as her hand grew near and she looked at him in surprise.

"It's impatient for yer touch," he told her, amused at the delight she took in this information. His amusement turned to panic as she wrapped a hand about him, holding him firmly and for a dreadful moment he feared he would not last above five minutes as sensation rocked him to his core.

"How do I touch you?" she asked curiously, staring as his erection pulsed in her grip.

"Slowly," he croaked, hardly able to catch a breath. "Stroke," he suggested, thinking that had been a stupid thing to say as she did just that and his mind turned to treacle. He groaned and crossed his arms over his face.

"So smooth," she said in wonder. "Does that feel good?"

"Mmmmhmmm," he said desperately, hardly daring to breathe. He let her explore him for a few moments more, swallowing a groan as her fingers tickled and stroked.

"My turn," he said, moving to sit up and startled when she put a hand to his chest and pushed.

"I'm not finished yet," she said crossly, taking hold of him with both hands now.

No, but he very nearly was.

"Enough!" he exclaimed, grabbing hold of her and pushing her down, climbing over her before she dismantled his plans for the night and his sanity.

"I'm going to kiss every inch of ye," he told her firmly, putting the words into action at once, starting with her forehead, her nose, her lips, and working his way down. He spent a long, lingering time over her breasts, biting gently on her nipples, licking the sweet swells and filling his hands with her softness. He painted pictures across her belly with his tongue, making her laugh and shiver, and bypassed the little thatch of curls for the moment, moving down her lovely legs to kiss her toes. That made her squeal again and kick, almost doing him a mischief.

"Dinnae be doing that, or it'll be the shortest wedding night in history," he said, laughing at the mortification in her eyes. "Ye daft thing, I'm only teasing ye," he said gently, kissing his way back up and this time turning his attention to the sweet place hidden in her curls with exquisite tenderness.

"If ye liked the touch of my hand, I think this will be a pleasure to ye," he told her, giving her a wink before he ducked his head and ran his tongue over the most private part of her, revelling in the sweet, tart taste of his bride.

Clara gasped, clutching at the bedsheets and squirming beneath him.

"Stop wriggling," he protested, laughing as he raised his head to see her gazing down at him with fiery cheeks.

"I can't!" she exclaimed. "N-not when you're doing… th-that!"

"Do ye want me to stop?" he asked her, all innocence.

"Certainly not," she replied tartly, laying back with a huff.

Chuckling to himself, Hamilton reapplied himself to the delightful task of making his bride squeal and thrash about and generally lose her mind. He held her hips firmly, keeping her still as she gasped and protested and demanded more all at once. It was a rewarding exercise and when she came apart, muffling her shouts by pulling a pillow over her face, Hamilton considered it time very well spent.

Deciding he'd been quite patient enough and his bride thoroughly prepared, he found his place between her thighs, nudging into the tender cove he had dreamed of possessing for what seemed like an eternity.

"I'll try to be careful, to—" he began, the words turning into a groan as the soft heat of her surrounded him, welcoming him inside. It was bliss of the purest kind, deeper than he'd ever known it before as they joined their bodies and their futures together.

"It's all right," she said, stroking his back, for all the world as if she was gentling him. "I know. I know."

Yet she stiffened when he pressed home, pushing all the way inside and he waited there, allowing her body time to grow used to him, the most excruciating, marvellous torture he'd ever experienced. The scent and feel and knowledge of her surrounded him, his body and his mind and he lost himself in pleasure. He kissed her, using his hands to soothe her once more and letting out a sigh of relief as her body relaxed. She moved with him then, tilting her hips just so, urging him deeper with such eagerness the pleasure of it almost undid him. Her breath was hot, fluttering against his skin, the soft sounds of pleasure she made so arousing he did not know how he managed to continue, forcing himself to pause at intervals to steady his resolve and not blow apart with the sheer joy of it.

"Hamilton," she whispered, her arms going around his neck, clinging to him and giving herself to him so sweetly and fiercely he knew he would never forget a moment of this night. "I love you."

Her voice, giving him the words that sang through him, settling in his heart to reside there until his dying breath, rang in his ears as he loved her, giving all of himself to her as she had done for him. The climax, when it came, shattered him, a pleasure deeper and more complex than anything he had ever known overtaking him, body and soul, until he knew he had been changed by the experience, remade into a man who would love only her until the end.

Epilogue

Dear Cara,

I have done the most ridiculous thing…

—Excerpt of a letter from the Hon'ble Miss Violetta Spencer (cousin and adopted sister to Lady Aisling, Lady Cara and Conor Baxter - Viscount Harleston) to The Right Hon'ble Cara De Vere, Viscountess Latimer.

One year later…

25th June 1851, New House, Wildsyde, Caithness, Scotland.

"Well, Jimmy, what do ye think? Wildsyde is fairly quiet, it's nae a busy town like Wick, but there is a grand school, and lots of boys yer age and plenty to do. Do ye think ye could like it?"

Jimmy studied the small cottage that sat in a private corner of the grounds of what had been called New House by everyone around. As neither Clara nor Hamilton could think of any finer name for the moment, it had stuck. The far grander building that was to be their home was well on its way to completion and Hamilton hoped he and Clara would be in for Christmas. The cottage, however, was finished entirely, and they both hoped it was pretty and well equipped enough to tempt Jimmy and Mrs Macready away from town.

"Do you like it, Ma?" Jimmy asked Mrs Macready, as his adopted mother stared dazedly at the cottage.

"Like it?" she said, her voice trembling, and then burst into tears.

Jimmy stared at her, and then at Hamilton with wide, panicked eyes.

"I think she likes it fine, Jimmy," Hamilton said, his tone dry as Clara rushed to hug Mrs Macready.

"It's beautiful," she said finally, her voice choked. "But I'll go nowhere if Jimmy disnae like it. If ye prefer to stay in town, laddie—" she began, but Jimmy only grinned at her.

"Did you see the all the fine horses Lord Buchanan keeps in his stables? He said there was a pony I might learn to ride on, provided I worked hard at school," he added with a roll of his eyes, as if this caveat was so obvious it hadn't needed mentioning. "And Hamilton said he'd have horses too, and that I can look after them and ride them too, if I learn properly."

"Would ye like that, Jimmy?" Mrs Macready said cautiously. "It would be a big change, all this countryside about us. There are nae shops."

"No," Jimmy said slowly. "But it's a fine house, and there's lots of places to explore, and the beach… and Lady Buchanan's brother, Jack, he said his dog, Skye, is due to have puppies. Do you think—?"

"Aye, aye, ye can have a puppy, though it will eat all my best furniture and ruin my rugs I dinnae doubt," the lady said, laughing and mopping her eyes at the same time. "But are ye sure ye want us both?" she asked, turning back to Clara and Hamilton.

"Of course we want you," Clara said, shaking her head at Mrs Macready. "I know it's been difficult for you with Flora in charge of the household, and the truth is, I'm scared to death about running such a large house. I've no idea how to go on, and I need you, Mrs M. Please, say you'll come and be our housekeeper."

“Clara winnae be satisfied until ye are here,” Hamilton said with a shrug. “And I winnae here the end of her nagging if ye dinnae come, so for the love of God, say ye will.”

“I do not nag, Hamilton Anderson,” Clara objected, glaring at him.

“Sure ye do,” he said equitably. “I just say nothing, ’cause I enjoy it for the most part.”

“Dreadful man,” Clara said with a sigh.

Hamilton winked at her, unrepentant as usual. “Well, why do ye nae go back into the cottage and make a list of anything ye might need that ye have nae?”

Mrs Macready leapt at the suggestion, and they watched, standing arm-in-arm as the lady chattered happily about all the things she would need to do before Christmas, including giving Flora Halliday her notice—something she sounded just a bit gleeful about.

“I think ye have pleased them,” Hamilton said with a snort.

“We have pleased them,” Clara allowed, leaning into him with a heavy sigh.

Hamilton glanced down at her with a frown. Turning, he held her by the shoulders, gazing at her critically. “Ye are looking a bit peely wally, love.”

“Why thank you,” Clara said dryly. “I suppose that means the honeymoon is over.”

He snorted at that, shaking his head. “Dinnae start fishing for compliments. Ye are still the bonniest girl in all of Scotland, but ye are as pale as a milk pudding. Are ye ailing?”

Clara swallowed hard, sucking in a deep breath before she shook her head. “No,” she said, “but I did want to ask. You are certain the house will be ready by Christmas?”

“Aye, I reckon,” he said, his frown deepening. “Why?”

"Because I would like our son to be born there in the new year," she said, the words trembling a little.

Hamilton stared at her. He'd heard the words. A part of him had been expecting the news for a few months, but hearing it now hit him a good deal harder than he expected. "Son?" he croaked, amazed he'd managed that much, for his tongue appeared to have been glued to the roof of his mouth.

"Or daughter," she said with a shy smile.

Hamilton made a choked sound, hauled her into his arms, and then let her go again with an exclamation. "Sorry!" he said, suddenly feeling the blood drain from his face.

"Don't be foolish," she laughed, shaking her head at him. "I'm not made of glass."

"But ye are with child! I… I…" He stared at her as his brain ran in addled circles.

"I'm perfectly well, just a bit queasy now and then," she added, swallowing again. "Goodness me, Hamilton! Lyall and Delia and Georgie have all produced babies, why should I not do the same?" Giving himself a mental slap and a command to behave like an adult, Hamilton nodded, clinging onto his wits and telling himself not to panic.

"Aye," he said, forcing his voice to sound normal, or close to it at least. "Aye, nae reason in the world. Ye will produce the bonniest babes Wildsyde has ever seen, that much, I ken very well."

Clara looked at him sceptically. "Do you need a lie down in a dark room?" she suggested.

"Aye," he said, wiping a hand over his face. "Aye, honest to God, Clara, I think I might. I dinnae want ye to think I am not glad, for I am. I'm so… so…" He made another choked sound and then cleared his throat vigorously. "I'm very, very happy," he said, the words strong and firm.

"But—" she said gently, taking his hands.

Hamilton stared at her slender hands holding his, knowing that she alone would bring their child into the world, a dangerous occupation for a woman. "But ye must promise me to take every care," he said, finding he was breathing hard. *"Every care,"* he said again, with added emphasis.

"Of course I shall," she said, sounding entirely too reasonable.

Hamilton shook his head and pulled her close, holding her tightly—but not too tightly. "Ye dinnae understand, *mo leannan*. Ye are dear to me… so… so very dear. I dinnae think I could survive it if ye were taken from me."

Clara looked up at him, stroking his cheek with her hand. "I'm going nowhere, Hamilton. I'm going to give you fine, strong sons and beautiful daughters to dote upon. We're going to live here and make this our home, and I shall be with you, beside you, every step of the way as we make our lives together."

"Aye," he said, his fears melting away at the certainty in her stormy grey eyes. She was a strong woman, no fragile creature that needed wrapping up in cotton wool, he had guessed that much from the start. Clara was the one who buoyed him when things got difficult, the one who made him smile when he wanted to bellow with rage, and the one who had calmed his restless spirit to find peace by her side. If she could do all that, she could do everything else she promised too. "I love ye, *mo leannan, mo chridhe, a thasgaidh, mo ghràdh."*

Clara smiled at him, looking rather smug, for she knew now what all those pretty words meant, and knew that he meant every one of them.

Coming next in the Wicked Sons Series:

Eight for Losing, One for Loving

Wicked Sons Book 9

Only cats have nine lives…

Leo Hunt has come to a crossroads in his life. A notable Corinthian, and a man who can never say no to a challenge, Leo has decided it's time to grow up. His friends are all marrying and settling down, and his sister's blissful if chaotic family life has given him the idea that he might like something of the sort himself. The woman who has inspired this volte-face is none other than his sometime friend, sometime nemesis, Violetta Spencer. Leo has known Vi since they were children and has never been in her company for above five minutes without vexing her.

Until now…

Cat got your tongue…

When Leo Hunt makes his intention to pursue her known, Vi thinks he's lost his mind. Either that, or he's doing it for a dare, or a lark, or, more likely, a bet. Whatever the reason, she's not about to fall for it. He might be the man she has secretly loved since girlhood, but she's no fool, and any connection between them would surely end in disaster. However, Vi has not reckoned upon her marriage minded adopted mama, Lady Trevick. The lady is determined to see Vi happily married, whether she likes it or not.

Finding herself out manoeuvred, Vi determines to endure Leo's courting like one would a bout of the measles, until he tires of the idea.

A catastrophe waiting to happen…

When Leo takes an unwilling Vi for yet another turn around the park, he is on his best behaviour, well aware that unlike his favourite feline, he does not have nine lives and his chances with Vi are running out.

Sadly, no one told his constant companion, *The Cat*, Mau. Unlike most cats, Mau's devotion is legendary, a superior feline, he is famous among the ton – and among those with nefarious intentions. Lured from his master's side, Mau is snatched by criminals determined to demand a vast ransom for the beloved and much-admired animal.

All does not go smoothly, however.

All nine lives…

When their diversion fails, the criminals scarper with Mau in their clutches, and Violetta and Leo in hot pursuit. On the adventure that follows, Vi discovers not only that she's rather enjoying herself despite imminent ruin, but that devil may care Leo is not at all what she expected.

Pre-order your copy here:

Eight for Losing, One for Loving

The Peculiar Ladies who started it all…

Girls Who Dare – The exciting series from Emma V Leech, the multi-award-winning, Amazon Top 10 romance writer behind the Rogues & Gentlemen series.

Inside every wallflower is the beating heart of a lioness, a passionate individual willing to risk all for their dream, if only they can find the courage to begin. When these overlooked girls make a pact to change their lives, anything can happen.

Twelve girls – Twelve dares in a hat. Twelve stories of passion. Who will dare to risk it all?

To Dare a Duke

Girls Who Dare Book 1

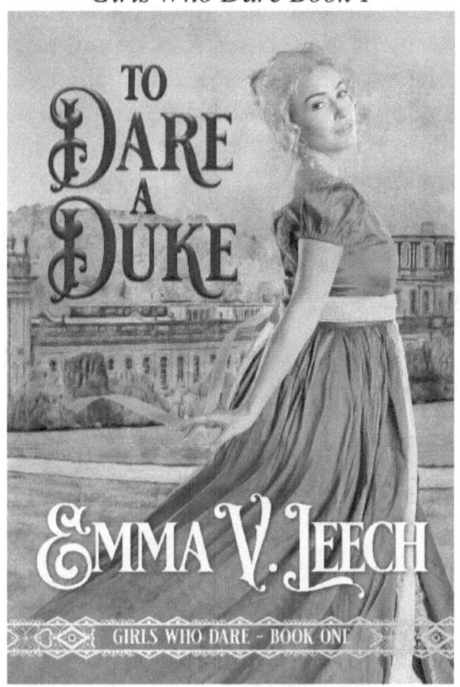

Dreams of true love and happy ever afters

Dreams of love are all well and good, but all Prunella Chuffington-Smythe wants is to publish her novel. Marriage at the price of her independence is something she will not consider. Having tasted success writing under a false name in The Lady's Weekly Review, her alter ego is attaining notoriety and fame, and Prue rather likes it.

A Duty that must be endured

Robert Adolphus, The Duke of Bedwin, is in no hurry to marry, he's done it once and repeating that disaster is the last thing he desires. Yet, an heir is a necessary evil for a duke and one he cannot shirk. A dark reputation precedes him though, his first wife may have died young, but the scandals the beautiful, vivacious and spiteful creature supplied the ton have not. A wife must be found. A wife who is neither beautiful or vivacious but sweet and dull, and certain to stay out of trouble.

Dared to do something drastic.

The sudden interest of a certain dastardly duke is as bewildering as it is unwelcome. She'll not throw her ambitions aside to marry a scoundrel just as her plans for self-sufficiency and freedom are coming to fruition. Surely showing the man she's not actually the meek little wallflower he is looking for should be enough to put paid to his intentions? When Prue is dared by her friends to do something drastic, it seems the perfect opportunity to kill two birds.

However, Prue cannot help being intrigued by the rogue who has inspired so many of her romances. Ordinarily, he plays the part of handsome rake, set on destroying her plucky heroine. But is he really the villain of the piece this time, or could he be the hero?

Finding out will be dangerous, but it just might inspire her greatest story yet.

To Dare a Duke

From the author of the bestselling Girls Who Dare Series – An exciting new series featuring the children of the Girls Who Dare…

The stories of the **Peculiar Ladies Book Club** and their hatful of dares has become legend among their children. When the hat is rediscovered, dusty and forlorn, the remaining dares spark a series of events that will echo through all the families… and their **Daring Daughters**

Dare to be Wicked

Daring Daughters Book One

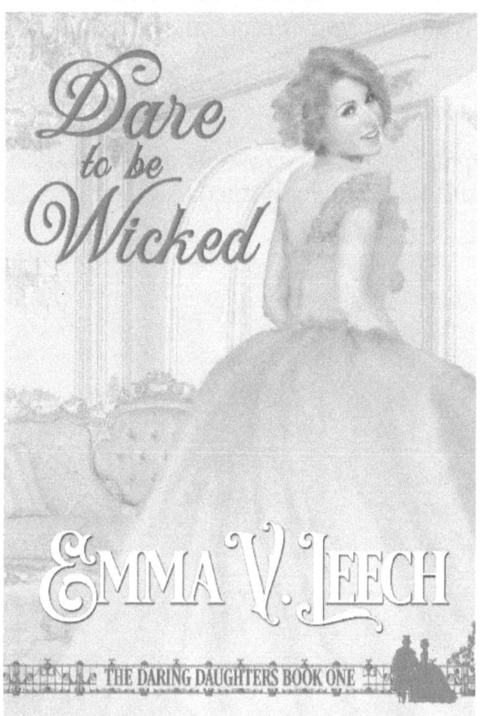

Two daring daughters …

Lady Elizabeth and Lady Charlotte are the daughters of the Duke and Duchess of Bedwin. Raised by an unconventional mother and an indulgent, if overprotective father, they both strain against the rigid morality of the era.

The fashionable image of a meek, weak young lady, prone to swooning at the least provocation, is one that makes them seethe with frustration.

Their handsome childhood friend …

Cassius Cadogen, Viscount Oakley, is the only child of the Earl and Countess St Clair. Beloved and indulged, he is popular, gloriously handsome, and a talented artist.

Returning from two years of study in France, his friendship with both sisters becomes strained as jealousy raises its head. A situation not helped by the two mysterious Frenchmen who have accompanied him home.

And simmering sibling rivalry …

Passion, art, and secrets prove to be a combustible combination, and someone will undoubtedly get burned.

Dare to be Wicked

Also check out Emma's regency romance series, Rogues & Gentlemen. Available now!

The Rogue

Rogues & Gentlemen Book 1

The notorious Rogue that began it all.

Set in Cornwall, 1815. Wild, untamed and isolated.

Lawlessness is the order of the day and smuggling is rife.

Henrietta always felt most at home in the wilds of the outdoors but even she had no idea how the mysterious and untamed would sweep her away in a moment.

Bewitched by his wicked blue eyes.

Henrietta Morton knows to look the other way when the free trading 'gentlemen' are at work.
Yet when a notorious pirate bursts into her local village shop, she

can avert her eyes no more. Bewitched by his wicked blue eyes, a moment of insanity follows as Henrietta hides the handsome fugitive from the Militia.

Her reward is a kiss, lingering and unforgettable.

In his haste to flee, the handsome pirate drops a letter, a letter that lays bare a tale of betrayal. When Henrietta's father gives her hand in marriage to a wealthy and villainous nobleman in return for the payment of his debts, she becomes desperate.

Blackmailing a pirate may be her only hope for freedom.

**** **Warning**: This book contains the most notorious rogue of all of Cornwall and, on occasion, is highly likely to include some mild sweating or descriptive sex scenes. ****

Free to read on *Kindle Unlimited*: The Rogue

Interested in a Regency Romance with a twist?

A Dog in a Doublet

The Regency Romance Mysteries Book 2

A man with a past

Harry Browning was a motherless guttersnipe, and the morning he came across the elderly Alexander Preston, The Viscount Stamford, clinging to a sheer rock face he didn't believe in fate. But the fates have plans for Harry whether he believes or not, and he's not entirely sure he likes them.

As a reward for his bravery, and in an unusual moment of charity, miserly Lord Stamford takes him on. He is taught to read, to manage the vast and crumbling estate, and to behave like a gentleman, but Harry knows that is something he will never truly be

Already running from a dark past, his future is becoming increasingly complex as he finds himself caught in a tangled web of jealousy and revenge.

A feisty young maiden

Temptation, in the form of the lovely Miss Clarinda Bow, is a constant threat to his peace of mind, enticing him to be something he isn't. But when the old man dies his will makes a surprising demand, and the fates might just give Harry the chance to have everything he ever desired, including Clara, if only he dares.

And as those close to the Preston family begin to die, Harry may not have any choice.

Order your copy here. A Dog in a Doublet

Lose yourself in Emma's paranormal world with The French Vampire Legend series….

The Key to Erebus

The French Vampire Legend Book 1

The truth can kill you.

Taken away as a small child, from a life where vampires, the Fae, and other mythical creatures are real and treacherous, the beautiful young witch, Jéhenne Corbeaux is totally unprepared when she returns to rural France to live with her eccentric Grandmother.

Thrown headlong into a world she knows nothing about she seeks to learn the truth about herself, uncovering secrets more shocking than anything she could ever have imagined and finding that she is by no means powerless to protect the ones she loves.

Despite her Gran's dire warnings, she is inexorably drawn to the dark and terrifying figure of Corvus, an ancient vampire and master of the vast Albinus family.

Jéhenne is about to find her answers and discover that, not only is Corvus far more dangerous than she could ever imagine, but that he holds much more than the key to her heart …

Now available at your favourite retailer.

The Key to Erebus

Check out Emma's exciting fantasy series with hailed by Kirkus Reviews as "An enchanting fantasy with a likable heroine, romantic intrigue, and clever narrative flourishes."

The Dark Prince

The French Fae Legend Book 1

Two Fae Princes
One Human Woman
And a world ready to tear them all apart

Laen Braed is Prince of the Dark fae, with a temper and reputation to match his black eyes, and a heart that despises the human race. When he is sent back through the forbidden gates between realms to retrieve an ancient fae artifact, he returns home with far more than he bargained for.

Corin Albrecht, the most powerful Elven Prince ever born. His golden eyes are rumoured to be a gift from the gods, and destiny is calling him. With a love for the human world that runs deep, his friendship with Laen is being torn apart by his prejudices.

Océane DeBeauvoir is an artist and bookbinder who has always relied on her lively imagination to get her through an unhappy and uneventful life. A jewelled dagger put on display at a nearby museum hits the headlines with speculation of another race, the Fae. But the discovery also inspires Océane to create an extraordinary piece of art that cannot be confined to the pages of a book.

With two powerful men vying for her attention and their friendship stretched to the breaking point, the only question that remains…who The Dark Prince is truly.

The man of your dreams is coming…or is it your nightmares he visits? Find out in Book One of The French Fae Legend.

Available now to read at your favorite retailer

The Dark Prince

Want more Emma?

If you enjoyed this book, please support this indie author and take a moment to leave a few words in a review. *Thank you!*

To be kept informed of special offers and free deals (which I do regularly) follow me on *https://www.bookbub.com/authors/emma-v-leech*

To find out more and to get news and sneak peeks of the first chapter of upcoming works, go to my website and sign up for the newsletter.
http://www.emmavleech.com/

Or follow me here…

http://viewauthor.at/EmmaVLeechAmazon

www.ingramcontent.com/pod-product-compliance
Lightning Source LLC
LaVergne TN
LVHW041151150826
845673LV00001B/132

* 9 7 8 2 4 8 7 0 1 5 3 3 3 *